Banished

LEE MAGNER

SILHOUETTE

Sensation

All the characters in this book have no existence outside the imagination of the author, and have no relation whatsoever to anyone bearing the same name or names. They are not even distantly inspired by any individual known or unknown to the author, and all the incidents are pure invention.

First published in Great Britain in 1995 by Silhouette Books, Eton House, 18-24 Paradise Road, Richmond, Surrey TW9 1SR

© Ellen Lee Magner Tatara 1994

Silhouette, Silhouette Sensation and Colophon are Trade Marks of Harlequin Enterprises II B.V.

ISBN 0 373 07556 1

18-9509

Made and printed in Great Britain

Other novels by Lee Magner

Silhouette Sensation

Mustang Man
Sutter's Wife
The Dragon's Lair
Stolen Dreams
Song of the Mourning Dove
Stand-Off

For my father-in-law, a son of the swordmaker, and
for my mother-in-law, a daughter of the samurai

Chapter 1

It was only a twin-engine jet. When the second engine failed, the silence inside the craft's tiny cabin was eerie.

Alyssa Jones yanked hard on the loose end of her seat belt, drawing it tight. Then she fought the upswelling of terror within her. *We're nearly at the landing field,* she thought, grasping at the first ray of hope that occurred to her. *Help will come.... If they survived the crash...*

The pilot shouted emergency instructions into the intercom. Alyssa obeyed them blindly. She felt light-headed. She was breathing too fast. *Don't panic,* she told herself urgently. *Don't panic...*

The wind roared past them as they plummeted through the dark, wintry night. Crouched in crash position, blood drumming loudly in her ears, she barely heard the distant voice of the pilot as he radioed a last mayday, giving their position, their horribly accelerating speed of descent, and their fearfully declining altitude.

Then they smacked into the sea.

Hard.

Alyssa felt excruciating pain. Against her head and neck and shoulders. Inside her chest.

Air whooshed from her lungs. A long-dead memory flashed briefly through her dazed mind. Of being knocked off a swing when she was five, of flying through the air and landing flat on her chest in the dirt, of thinking she had died because she couldn't breathe and felt as if she were turning blue from lack of oxygen....

Alyssa fought to inhale, to expand her lungs, to suck in air. To survive.

Blackness swirled around her. She tried not to pass out. Had she already? she wondered dizzily. She felt very disoriented.

Something cold was wrapping its clammy hands around her ankles and gliding up her stockinged calves. It felt wet.

Water.

Seawater.

Cold, relentless fingers of the vast North Pacific.

Come to pull her down into a silent, final voyage into oblivion.

Alyssa struggled for another breath. Her lungs expanded a little.

She wasn't ready for a watery grave. Not without a fight, anyway. Air filled her and oxygen shot into her. Never had breathing felt so good.

She moved. Testing to see if she were seriously hurt anywhere. Hands...arms...head...back...legs... She was sore. There were some badly wrenched muscles. But she was whole.

Relief flooded her. Followed immediately by a huge burst of adrenaline.

She had to get out of here—fast.

She released her seat belt and looked around. The emergency lighting was on. Except for that, it was pitch-dark inside the sinking aircraft.

"Captain Waylon?" Her voice was shaky. It didn't quite sound like hers. She tried again. "Captain Waylon? Are you all right?"

There was no reply from the cockpit. Just water gushing through the cockpit doorway and into the cabin.

Except for the pilot, Alyssa was alone in the plane. This had been a special run, just for her. The company had chartered the jet to take her to Onijima Island. The cabin attendant who usually flew with Captain Waylon had unexpectedly fallen ill with food poisoning just hours before takeoff. There hadn't been time to get anyone else. Besides, it was a short hop, the pilot had observed with a shrug. They could manage on their own, he'd said cheerfully.

Alyssa fervently hoped that he would be proved right about that.

She staggered to her feet as icy water sloshed around her knees and inched ever higher. She felt around her until she located her briefcase under the seat in front of her. Then she slipped off her leather belt and slid it through the briefcase handle. The fine, supple leather was dripping wet. She refastened the belt, securing the briefcase against the small of her back. It was a little awkward, but at least it didn't weigh much.

Shivering, she yanked a flotation pad and a life vest out of the overhead compartment. By the time she had the vest on and strapped in place, the water was lapping at her thighs.

They were going down fast, she thought. The plane must have a horrendous hole in it somewhere to be taking water at this rate.

She tried to remember how it felt to be calm. To be focused. She still hadn't heard any sound of life from the pilot. She had to depend on herself, on her own judgment, on her own survival skills. A fragment of a childhood prayer filtered through her fear-frozen mind. And with it came the faith that anything could be overcome. Life had seemed very simple and very safe back then. And she'd been fearless.

Her legs stopped shaking quite so badly. With numbed fingers she gripped seat backs and pushed her way through the deepening water in the aisle. She was going to the cockpit. And the front exit.

"Captain!" she exclaimed as she saw the pilot. He was slumped facedown against the control wheel. He wasn't moving. He didn't appear to be conscious. The water was nearly up to his face. If he wasn't already dead, he would drown soon.

Alyssa shoved through the water and reached his side.

She gently lifted his face away from the water, praying he didn't have a spinal injury. Then she fumbled beneath the icy water until she located the fastenings of his seat belt. As soon as she freed him, his weight sagged heavily. Desperately, she struggled to hold him above water.

"Captain, can you hear me?" she shouted frantically. "You have to help me! You're too heavy for me! I've got to get a life jacket on you. Where is yours?"

The plane lurched. Downward. Water was up to her rib cage. Ironically, as the water rose, it became somewhat easier to manage the man's weight. The sea buoyed him up.

However, water was pouring in through a hole or holes somewhere in the flooring beneath their feet. She felt the rushing currents against her ankles just before they went numb.

If they didn't drown, they'd die of hypothermia, she realized bleakly. They had to get out of the plane and into something dry. She prayed that someone had heard Captain Waylon's mayday calls. Someone close to them. Maybe someone on Onijima Island. That couldn't be too far away. They had been descending in preparation for landing when the second engine had died.

Alyssa caught sight of the captain's life vest and pulled it loose. It required a lot of contorting to get the vest over his limp body while trying to support him against the side of his seat. She blew a little air into the inflation tube, just enough to help ease the burden of his deadweight while she tried to get them both to the exit. If their life vests were fully inflated before they got out of the craft, there was always the possibility they might get stuck trying to escape through jammed or narrowed passageways.

Alyssa had to take her chances with the sea. Once they were free of the aircraft's door, she'd pull the automatic inflation cords on their vests.

With the captain's unconscious body to maneuver and the seawater now nearly up to her shoulders, the going seemed painfully slow. She thought she heard the sound of an engine in the distance, but suddenly the craft lurched to one side, sending her off balance and she struggled with a renewed onslaught of terror.

The plane was sliding into the sea at an angle, leaving the small jet's front exit nearly submerged. Alyssa thought she could probably swim out and get away from the plane before being sucked back when the aircraft sank beneath the waves.

But what about Captain Waylon?

"Where are the cavalry when you need them?" she muttered, exasperated and very much afraid for the pilot. She tried to find a pulse in his neck, but she didn't feel anything. Her fingers were so cold and slippery, though, she might be unable to detect it. She had to assume he was alive and try to get him out, if she could....

She pulled hard on the emergency cord on his vest and it inflated immediately. She decided to wait to pull hers once they were out of the plane. With any luck, one inflated vest wouldn't create a major problem—she hoped.

Water was now curling dangerously around their necks and Alyssa was starting to tread water. The plane settled gently down into the sea, rolling like a watery cradle with the rising and falling of the waves.

Alyssa reasoned it was as good a time as she was likely to get to try to open the door. The water was lapping near its top. Hopefully the pressure would be about equal inside and outside of the aircraft, and there would be no catastrophic inrush of seawater when the hatch opened. Anyway, she couldn't think of an alternative escape route that they could both get through in time. This would be their only chance.

"Hold your breath, Captain," she said shakily.

She couldn't tell whether he heard her or not.

Then she noticed the ribbon of blood that had begun trickling from his left ear. She felt sick. His slack lips were gray, but there was now an ominous rivulet of blood staining them dark pink.

Serious head injury, she thought, her stomach clenching.

Alyssa steeled herself to do what had to be done. She knew that she wouldn't be any good to either of them if she panicked now.

"You'll bob up in the water like a cork, Captain," she said, trying to inject some confidence and hope into her voice. She didn't know if he was listening. She wasn't even certain he was breathing. "You'll feel the ocean splash you in the face in a few moments. Hang on. It won't last. You'll have air again before you know it. Just…take a deep breath when I tell you to, if you can…. Okay now…here we go…."

Alyssa located the emergency handle beneath the rising waters. As she yanked the handle she shouted, "Hold your breath!"

The door sprang open.

For a split second, the cold, merciless sea relented and sucked them out through the door, into the ocean's waiting embrace. As the frigid waters closed over her head, Alyssa struggled to shove the unconscious pilot ahead of her. She felt him being pulled out of the airplane and floating free just ahead of her. His legs brushed her outstretched hands and she knew he was rising, not sinking into oblivion. She'd done what she could. She could only hope that the life vest would do the rest and carry him up to the surface. She thought it was just a few feet over their heads. The captain had a fighting chance.

Which was more than she might have.

Her lungs were aching for fresh air. Water was all around her. And the sea had shifted direction.

Having sucked water out of the aircraft first, it now rushed back in to fill the vacuum.

And it was shoving Alyssa back inside with it.

She surfaced inside the plane. Her head banged against the ceiling, where the last few inches of air inside the jet could be found.

Alyssa didn't dare inflate her vest now. She needed all her energy to dive through the water and swim out the emergency exit. But she'd need the vest inflated to help her find the surface quickly when she got out.

She inhaled deeply, dove and swam with all her strength away from the exit. When she'd gone a few strokes out into the ocean, she pulled the cord.

The vest expanded. Thank God.

When her face broke through the rolling waves, she was gasping for breath.

Numb with cold, she treaded water, turning slowly to search for any sign of Captain Waylon.

He was about twenty feet away from her. He didn't appear to be any better. He was slumped in the vest, as limp as a dead man.

The ocean swelled, raising her up on its shifting palm. Alyssa thought she heard the sound of a motor. Desperately, she tried to turn toward the thin, metallic rumble. A great, whalelike roll of seawater heaved itself upward, dumping her over its watery back and obscuring her frantic view.

Her mouth tasted of brine and her ears ached from the blood-freezing cold. Thoughts were harder to form, as her mind became saturated by a deadly, numbing lethargy.

She managed to splash and paddle around until she was again facing the spot where she'd last seen Captain Waylon's inert body floating. Now there was nothing.

"Captain!"

Alyssa swam stiffly in the direction where he'd last been, hoping that she hadn't lost her bearings and wasn't going the wrong way. With no landmarks but the ever-shifting surface of the ocean, she only had instinct to guide her.

If she could get to him, she hoped they could hug each other for a little body warmth. She was so cold, she didn't think she had any body warmth left, and she imagined that the poor pilot probably had even less, if he was still alive.

She had nothing to lose, however. And nowhere else to go. God, had anyone heard their radio cry for help?

Her arms were leaden. With each stroke she felt as if a hundred-pound weight had been added to her hand. She thought her legs were moving, but they were so numb, she couldn't be certain.

This must be what it feels like just before you die. She was too tired to be afraid anymore. She just wanted to rest. To lay down her head and sleep. Her arm barely lifted out of the water now. Water splashing on her face began to feel warm. She closed her eyes and remembered a fragment of her childhood...swimming with her family in the warm, shallow sea...

A large black-and-silver creature broke through the wave next to her. Its face had an oval window. Inside the window were eyes like a man's. There was a big black plug in his mouth and two tubes went from the plug over his shoulders to a hump on his back.

"Got to get the captain...." Alyssa mumbled, splashing water as she feebly attempted to swim through the sea beast in front of her.

It wrapped its tentacles around her and pulled the plug out of its mouth.

"Hold still. I'll pull you in," it said.

Strange that a sea creature spoke such impeccable English, she thought. Perplexed but too numb to be able to make any sense of it, Alyssa tried to swim along with him as he towed her away.

"Nice of you to come and get me," she said. His head was close to hers and miraculously, he heard her.

She thought he looked startled. But with the plug back in his mouth, it was hard to tell. His tentacles were firmly wrapped around her, though, and he was pulling her along with strong, steady strokes.

"You're very strong," she murmured. "But I don't think you can pull both of us."

The sea creature pulled the plug out of his mouth, but he kept on swimming, towing her along.

"Who else is out here?" he shouted. The words were as sharp as the sea wind.

"Captain Way-lon..." Her teeth chattered. Her lips were stiff from the cold and glistening with saltwater. "I have to find Captain Waylon...."

The sea creature tangled a slippery black arm around her more firmly and kept swimming.

"Just a minute...."

There was no sound from the creature.

"Captain!" she cried, not so much in fear for herself but out of fear that the poor pilot would be lost in the sea forever.

She was nearly unconscious when she felt herself being unceremoniously shoved up out of the water. Other hands pulled her into the air. She shivered violently. The air felt brutally cold in comparison to the numbing warmth of the sea. She protested, tried to fall back into the water.

The sea creature shoved its flippers against her bottom and Alyssa fell into the beast's floating house. It was hard, and it bruised her body. And there was a rumble in it. Like the one she'd heard earlier.

"Cap-tain Way-lon..." she whispered through violently chattering teeth. Something stiff and scratchy and hot was being wrapped around her. Too exhausted to raise even her eyelids, she curled into a fetal position, instinctively trying to husband the last tiny bits of warmth deep inside her body.

She heard someone next to her call out to the sea creature as he slithered away from the floating house.

It sounded like they shouted "Be careful."

In Japanese.

The sound of the engine was in her dream. And then she crossed over the edge of the dream and into the fringe of consciousness.

There was an engine. It sounded like it belonged to a boat. A fairly large boat. It was close. All around her.

She was swaddled in a cocoon of blankets. Someone was trying to lift her head and wake her up. A voice was urging her to do something.

"Drink this. Open your mouth and swallow...."

She opened her eyes and saw the sea creature. Dressed in black. A wet suit. The suit looked as if it had been poured over his large body. His eyes were a fierce, dark blue.

"That's good. Now, open your mouth and swallow some of this. It'll warm you up."

She opened her lips and he pressed a thermos against them. He lifted her shoulders, bracing her against his chest and arm. The liquid he poured into her mouth felt so hot, she thought she was burned.

"It just feels like fire because you're nearly frozen," he said curtly, refusing to let her flinch away. "Drink some more. It'll thaw you from the inside."

She stared at him, unsure whether to trust him or not. There was something overwhelming about him. He was too sure of himself. Alyssa had never been one to blindly follow orders, especially from total strangers. And this stranger frightened her. More than the sea did.

His eyes narrowed and his lips thinned angrily.

"Drink it or I'll pour it down your throat!" he threatened in a low, warning growl.

She felt his fingers tighten on her jaw. Anger flared up inside her, thawing her out a little.

"G-get your hand off my j-jaw!" she flashed back.

He relaxed his hold.

Alyssa struggled to free her hand from the layers of blankets and took hold of the thermos. He didn't let go. Her fingers bumped against his. Together they tilted the thermos and hot, sugared tea filled her mouth.

This time when she swallowed it, she could taste it.

"That's wonderful," she admitted gratefully. "Thank you."

The hard lines in his face softened slightly.

"You're welcome."

"After you b-brought me in, you went b-back, d-didn't you?"

"Yes."

"D-did you find the p-pilot?"

"No."

Alyssa closed her eyes. Tears welled up and trickled down her face. They felt scalding hot against her icy cheeks.

"I'm sorry," the man said softly. "We did everything we could."

"So did I. . . ." she said, the words choked with sorrow.

The tears fell harder. She didn't know why she was crying. She had just met the pilot, barely knew him at all. But she had tried so hard to save him. And it didn't seem fair that she had made it and he hadn't.

Alyssa remembered him mentioning something about a wife and a little girl waiting for him. She began to sob. Dismayed, she searched for the icy blue eyes of her rescuer.

"He had a family. . . ." she managed to say, struggling hard to stop the tears.

Grim-faced, the man pulled her up into his arms and pressed her head against his hard, rubbery shoulder. Her cheekbone hurt from the pressure.

"We'll keep searching," he said. His voice was rough, but the words were meant to soothe her.

Alyssa knew in her heart that nothing short of a miracle would undo what nature had already done. But it was kind of him to try to offer her that last, faint hope. He didn't seem quite so frightening now. Mysterious. Dangerous. But not frightening.

Nearby, a woman spoke.

In Chinese.

Alyssa heard him answer with a few, succinct phrases. In the same, singsong language.

The old legends told tales about the waters surrounding Onijima, the island of devils. The sea was infested with dragons and sea serpents and the ghosts of warriors lost at sea. Alyssa turned her head to stare into her rescuer's harsh, sea-washed face.

Was he a Chinese dragon? Or the ghost of a long-dead warrior?

He stared back at her, as inscrutable as the dark winter sky.

Though neither of them spoke, there was a peculiarly intimate contact beginning to be formed between them. Intangible. As fragile and as strong as a single strand of the finest silk. Alyssa's body relaxed. She closed her eyes and rested her head in the hollow of his shoulder.

He laid his hand across her cheek.

The engine changed pitch.

The "floating house" headed back toward its island home.

Slowly the seductive warmth of unconsciousness stole over Alyssa, sending her into the silent depths of sleep.

Wrapped in the arms of the devil from the sea, she felt strangely protected and safe.

For the moment.

"Can you walk?"

Alyssa shook the fog from her mind and groggily dragged open her eyes. The floating house had become a deep-sea fishing boat and they had arrived at the small dock of a local fishing village.

"If I have to carry you, I think we'd better get rid of some of these blankets," said the man with the icy blue eyes and comforting shoulder in whose arms she was still very much wrapped.

Alyssa struggled with the bundling and managed to loosen herself from the layers of blankets. When she staggered to her feet, she sent her rescuer sprawling onto his back clutching a chest full of damp wool and cotton where she had once been. He scowled at her and curled up to stand on his feet in one, lithe motion. The blankets dropped to his feet in a sodden heap.

"It looks like you can walk just fine," he said, still frowning. He swung over the rail and dropped down onto the old wooden planking that served as a walkway from the boat to the shore. He held out a hand to her and Alyssa took it as she gingerly followed him.

He released her hand as soon as it was obvious that she wasn't going to fall down.

"This way."

It was then that Alyssa felt the cool breeze on her back. Quickly she felt her waist and hips. She knew it wasn't there anymore. There was no bulky weight hanging from her belt, banging against her body with its sodden leather.

"My briefcase . . ."

He turned to face her.

"What the hell's the matter?" he demanded impatiently.

"My briefcase is gone. I belted it to my waist. I had it on when I was out in the ocean. But now it's gone."

He looked both amazed and infuriated.

He walked over to her, grabbed her by the shoulders and pushed her ahead of him on the wooden planks.

"I didn't see it on you when I shoved your fanny in the boat."

Alyssa heard the tightened fury in his voice and balked. He slammed into her back. And cursed shortly and brutally.

She turned to face him, hands on hips, eyebrows dropped and threatening. Since she only weighed a hundred and fifteen pounds dripping wet, she had developed threatening looks as a form of self-defense.

The man standing toe-to-toe with her did not appear the slightest bit intimidated, she noted. The sea breeze sprayed ocean foam across her and her skin rose in goose bumps. She shivered and rubbed her arms. That ruined her threatening posture. It also deepened his obvious irritation.

"We can look for the damn briefcase tomorrow. I'm sure most of the contents can be duplicated, so if it's lost for good, don't sweat it. Now, for God's sake, can we go inside? I'd like to get out of the wet suit and have dinner. You, obviously, are made of hardier stuff and would prefer to stand out here and revel in winter!" he snarled sarcastically.

He ran his gaze down her shivering body and back up again, as if daring her to deny the obvious fact that she was freezing and needed warmth much more than he did.

"But I can't duplicate everything that was in it!" she cried out, stamping a foot in frustration. "There was something irreplaceable in that briefcase...." A note of despair crept into her voice as she realized the enormity of what had just happened. "Oh, no...."

Muttering something uncomplimentary about her priorities, he shoved her ahead of him down the planking, pointing her in the direction of the outskirts of the village.

Alyssa glanced over her shoulder, desperately wondering what had happened to the precious cargo she had brought with her. There were several people standing on the deck of the boat, watching her leave. Two were men. One was a woman. Her other rescuers. If only they had been able to find that lonely leather briefcase, she thought despairingly. Now it was no doubt far beneath the sea. Oh, God...

"Watch where you're going or you'll end up in the water again," her chief rescuer pointed out sarcastically.

"Thank you. I'll do that," Alyssa said bitingly. The man certainly wouldn't win any sensitivity contests!

She abandoned the view of the boat and paid close attention to where they were going. Apparently, he was taking her to a residence at the ragged edge of town. After struggling across some boards slick with seawater and gritty with sand, they finally reached the deserted shoreline and made their way up the slope to the edge of town.

When they reached the house he intended to take Alyssa into, a middle-aged Amerasian woman opened the door and ushered them inside.

Alyssa saw the radiant happiness on the woman's face.

And she saw that it was directed to the man angrily pushing her inside.

"John! We're so glad you got back safely! Everyone was so worried!"

So the sea dragon's name was John— Then an awful feeling settled in the pit of her stomach. She turned to face him. He was standing in the middle of the room, stripping off the rubberized helmet-style head covering. Black hair glistening with water sprang free and a few strands fell across his forehead. Oh, no. How many people named John could there be here on little Onijima, she wondered, fearing the worst. And how many would look like a pirate and act like he was in charge of everything in sight? Not many. Probably, only one. Her stomach felt like it had been given an angry porcupine to digest on short notice. There was only one way to find out if he was who she feared he was.

"John . . . Mori?" she ventured cautiously.

He scowled at her again.

"At your service," he acknowledged curtly. He lifted a dark brow as a pained expression crossed her face. "You were hoping that someone else would swim out in that weather to haul your butt in here?"

"Of course not!"

"Well, then?" When she hesitated to explain how she guessed his last name he growled, "Who are you?"

"Alyssa . . . Jones."

She saw his irritation transform into cold fury.

"I thought I told you not to come here."

Alyssa blinked at him in confusion.

"But . . . that was last year. . . ."

"And the year before. And the year before. And every year before that anyone's asked."

"But my brother said that he and George had gotten permission from your father."

John Mori looked as if he could have breathed fire. His hand clenched until the skin was white. The woman who had let them into her home looked genuinely alarmed.

"You have been misinformed," he snarled contemptuously.

Alyssa realized he thought she was lying to him. Shocked, she held out her hand in apology and shook her head.

"I'm telling you the truth," she swore. "The proof is in the briefcase...."

Mori laughed harshly.

"How convenient for you. It's under quite a bit of ocean water by now. And I'm fresh out of submarines to go looking for it."

He stripped off the wet suit and stood in the cold air, magnificently male and thoroughly furious.

"Mariko-san, would you do me the kindness of warming up my...*guest*...?" He gave Alyssa a contemptuous look.

The lovely woman, wearing a light woolen *kimono*, bowed slightly and smiled.

"Of course, John. The hot water is already drawn for the bath. Help yourself."

When he looked at Mariko, his expression was much less harsh. Alyssa would have described it as almost tender but for the toughness that still radiated from him.

He walked back into one of the nearby rooms. There was a sound of his remaining clothing being stripped off and water splashing as he stepped into a tub of bathwater.

"What about notifying the authorities?" Alyssa called out.

"I'm the *authority* here," he said tersely. Then, as if relenting a little, he added brusquely, "We contacted everyone else from the boat's radio. There isn't anything else that anyone can do until the weather clears. I've left three other boats and a helicopter out there to continue looking for your Captain Waylon. Just in case."

Mariko smiled shyly at Alyssa and led her into another room. There was a bath there, too. This one was large enough for quite a few people to use at once.

"This is the bathhouse," Mariko said with a soft laugh. "If you'll permit me, I'll show you where everything is...."

Alyssa would have died for the comforting warmth of a nice, hot bath just then. Gratefully she washed herself off with Mariko's assistance and sank into the luxuriously heated waters.

She didn't give a thought to her nudity until she heard voices down the hall.

Mariko had gone to scrub John Mori's back. From their laughter, Alyssa decided it was not the first time Mariko had done so. She sank deeply into the water, clutching the small white washcloth to her body. It didn't cover much, she realized despondently.

The laughter faded into an embarrassing silence and Alyssa hastily stepped out of the bath and dried herself off. She put on the cotton *kimono*-style undergarment, the fine wool *kimono* and the white cotton *tabi*, Japanese-style socks that Mariko had generously laid out for her.

Then she returned to the main room to wait.

As soon as Mariko and John finished whatever they were doing, she'd ask them if she could borrow their phone. She needed to tell her brother that the plane had crashed and that she was all right, before he heard it from someone else.

Poor Alasdair. Catastrophes unnerved him. That was why he kept her around, he always teased. She was the cool head in the family. He supplied artistic temperament and vision. Not to mention enough spending for both of them.

Alyssa couldn't help smiling, though, as she imagined her poor brother running around the office like crazy, demanding that something be done. He wouldn't pull himself together until he knew she was all right. That was her brother, Alasdair. Dair, as she affectionately called him.

The world could be a harsh and lonely place, she had discovered. She and Dair had stuck together, fused in part by two tragedies: the suicide of their mother and the death of their father in a boating accident almost a year later.

Poor Dair. He'd be worried sick if he knew the plane had gone down. He'd been nervous about this trip to begin with.

Alyssa looked around the room with a growing sense of concern. What if Mariko didn't have a telephone? The place looked like it was a hundred years old. Did they have phones on Onijima back then? The wooden doorframes were dented and stained from years of use. A heavy, old-fashioned iron pot simmered over the charcoal fire nestled in the traditional square pit. From sliding wall to sliding wall, worn *tatami* mats covered the floor.

The soft sliding of a *shoji* door told her she was no longer alone in the room. Unaccountably, the hair stood up on the back of her neck. She turned to see who was there.

Chapter 2

"Feeling better?"

John Mori looked Alyssa over with a critical, experienced eye. He was alone. There was no sign of Mariko.

"Much better, thanks to you and your friends." Alyssa stood, feeling a little shaky in the legs, sore around her head and neck but very thankful to be alive. Her voice shook a little, too, when she said, "Saying thank you is a pitifully small thing to offer someone who's just saved my life."

She would have held out her hand in friendship to him if he'd been closer, but he was standing several feet away and making no immediate move to close the distance.

He made a dismissive gesture with one hand.

"I'd have done the same for anyone. It's nothing personal, if that's any help."

Alyssa blinked. She'd been close to tears, realizing how much he had done for her, and he had deftly killed those tears by uttering two clipped sentences. Well, if he could shrug off saving her life as a minor act, she supposed she could, too. She went back to the problem she'd been worrying about when he'd come onto the scene.

"Could I use a phone? I wanted to let my brother know what's happened, and that I'm all right."

Mori walked across the room in slow, measured strides. He didn't answer her at first. He seemed to be considering the request, weighing it along with several possibilities. And he was looking her over with a penetrating scrutiny that made her want to turn and run.

Alyssa felt something cold tiptoe around the region of her heart. John Mori was looking at her the way a barracuda once had when she'd been scuba diving. Her heart had chilled the same way then. She had escaped serious injury, but the barracuda had hunted her with a fearsome vengeance for several terrifying seconds before she managed to escape its sawtooth jaws.

Instinctively, Alyssa kept her eyes on the man circling closer to her.

"Do you have problems with the phone service here on the island?" she asked.

"Not generally."

"Then I can use a phone?"

"Later."

Alyssa frowned.

"My brother will be worried sick!"

"Maybe."

"Maybe?" Alyssa exclaimed. She was shocked that a total stranger could be so cynical that he would doubt the natural bond between a brother and a sister. "Believe me, Mr. Mori, there's no *maybe* about it!"

Mori shrugged and knelt by the bubbling pot. There were two large pottery bowls next to a large wooden dipper. He ladled some thick winter stew into each bowl. He motioned for Alyssa to sit next to him, nearer the warmth of the burning charcoal.

"Eat this first. You were pretty cold when I brought you here. The bath probably helped, but, like I said in the boat, it helps to get warm from the inside."

He handed her a large, hammered metal spoon.

She stared back at him as politely as she could while trying to keep calm. What kind of a life did John Mori have that he could assume one's closest relative wouldn't give a damn whether you'd sunk to the bottom of the Pacific?

"Look, Mr. Mori, I truly appreciate all that you've done for me, and I agree that the bath did wonders and the hot tea was great, but right now I'd really like to call my brother, if you don't mind."

"I do mind."

"I beg your pardon?"

"I said that I mind, Miss Jones."

Alyssa couldn't believe her ears. Surely she was misunderstanding the man, she told herself. No one would be so churlish as to refuse to let someone call their family under these circumstances!

"You're refusing to let me call my brother?" Her measured tones made the question seem more like a threat.

"More or less." He spooned the soupy stew into his mouth and ignored her furious dismay.

"I don't believe this," she muttered. She leapt to her feet. If this arrogant Neanderthal wouldn't show her to the nearest telephone, she'd darn well find one herself!

Her progress was abruptly stopped as Mori's hand closed over her wrist like a steel handcuff being snapped shut. With her forward momentum unexpectedly halted, Alyssa lost her balance and fell down next to him onto her hands and knees. She glared at him, feeling thoroughly humiliated.

"Eat," he ordered. "It's good for you. Then we'll talk about why you came to Onijima. If I'm satisfied that you're telling me the truth, I may let you make that phone call."

Alyssa stared at him as if he had lost his mind and was running around headless. *If* he were satisfied? What was going on here?

"Let go of my wrist, Mr. Mori," she demanded, blushing in anger.

He eyed her over the bowl of stew, which he was polishing off with relish by drinking out of it as if it was a large, steaming cup. When he'd finished the stew, he put the bowl down. Slowly.

"I'll let go of you. But don't take advantage of my patience by trying to leave before I'm ready for you to go, Miss Jones. There are many ways to keep you in one place. I know them all. Don't provoke me to a demonstration."

It was ludicrous, Alyssa thought. He was speaking in a conversational voice, but he was threatening her!

The man was obviously a criminal, she thought. The cold shiver of fear rippled through her heart again. She had no doubt that he could overcome her physically if she tried to leave. She was unarmed. He was big and strong, and from the way he moved, she guessed that he might be an experienced fighter. She was on *his* island and therefore unlikely to get much help from the locals.

"What do you want from me, Mr. Mori?" she asked, trying not to show any fear. She met his gaze fully without flinching or shrinking back.

"The truth about why you're here."

She frowned.

"I've told you...my brother and our business partner arranged the trip...."

He swore and narrowed his eyes angrily.

"Try again, Miss Jones. That one didn't work the first time, and it's not going to work now."

"But it's the truth!" she protested in frustration. "You can't keep me incommunicado just because you don't like my answer! There are laws..."

"None of which apply here."

"Even an independent island has to live within the community of laws, surely," she said brashly, gambling she could at least make him pause and consider the consequences of what he was doing.

A lethal smile containing not one drop of humor spread slowly across his angular face, making him look every inch the ruthless pirate.

"Why, Miss Jones, surely you know that Onijima Island has lived outside the bosom of civilization since the dawn of history? We like it that way. And so, it appears, do the more enlightened countries of the world. It serves their purposes to have a port that's beyond the rule of civilized laws. And tonight it serves mine. Now, take my advice and eat your soup. You're going to need your strength. We're going to have a long talk, you and I."

He released her wrist.

Alyssa couldn't believe this was happening. She stared into the bowl of soup and held it with both hands. It felt real enough.

"I *must* have passed out in the sea," she muttered despairingly. "This is some sort of nightmare and John Mori is the demon." Of course, she'd never met John Mori, never even seen a picture of him. She peered at him. "You probably don't look like this," she told him.

He looked irritated at her comments. She was delighted. *His* comments had certainly irritated *her!*

"I've heard you feel warm when you're frozen, and it's nice and warm in here, so if I'm still floating in the Pacific, I'm obviously frozen and hallucinating all this." She'd no idea she had such a gift for vivid imagining.

Mori's teeth flashed in a small snarl, and he pointed at her bowl of stew.

"Eat! I don't have all night."

Alyssa had always disliked being pushed around. Especially by overbearing men. John Mori was doing an excellent imitation of overbearing at the moment, even if he was a figment of her comatose imagination, although he seemed awfully solid for a figment.

Reluctantly, she ate the stew. It tasted as good as it smelled. She didn't really think her imagination was *that* vivid, so it was unlikely that this disaster was just a bad dream.

Well, maybe eating the stew would humor him. Maybe she could buy herself some time. She needed time. Time to think, and time to come up with a plan to get out from under John Mori's overbearing, paranoid thumb. She ate slowly. Down to the last drop.

"Could I have some more?" she asked hopefully, offering him the bowl.

"No! We'll be here till dawn," he growled. He took the bowl and faced her grimly. "I don't suppose you normally eat that slowly?"

Obviously he'd figured out that she'd been stalling. Rats. Well, she hadn't really expected him to be stupid enough to be taken in by her snail-paced eating. So, what else could she do to try to wrest a little control from this unpredictable man? Maybe a little saccharine femininity? Maybe she could convince him that she was a harmless bubblehead and then he'd let her get to a phone. Alyssa tried not to smile.

"Go ahead," she said, bravely lifting her chin. She opened her eyes wide, so he could see how honest she was inside. She didn't think he looked too impressed. Her spirits sank a little. Well, you had to give this time, she reminded herself. Rome didn't fall in a day. "Ask away."

His lips twisted into a cynical smile.

Alyssa's optimism wavered a little again. Surely he couldn't see through her ruse so easily? She wasn't *that* inept, for heaven's sake! Still . . .

His eyes locked with hers and for a split second she forgot her plan. She felt as if she'd been touched by fire. For a moment, she thought he looked as if he'd felt it, too. But the subtle shift in the depths of his eyes vanished almost as quickly as it had appeared.

He was just a hard man with opaque eyes asking blunt questions.

"Why are you here?"

"I came to see your father."

"Why did you think my father would meet with you?"

"He wrote a letter to my brother and our business partner saying that he was willing to discuss our long-standing— but often refused—proposition."

"When did you receive this . . . letter?"

"Just last week." She wondered why Isamu Mori had not confided in his son. "Perhaps you should ask him these questions," she said cautiously. It was hard to know what to make of John Mori's lack of knowledge. Had his father cut him out of the information loop on purpose? Did the older man not trust his son? If so, maybe she shouldn't trust him, either.

Mori's eyes narrowed.

"How did you get the letter?"

"By fax."

"From Onijima?"

"No. From Japan. There's a seaside resort, a private golfing and recreational club, near the ferry dock. . . ."

"I'm familiar with it."

"It was sent from there."

"By whom?"

"Your father, or someone he sent. The letter bore his signature, though.... And his seal."

"His *hanko?*" Mori was obviously surprised. Then he became dubious. "How would you recognize his *hanko?* Or his signature?"

Alyssa hesitated.

"We've seen it before."

"We?"

"My brother, Alasdair and I."

"Where have you seen it?"

She blinked and looked away, frowning slightly.

"I'd rather not say."

"And *I* would rather that you *did,*" he said, his voice heavily gilded with dangerous undertones.

"It's personal, Mr. Mori. I'm sure you understand *personal.*" Hang feminine! she thought, disgusted at her flare of temper. Well, John Mori probably wasn't easily swayed by traditional wiles anyway.

He leaned back on one hand and studied her for a long time through narrowed eyes. Alyssa felt her heart beating like a drum.

"Personal," he murmured thoughtfully, rolling the word over his tongue as if measuring its various meanings. "Personal between my father and you?"

Alyssa blushed. The insinuation was insultingly clear.

"Not that kind of personal," she said defensively. She sat up straighter and tucked the *kimono* around her legs protectively.

Mori glanced at her legs and then let his gaze drift over her in lazy exploration. His lips flattened and his eyebrows lifted once, as if considering her physical attractions on a purely research basis.

"No. I think you're a little young for him," he mused detachedly. His eyes met hers.

She wasn't too young for John Mori, however. Alyssa was horrified that the thought had entered her mind. She wondered if she'd somehow sensed it in him. That had to be it. She wasn't neurotic enough to feel attraction for a man who was basically holding her hostage until he finished grilling her, assuming he truly intended to let her make her phone call *then!*

"Tell me, Miss Jones," he said coolly. "Where is this faxed letter bearing my father's signature and *hanko* seal?"

Alyssa rolled her eyes and looked at the beams in the ceiling overhead before forcing herself to face him with the answer.

He lifted an eyebrow and waited.

"I told you— It's in my briefcase. The one that I tied to my waist with my belt but that got lost between the airplane and your boat."

His teeth showed when he smiled this time. The smile was even more frightening than the last one had been.

"And I told you how incredibly convenient that is for you, Miss Jones." He shook his head and laughed sarcastically. "It's not too original, but it certainly is a convenient coincidence."

"Be as sarcastic as you wish, Mr. Mori," Alyssa said angrily. "But it's the truth. I swear it. On my honor."

He looked into her eyes and this time a peculiarly charged current flowed between them. It held a quality more disturbing than mere distrust or dislike. And Alyssa was afraid she knew what it was.

"Do you have a lot of honor, Miss Jones?" he asked softly in that deadly voice that traced a silver trail of fear down her spine.

Alyssa gathered her courage and looked into the face of the barracuda.

"Yes, Mr. Mori. As a matter of fact, I do."

The look he gave her became speculative, then shuttered as it covered every inch of her body. She was grateful for the kimono's concealing folds, because that last current had held a strong charge of sexual chemistry in it. Alyssa knew she had enough trouble on her hands without adding that.

Mori rose to his feet and, as if on cue, Mariko appeared at the door that led back into the bath areas. Alyssa wondered if Mariko had been there in the shadows all along, listening.

Mori frowned. He stared hard at Alyssa, but he spoke only to Mariko.

"Would you keep an eye on her for me tonight, Mariko-san?"

"Of course, John." Mariko smiled and bowed slightly. It wasn't obeisant. It came naturally to her; it was done as a relaxed expression of friendly courtesy.

"Don't give Mariko any trouble," Mori warned Alyssa. "If you need a sterner baby-sitter, I'll replace Mariko with one of my Indonesian sailors. They don't speak English." With cool amusement he added pointedly, "And they're not nearly as clean and polite."

Alyssa shot him a venomous look. The pirate was without a conscience! She stood up and lifted her chin with defiant pride.

"Just let me know when I can call my brother," she said icily. At that moment, she would have preferred calling the navy, if she could have figured out how to get them to come to her rescue.

Mori's expression was not encouraging.

As he left them, Mariko smiled and motioned for Alyssa to accompany her down the narrow hallway.

"I have prepared a room for you," she said kindly. "And there is some hot tea waiting. You must be exhausted," she murmured sympathetically. "Come. Sleep. Everything will seem better tomorrow."

"You're an optimist, Mariko-san." Alyssa sighed, feeling discouraged. "I always used to try and look on the bright side of things. My brother complains I need to be more of a 'brutal realist.' This is really putting a strain on my optimistic tendencies."

"Here we are. Please excuse the smallness of the room," Mariko said graciously, kneeling at the entrance as she slid open the *shoji* door and motioned for Alyssa to go inside. She smiled and her face was illuminated with an inner loveliness. "It is cool and damp here on Onijima at this time of the year. We have found that the smallness of the room brings warmth."

Alyssa smiled at Mariko and went inside.

"The room is lovely," Alyssa assured her. "As is your generosity for letting me stay on such short notice."

Mariko put her hands on the floor and performed a traditional bow.

"It is an honor," Mariko replied smoothly. There was a twinkle in her eyes as she added, "Besides, if our positions were reversed, I would prefer to be here than with John's alternative hosts."

Alyssa sank down onto the *futon* spread out on the floor. She groaned and nodded her head.

"From one woman to another, I thank you, Mariko-san."

Mariko laughed softly and motioned toward the tea on the black lacquer tray next to the bedding.

"If you need anything, please call out. I will be sleeping in the room next to you. The bathroom is just on the other side of my room."

"Thank you."

"Sleep well, Alyssa." She hesitated, as if wanting to say something, but feeling that perhaps she was not free to.

"What is it?" Alyssa coaxed softly.

"John is a man I would trust with my life," Mariko said softly. Her dark brown eyes were steady. "But he is a dangerous man to cross, Alyssa. Please tell him the absolute truth."

"I have," Alyssa said, leaning forward and reaching out her hand in supplication. God, would none of these people believe her? "I swear to you, I've told him the truth and nothing but the truth!"

Mariko bowed slightly and withdrew without commenting further. As the *shoji* door quietly slid shut, Alyssa was left to wonder why Mariko had spoken. Alyssa had been under the impression that John had more or less told her to keep quiet. Was Mariko willing to befriend her, then? Or, perhaps, help her?

Alyssa caught her lower lip between her teeth and worried it thoughtfully. Could it be some sort of trap? She sighed and rubbed her throbbing temples. She was too exhausted to do anything more tonight, including think.

Much as she would have liked to slip out and search for a phone somewhere in the village, she doubted that she could move far without being noticed. Being a stranger, she would probably be very conspicuous. Especially if word had gotten around that she had been pulled out of the sea and put into solitary confinement by the head man around here.

She tried to take heart from Mariko's reassurance that she got along well enough with John Mori and thought highly of him. At least the man didn't alienate all women the way he had her, Alyssa thought, begrudingly granting him that small plus for his character. And he had saved her life, not a small consideration. From the way he was behaving, she couldn't help wondering if he was regretting that bit of heroism.

Alyssa's eyes sparkled with renewed determination. Maybe Mariko could be persuaded to help. She seemed to have a kind heart. If John Mori continued to act like an unreasonable, roguish ogre, then perhaps softhearted Mariko could be cajoled into extending some small kindness... such as looking the other way when Alyssa finally came across a telephone on this wretched island.

Alyssa smiled and sipped the hot green tea that Mariko had left for her.

Yes. Tomorrow, she'd keep on the alert for a telephone. Or an arriving plane. Or boat. Anything that connected with the outside world. Maybe she could convince someone to take her to Isamu Mori himself. She brightened. Now that would stick a wrench in John Mori's plans, she thought, cheered. He couldn't very well isolate her if she received his father's protection!

Alyssa put the small Japanese teacup back on the tray and lay down. She wrapped the thick, quilted *futon* comforter around her until she felt snug and warm in its soft cocoon. She was smiling as she fell asleep, with images of victory dancing in her head. She'd find Isamu Mori and he'd hand her a telephone and she'd be off the island with her business successfully concluded in no time at all!

The smile faded, as the dream began to blur. Hard, blue eyes of a watchful barracuda haunted the shadows of her mind. He was laying in wait to hunt her down.

Alyssa shivered in her sleep and huddled under the thick folds of the comforter.

That barracuda was dangerous.

And he was swimming straight toward her with his teeth bared.

"Hey, boss!"

John Mori turned to stare through the darkness at the man hurrying toward him.

It was Henry Chan. Henry had been on the fishing boat when they'd pulled Alyssa out of the sea earlier in the evening. Henry and the others had gone back out to continue searching for the pilot. From the way Henry was hurrying, it appeared that he had some exciting news to share.

John could see the fishing boat tied up at her berth down at the dock, which was kept modestly well lit all night to discourage some of the less responsible members of the community—or their acquaintances—from making off with a boat. No one was moving around the vessel, so he assumed it had been tied up for a while.

When Henry arrived, he was grinning broadly. Light from a lamppost glinted off his gold front tooth.

"Henry, you look like a gunrunner who just got contracts with both sides in a war."

Henry, who had been known to carry a contraband weapon or two among his various business transactions, took no offense.

"What will you give me for a half-drowned pilot?" he bartered with a shrewd leer. Mori had driven a lot of hard bargains with Henry over the years. Henry was delighted to have something that John wanted. He rubbed his hands enthusiastically.

"Where is he?"

"At the doc's. Suzie's helping out. And a couple of the others who were searching for him."

"Who found him?"

"That was kinda funny, John." Henry's smile faded and his weathered parchment brown skin wrinkled into a frown. "He was floating awful low in the water. That must be why we didn't see him the first time, when you were with us. The waves rolled him away from us and hid him in the troughs."

"So? What's strange about that?"

"Esau Holling was out in his boat. I don't see how he and his crew didn't see that orange life vest. Hell, John, they're used to finding things in the sea at night! And they must have been within fifty yards of him most of the time. We didn't search there at first, cause we thought Holling's boat had swabbed the area good. When we went back and widened the pattern, we found him, more dead than alive, floating there like a little orange cork. We'd have found him sooner if Holling hadn't helped!" Henry spat in disgust.

"Good work, Henry. Name your bonus."

"Hey, boss, I was just kiddin'." Henry slapped John on the arm in a friendly way. His grin was back. "I kinda like having you owe me something."

John kept a stone face but inside he grimaced. Henry would ask for something eventually. Henry rarely did something for nothing.

"Is everybody back in?"

"Yeah, boss. Tucked in their beds." Henry chuckled. "Except you, me, the doc and my talky sister, Suzie. Now I'm goin' to bed, so that leaves you and the others. 'Night, boss."

"'Night, Henry. And thanks."

"You bet, boss. I send you my bill someday." Henry's laughter echoed in the air as he hurried into the darkened village, heading toward home.

"I'm sure you will," John muttered under his breath.

John turned down the wooden planking, which was damp from the moist sea air, and he went in the direction of the village's emergency infirmary where the pilot had been taken.

The lights were on when he arrived. He found the doctor bending over his patient, listening to his chest with a stethoscope. From the look of the metal stand with its clear plastic bags and tubing running up to the unconscious pilot's arm, intravenous fluids had been started.

Derrick Alsop, Onijima's only resident physician, was visibly relieved to see John.

"Thank God you're finally here! I told Henry if he didn't get you down here in the next ten minutes I was going up to Mariko's myself and get you!"

John approached the examining table as the doctor covered his patient's chest with a thermal blanket.

"How is he, Derrick?"

"Not good. He hasn't regained consciousness yet. There's some fluid in the lungs. Cracked or broken bones in the rib cage. Probably concussion. Probable head injury. And hypothermia. We need to get him stabilized."

"Do you want him flown out to a trauma center?"

"Not right now. If he makes it through the next few hours, however, that might be a good idea."

"I'll put Mick and the plane on standby."

"Thanks, John."

"I want to talk to him first, if he comes around, Derrick."

The doctor raised an eyebrow.

John didn't elaborate.

The doctor's face was a picture of exasperation. "Damn it, John, you don't have to play everything like a poker hand! This man is my patient. I put his well-being before anything else."

John patted the irritated doctor's stiffened shoulder.

"If I didn't believe that, Derrick, you wouldn't be here."

Derrick rolled his eyes and turned back to his patient.

"I'll call you if there's any change."

"I'll be at the house." John frowned. "Where the hell is Suzie? Henry said she was helping you."

The doctor continued monitoring his patient and kept his back to John.

"I told her to go get warmed up and get some sleep. One of the midwives is coming over to help me out. She should be here any minute now. After all the training I've given them, they're fighting for the chance to do some emergency room nursing."

John nodded and his mouth relaxed into a partial smile. Derrick had put the women through medical boot camp but they had thrived on it. Fortunately, Onijima hadn't had many accidents or medical conditions to test their training.

The pilot was the first in months. Lucky for him that Derrick Alsop was around.

"Call me as soon as he regains consciousness," John repeated as he turned to go.

"You already said that," the doctor pointed out in irritation.

"If you need anything, let me know."

"I will. By the way, shouldn't you notify the pilot's employer that he's been found?" Derrick looked over his shoulder and stared pointedly at John. "I'm a little busy right now, but I can talk to his family if they're anxious for news. And it wouldn't hurt to get a quick medical history on him, though most pilots are in good shape, especially at his age."

John thought hard on that. The pilot's life was still in danger. He should contact his next of kin. Still, there was something suspicious about the plane's sudden crash. It shouldn't have been coming here in the first place, either.

"I'll take care of the notifications," John said abruptly. "Don't discuss the pilot's condition with anyone but me. And . . . I'll send Kojiro down to keep you company as soon as I can."

Derrick Alsop looked around in surprise.

"Kojiro? The bodyguard? Why the hell do we need muscle?"

"I'm not sure that you do, Derrick. Think of it as an insurance policy."

"Great," the doctor muttered darkly. He shook his head.

Just then a small, wiry Japanese woman came through the door. She was grinning cheerfully and bowed in greeting to both of them. Hastily removing her shawl and donning a light green surgical gown, she came over to the doctor's side.

"Ready Dr. Alsop," she announced proudly. "We gonna operate?" she asked hopefully. "I ready to scrub up."

Derrick grinned at his enthusiastic and experienced assistant.

John left them busily attending to the unconscious man and went in search of Kojiro. He found him at his home, sound asleep in bed. His wife, Chisako, woke him up at John's request.

"Don't leave the pilot alone with anyone. If you have to go to the bathroom, make sure the doctor and one of his nurses are with him."

Kojiro gave a short bow and uttered the guttural Japanese meaning yes.

"And keep an eye on your own back, Kojiro-san," John added quietly. "Your wife won't forgive me if anything happens to you."

Kojiro grinned and waved off the warning.

"Not to worry. I take care of everything. You go to sleep."

John rubbed the back of his neck. He was tired. He wasn't sure how well he would sleep, though, until he got some answers to some questions.

Before he went to bed, he placed a call to the charter airline and another to the pilot's wife. Later, he dialed up an old friend who specialized in deep-sea salvage.

Finally he went to bed. A man who rarely dreamed, he was startled to find that a gray-eyed sea siren followed him into the depths that night. She wrapped her silken arms around him, rubbed her soft body against his and leaned forward offering her lips for his tasting.

He wanted to kiss them. He ached for it more each time she dissolved away, only to return, smiling that haunting smile of hers.

He hadn't had a woman in a long time.

Deep inside, something long buried roused back to life.

Chapter 3

It was the whispering that awakened Alyssa.

The faint light of early dawn was just filtering through the thin white paper of the *shoji* window shutters. Alyssa ignored her bruised and aching muscles and turned, straining to hear what was being said.

The sea breeze tickled bamboo wind chimes outside her window just as the whispering started up again. She couldn't hear a thing over the delicate musical patter.

Alyssa wanted to groan in frustration. She quietly rolled back the thick comforter and crept closer to the window, hoping to hear who was standing there at dawn having a suspiciously hushed conversation.

"I take care of it," whispered someone. "Don't worry."

There was a faint scraping sound of someone walking away.

Alyssa carefully slid open the *shoji* window until a tiny crack formed, permitting her to peer outside.

She saw no one.

Just the old bamboo wind chime, swaying in the breeze, clinking softly on the breath of the sea.

Had that last whisper belonged to a woman? If she had to bet on it, Alyssa would have said it did.

But what was she going to take care of? And who had she told not to worry?

And what in the devil were they doing whispering about all this outside her bedroom window a few minutes after dawn? she wondered, perplexed.

Of course, maybe they didn't know she was there, Alyssa thought.

Alyssa sighed and shook her head. What was the matter with her, anyway? This probably had nothing to do with her at all. It was all John Mori's fault, she thought, somewhat self-righteously. That man was suspicious to the point of paranoia, in her unlicensed opinion. And his behavior last night had obviously had a very bad influence on her normally calm and rational thinking processes.

She looked around the room and located her clothes, neatly folded on the floor in a corner.

Heavens, this was a fishing village! People undoubtedly got up early to fish. And why wouldn't they whisper? They probably didn't want angry nonfishermen throwing cold water on them for being awakened at an early hour.

Alyssa shrugged out of the *kimono* she'd been sleeping in and went over to get into her own clothes.

The sooner she got to a phone and asked her brother to fly in a plane, the sooner she'd leave Onijima Island!

She smiled, feeling cheered.

And while she'd be waiting for her ride out, she'd wander around and ask where Mr. Isamu Mori's house was. Someone was bound to tell her.

"Then it's *'Sayonara,'* John Mori!" Alyssa murmured with determination.

The next time she tried to cajole the Mori family into loaning her that magnificent art treasure that she was after, she'd have her lawyers do her talking for her. And her traveling!

The old wooden house was silent except for the occasional creak and groan of its timbers in the wind. Apparently Mariko was still asleep.

Alyssa tried not to make any sound that would awaken her unsuspecting hostess in the adjoining room. They were separated only by a thin, sliding wall of white paper. The slightest rustling might be enough to awaken a light sleeper.

Gingerly she stepped into her green silk dress. She held her breath and listened.

Nothing.

Just the soft clacking of the bamboo and the aching of a pine bough nearby as it arched and dipped in the breeze.

Cautiously, Alyssa slid open the *shoji* door and crept out of her room. Seeing no one, she tiptoed down the hall toward the front door.

The heavy wooden door was bolted from the inside. No brass doorknobs or steel dead bolts for Mariko, it seemed. The bolt was a huge beam laid across the door and resting in sturdy wooden cradles.

Normally, Alyssa would have been thrilled. She deeply admired the old architecture of Japan. She was a student of Japanese art history, and ancient woodworking and joinery had always fascinated her. From the look of it, the door and its bolt, like the rest of the house, had to be a hundred and fifty years old or more.

Well, she certainly didn't have time to stand around and admire the surroundings! She had to get to a phone and let her brother know where she was and what was going on. It made her nervous to be out of touch with everyone she knew. She felt as if she'd been kidnapped by John Mori and was being held captive on his island of devils for having trespassed on his privacy!

The old, worn beam was smooth against her palm and it creaked softly as she lifted it. She opened the door and closed it after her as quietly as she could. She didn't know if she'd awakened Mariko, but she wasn't going to stick around and find out!

Her shoes were gone, so she slipped her feet into a pair of wooden platform clogs called *geta* sitting just outside the door. There were several other pairs of *geta* in the small niche where shoes could be left before entering the house. Some were big enough for grown men to wear, she noted. Did Mariko have a man under her roof? Other than occasional visits by John Mori? From what she had seen so far,

Alyssa assumed that John Mori came and went as he pleased and that Mariko was happy to have him whenever.

Mariko's house was set off from the edge of the village. It lay a few hundred yards up a gently sloping hill covered with pine trees and huge rocks. The docks lay down toward the water's edge and the town was nestled between the water and a rising hill that abruptly jutted upward to form a ragged cliff.

Alyssa could see quite a bit of the village from Mariko's front step. Some of the closer houses were just a few hundred feet away, along a wide trail of flat stones that served as sidewalk. There were sounds of conversation in the distance. Alyssa couldn't tell if they were people just getting up for the day or not. The unhurried feminine voices coming from town sounded like women beginning their work for the day, she decided.

The voices closer to the docks sounded more urgent. And they were masculine.

She followed the stone trail, keeping close to the houses and trees. She wasn't hidden, but she was less easily visible than if she walked down to the docks.

She saw what looked like telephone lines running from house to house. She followed the lines, hoping to locate a pay phone. Since it was a small village, she thought it more likely there would be a pay phone closer to the docks. She imagined commercial fishermen coming in with their hauls and needing to communicate quickly with their families or their wholesale buyers. Or maybe even with the local doctor. After all, fishermen got hurt at sea.

Commercial fishing was dangerous, hard work. Alyssa had been born near a little fishing village much like this one. Her parents had spent several years there while her father expanded his powerful business empire. Alyssa vividly remembered one bitter winter when a shark had attacked a small boat. The fishermen had tried desperately to fight it off and save their catch. Their catch was their livelihood, the food for their children for the next month. But the shark had taken a toll on them.

Alyssa had just turned four, but she remembered the fishermen being carried on stretchers to the local doctor's house. Down by the sea.

There was a convergence of power lines on one building not too far from the center of the docks.

"If there isn't a phone in that place, I'll eat my stockings," Alyssa muttered to herself.

She was only a few feet from the back of the building when the front door opened and people came out. She shrank against the back wall and listened. Her heart sank when she heard the first voice. He was speaking with great clarity, so there was no doubt in her mind who it was. John Mori.

"When you get back, we'll see if we can get the new lab equipment ordered," Mori was saying. "Is that soon enough for you, Derrick?"

"Better late than never, John," the second man replied briskly.

"And, Captain, you hang on. You'll be at that hospital within the hour. Your wife and daughter are waiting for you along with the doctors."

"Thanks, Mori," whispered the third man. "I'll never forget this. And please, thank Miss Jones for me."

Alyssa felt weak in the stomach and faint with shock. That whispered voice belonged to Captain Waylon. He had survived! She closed her eyes in thanksgiving.

Then she bit her lip, thinking hard. Should she join them? If they were helping the pilot get to a hospital, maybe she could accompany him? Then she could call her brother and her business partner, and they could regroup and come up with Plan B for getting that objet d'art for the exhibit.

The engine of a small jet revved into life in the distance. Alyssa went around to the side of the building and saw a small plane sitting on a runway at the far end of the beachfront. Then she saw the ambulance in front of the house. A man on a stretcher was being loaded into it. The man was Captain Waylon.

"Thank God," she whispered fervently.

Alyssa's hands trembled and for a second time she felt faint. It wasn't every day you witnessed someone's return from the grasp of death. She shook her head in an attempt to rid herself of the terrible weakness saturating her.

"Snap out of it," she whispered to herself fiercely.

Seeing the ambulance and the captain provided her with some unexpected and welcome reassurance. John Mori might have a very inhospitable way of receiving unexpected visitors, but he obviously was willing to help out a person in need. He had saved her life. Now it appeared that he had saved the pilot, or at least helped.

She was willing to gamble that he wouldn't harm her. Though late last night, as he'd manacled her wrist and stared her down over dinner, she hadn't been entirely certain of that.

So...if she stuck around long enough to try to speak with Isamu Mori, she might not be risking bodily harm at John Mori's irritated hands. She had high hopes that Isamu Mori would be more reasonable than John.

However, she still needed to find a telephone.

The quiet roar of the airplane's engines helped cover the sound she made as she clattered over the rough stone paving along the side of the house in her wooden *geta*. She hurried inside, praying that no one was there and that the house possessed a telephone.

The first thing she saw was a black console-style multi-button telephone sitting proudly on a large desk inside the main hallway.

"Thank you, Mother McKree!" Alyssa whispered fervently.

She picked up the receiver and dialed the operator. She'd lost her telephone credit card. It was littering the bottom of the Pacific inside her briefcase along with everything else of any importance.

But she could always call collect....

"Operator? I'd like to place a collect phone call to Alasdair Jones in San Francisco. Yes. The number is..."

Alyssa gave the operator the phone number at the apartment that she and her brother owned. It was late Sunday night in San Francisco. Alasdair was probably asleep in bed. She waited eagerly for his voice at the other end of the line. It never came. Her heart sank.

"I'm sorry, miss, but no one answers. Is there anything else?"

Where could he be? Alyssa frowned. She had no idea.

"Operator, could you dial another number for me? Collect? It's..."

This time Alyssa gave her the home phone number of her business partner, George Bodney. George tended to wine and dine the ladies, but surely even George would be home in bed by now, she thought. Only, George wasn't. Alyssa felt a stab of despair.

"No one answers, miss. Is there any other number you would like to call?"

Work? Surely George and Alasdair wouldn't be at the office. Not this late on a Sunday night, for heaven's sake. Still, she couldn't think of anywhere else to call. Alasdair wouldn't have gone down to her place on the ocean. And George disliked the beach. Said he hated getting sand in his expensive shoes.

Alyssa asked the operator to call George Bodney's office phone number. When no one answered, she gave the operator Alasdair's work number. To no avail. She couldn't remember his pager number.

"Damn!" she muttered as she hung up the phone in defeat.

"Who are you sending to hell?"

Alyssa whirled to face John Mori and the man wearing a white lab coat who'd been attending Captain Waylon. Alarm rippled through her like a swallow of ice water on a hot summer day.

"Damn my brother and my partner for not being there when I need them," Alyssa replied defiantly. She was embarrassed for using someone's phone without permission and for being caught in a private moment of defeat. She was willing to bet that John Mori wouldn't be embarrassed in the slightest if their circumstances were reversed. The pirate! She blushed deeply.

John's eyes turned a darker shade of blue. A hint of amusement played about his hard mouth.

"Are you blushing in anger or in embarrassment?" he asked, leaning against the door as if he intended to stay there all day.

"Both, Mr. Mori. It seems I'm reduced to sneaking into a stranger's house and borrowing his phone without permission."

"And that embarrasses you?"

"Yes!"

"You sound more angry than embarrassed," he pointed out lazily. He surveyed her appearance. Slowly. "It looks like Mariko's laundress forgot to press that dress before she returned it to you."

"I can't help looking like I've just walked through a car wash, Mr. Mori," she said, bristling. "It's been a difficult twenty-four hours...."

"Difficult? That's a mild description for a plane crash at sea, Miss Jones," he observed dryly.

Alyssa's cheeks reddened more but she ignored his sarcasm.

"As I was saying, it's not been the best twenty-four hours of my life, so please excuse me if I'm angry and embarrassed for trying to get things back under control."

The man in the white lab coat who was standing behind John stepped forward. He gave John a sidewise look and cleared his throat.

"Since John obviously has forgotten his manners, let me introduce myself. The name's Derrick Alsop. I'm the doctor here."

Derrick Alsop's sherry eyes were warm and appreciative as he looked her over. When he extended his hand in friendship, Alyssa shook it gratefully.

Then he squinted his eyes a little and looked at her with a more professional interest.

"How are you feeling, by the way? I asked John if I should look in on you last night, but he thought that he and Mariko had you well in hand, warming you up and so forth." Instead of releasing her hand, he turned it over and examined it. "No tingling or numbness in the extremities?"

"No. Just a few bruises and wrenched muscles."

He went over a few other questions, looked into her eyes, checked her pulse. He looked up and grinned crookedly.

"Your pulse is a bit fast, but I imagine it's from being in a wrestling match with John here."

Alyssa pulled her hand back.

John looked on implacably.

The doctor stuck his hands in his lab coat pockets and sat on the edge of the desk with the phone on it. His walnut-brown hair was thinning at the temples and needed a fresh trim. The man was lanky and tall. And there was a friendliness in him that reached out to her.

Alyssa smiled at him warmly.

"Thank you for being concerned, Doctor."

"Call me Derrick."

"Derrick."

John Mori's eyes narrowed ever so slightly.

"Where is Mariko?" John asked abruptly. "I thought I told you to stay with her."

"I did," Alyssa pointed out innocently.

"You left."

"As soon as I could."

Derrick was looking back and forth between them, becoming increasingly bewildered.

John ignored his bafflement and leaned forward threateningly.

"And I asked you not to make any phone calls unless I gave my permission," he pointed out.

"Every prisoner is permitted one phone call."

"You aren't a prisoner, Miss Jones."

"Then you don't mind my using the phone?" she said, feigning cheerful surprise.

"I didn't say that."

Derrick raised a hand, halting the exchange and turned to face John.

"Why in God's name aren't you letting her call anyone, John?"

"It's a temporary precaution."

"Precaution against what, damn it all?" Derrick asked crossly. He ran both hands through his thin hair and glared. "You've taken distrust to a new level, John. The woman's barely survived a plane crash and near drowning. Why are you afraid to have her call her next of kin?''

''Because they may have planned it,'' Mori said through gritted teeth. His eyes burned with anger. He didn't like being forced to admit things before he was ready. ''Mind your medical business, Derrick. Let me take care of this.'' He gave Alyssa a look as hard and cold as diamonds on ice. ''And leave Miss Jones to me.''

Alyssa was staring at him with her mouth open.

They may have planned it? Her brother? And her business associate? Maybe John Mori was mad after all. She snapped her mouth shut.

''You've been living in isolation for too long, Mr. Mori,'' she said carefully. ''I can assure you that no one would want to harm me, least of all, my own brother.''

He stared at her for a long, silent moment. Then he shrugged.

''You never know, Miss Jones,'' he said softly.

Outside, the plane carrying the injured pilot was taking off. They all turned and watched it rise into the sky and turn toward Japan.

Derrick slapped his hand on his thigh and stood up.

''Well, I'd like to stay and help you two unravel this tangle you've gotten yourselves into. Sounds fascinating to me. But as John knows, I've got to take the mail plane over to Tokyo.'' He looked at John seriously. ''I'll be back in two weeks, barring complications.''

John nodded curtly.

Derrick turned to Alyssa and considered her thoughtfully.

''I'd listen to John, if I were you, Alyssa Jones,'' he said. ''If he's suspicious of your associates, don't be too hasty in coming to their defense.''

Alyssa wasn't about to abandon her loyalty to her own brother or business partner just because two strangers she had never met before last night were suspicious of them.

''I'm not the person running hastily to a rash judgment,'' she said.

Derrick sighed.

"If you don't get to the airfield in ten minutes, Derrick, you'll miss the flight," John pointed out. "The mail pilot doesn't slow down for anyone."

"How well I know that!" Derrick exclaimed mournfully. He leaned toward Alyssa conspiratorially. "I was dashing down the runway after the little jerk six months ago, and he took off without me! Can you believe that? And to think I thought Onijima would be a haven from rigid, unimaginative bureaucrats!"

Alyssa laughed.

Derrick grinned, pleased with himself.

"I'm off, then."

He retrieved a suitcase from the adjoining room and headed for the door. Outside, he got into a small European car that could have served as a dented flying saucer prop in a movie. Miraculously, the vehicle started, Derrick waved goodbye and drove off.

"He isn't going to the airfield," Alyssa said, confused when Derrick went in a different direction.

"Captain Waylon was evacuated from our emergency field," John said. "The mail plane uses the island's main airfield. It's ten minutes inland." He added dryly, "We can land jumbo jets and military cargo planes on our main airport runways, Ms. Jones. If your plane hadn't ditched, that's where you'd have arrived. And by now departed."

Just then Mariko rushed into the house. Upon seeing Alyssa, she stopped dead and gasped for breath.

"Oh, there you are, Alyssa!" she exclaimed with great relief. "I've been so worried!"

Alyssa couldn't help but feel a small stab of guilt. She liked Mariko. And Mariko had extended her friendship, as far as John would let her.

"I'm sorry, Mariko-san," Alyssa said.

Mariko turned to John and bowed apologetically.

"So sorry, John," she murmured. "I failed you."

His expression softened, the way it had last night when he looked at Mariko. Alyssa watched in fascination as the hint of tenderness transformed his stony masculinity into warm strength.

"Don't worry about it, Mariko-san. I shouldn't have asked it of you. You're too gentle-hearted to be a jailer."

Mariko laughed, embarrassed.

"I'm afraid you're right, John."

"Don't worry about Alyssa," Mori said, his eyes returning to her. Predatory, barracuda eyes. "I'll take care of her. Personally."

Alyssa swallowed. She didn't like the sound of that.

Mariko left, bowing.

And John ushered her through the door. As he locked up the doctor's office and pocketed the key, he motioned for her to go to his car.

He held the door for her and locked her in. Then he slid into the driver's seat and turned on the engine. It was a small silver sports car with black leather interior and everything Alyssa had ever heard of on the dashboard.

He pulled onto the narrow street and drove through town. People waved to him when he passed by; he acknowledged each one. Alyssa studied him out of the corner of her eye. She might not care much for John Mori, but the denizens of Onijima seemed positively smitten with the man.

He was looking straight ahead when he said, "Are you memorizing my features so you can give my description to a police artist when you get back to the States?" His mouth curved slightly in amusement.

Alyssa blushed. Damn the man. She hadn't blushed this much in years.

She folded her arms and crossed her legs and looked straight ahead with a vengeance.

"I don't know what you're talking about," she said blithely.

The hint of a smile was joined by a raised eyebrow.

"No?" he countered dubiously. "You were staring at me, Miss Jones. Didn't anyone ever tell you that was rude?"

"Are you intentionally picking a fight with me, Mr. Mori?" she asked in amazement.

He laughed.

"No, Miss Jones. I'm distracting you."

"Distracting me? What for?"

"So you won't remember which roads to take if you want to hike down the mountain when my back's turned."

Alyssa turned around and bit her lip in dismay. Heavy vegetation had swallowed them up. They had made several turns onto roads that crisscrossed. She gave him a malevolent look. To think she had been considering giving him the benefit of the doubt because he'd saved her life and Captain Waylon's. The man was definitely missing a screw or two.

"Am I allowed to know where I am going?" she asked sweetly. "Or will that compromise Onijima's national security?"

"To my home."

"And what are we going to do when we get there?" she asked coolly.

He looked over at her briefly. Something altered in the depths of his eyes. Alyssa felt a frisson of alarm sizzle down her spine. Her eyes must have shown some of her uneasiness because he tightened his jaw and looked away, as if annoyed by something unexpected.

"We're going to talk," he said curtly.

"So far our 'talking' hasn't gotten us very far, Mr. Mori," she pointed out. She added, tartly, "Are you prepared to believe that I'm telling you the truth this time?"

"Words are easy to say," he said softly. "People use them to further their own ends all the time. You'll need something besides that to convince me you're being completely honest, Miss Jones."

"That's just great," she muttered sarcastically. "What can I do? Swim down to the bottom of the Pacific and retrieve my briefcase?"

"That's a thought," he said with a shrug.

Alyssa turned her head and stared at him as if he'd lost his mind.

"I'm hungry, Alyssa Jones," John said. "So we'll do our talking over breakfast. If you care to join me..."

"I'm so famished, I'd eat with a sea snake across the table from me, Mr. Mori," she said.

She'd nearly said barracuda. She sidestepped the word just in time. She knew he had no idea what she'd been dreaming last night, but it seemed like too revealing a comment to her, all the same. John Mori had too predatory a nature to be given any more insight into her than necessary.

His mouth twisted into a bitter smile.

"Sea snake?"

But that was all he said. He seemed to lose interest in any more conversation for the moment. He just focused on his driving.

He was a very good driver, Alyssa realized. He turned the wheel smoothly. And he drove fast. Like a race-car driver. The tires had squealed softly on the hairpin turns but he accelerated out of them as if he had driven the road blindfolded for years. His hands were lean and capable. His body relaxed. Yet, there was an aura about the man. A sense of alertness.

"Here we are," he said, as they surged out of the woods and pulled into a garage. Nearby was a house. Moderate in size. Built of dark brown beams and whitewashed walls. A huge pine bonsai sat in a large pot beside the stone gravel walk that meandered around to the back of the house.

He opened the door for her and took her hand as she got out of the car. Their eyes met. Something sizzled between them. Alyssa stared at him in surprise. She thought he seemed disconcerted. He had felt it too, she realized. Well, at least she wasn't alone in being disgusted by their unfortunate chemistry.

"Breakfast will be served near the garden," he said, frowning.

"Just so long as it isn't me," she murmured, as she followed him down the garden path.

Chapter 4

He watched her as she moved about the garden. The jade-and forest-green colors of her dress made her blend in with the rustic setting. The graceful curves beneath the silk reminded him that she was a woman.

A very attractive woman.

Sunlight burnished her light brown hair, igniting the auburn color within each silky strand. Her face had a healthy, clean glow. The skin was as smooth as a pearl's. She walked with easy grace in the *geta,* bending now and again to admire one of the numerous *bonsai* that inhabited his private Eden.

Eve in the garden of Eden, he thought, with bitter irony. And she thought of him as the snake. He found that amusing. Maybe she wasn't too far off in that assessment. He would concede that he had been hissing at her ever since he realized who she was.

When the air-traffic control tower had phoned him to alert him to her plane's emergency, he hadn't had time to find out who the hell they were. He'd been engaged in a lengthy telephone conversation on another line with an old business acquaintance, discussing some possible stock transactions in Hong Kong. He'd cut off that conversation with the terse explanation that he had to attend to an emergency and would get back to his friend in a day or two. Then he'd driven to the dock in record time, using his car phone to shake Henry out of his Saturday night game of mahjongg at Mariko's.

Henry and the others were waiting for him when he reached the fishing vessel.

He hadn't thought about Alyssa as a woman when he'd found her in the sea. He had been impressed that she hadn't panicked, though.

It was when he held her in his arms on the damn boat that he realized there was more to her than drenched hair, a fighting spirit and eyes the color of fog on a winter sea.

Even through the blankets he'd felt her enticing shape.

He couldn't remember the last time he'd held a woman like that. Holding her head close to his shoulder, trying to comfort her when they believed the pilot was lost.

Maybe he'd never held a woman like that.

Of course, he had women acquaintances. He knew some of them through his extensive business activities throughout Asia, the Pacific and Europe. Women of different races, of different cultures, of different ages.

He never got intimately involved with any of them. He made it a practice to keep his personal needs separate from his business activities. That made for cleaner, sharper judgments. In both spheres.

He'd been tempted, of course.

But he had never yielded.

He was made of steel where women were concerned. He never engaged in intimate relations with a woman who might not be willing to let him go when he was ready to leave. Even years ago, when he was a student at Oxford, he'd made it brutally clear to a couple of successive ladies that he was interested in sex. Period.

Not that he was cruel to them. They'd gone into the affairs with their experienced eyes wide open. They'd been wined and dined and provided with suitably discreet and impressive gifts. He'd been a highly attractive and titillating man, a conquest for them to display in the stodgier parties of England's upper crust. No one could decide if he was a modern-day soldier of financial fortune or just a mysterious, moneyed man who rarely discussed his past.

He'd found that women were fascinated by the mystery that hung about him.

And that had suited him fine.

Because he had no interest in telling them a damn thing about himself.

He wasn't going to lay open his guts for their greedy gaze. He was nauseated by shows of sympathy from pale little city girls who'd never experienced anything more traumatic than a fired nanny in their well-polished lives. He didn't need their pity. And he didn't want it.

He should have felt a certain disdain for a woman like Alyssa Jones. She was wealthy, primarily through inheritance, and not by the sweat of her own pretty brow. She was determined to have her way, no matter what he or his father said to try to dissuade her. That stubborn arrogance irritated him in anyone. But for her to come here under that lame excuse that she'd been invited . . . !

Hell, he wasn't that naive. He'd been manipulated by women often enough to see through an old ruse like that.

Then, last night in Mariko's house, he had seen Alyssa clearly for the first time. She had looked pure and clean, sitting there with her freshly washed hair dampening the tops of her shoulders, her slender feet tucked neatly beneath her hip.

And those eyes . . . wide and gray and clear of pretense. . . . He vividly recalled the feel of her wrist when she'd tried to leave, and he had grabbed her and forced her to her knees beside him.

Slender bones. Smooth skin. Alyssa Jones was as warm and soft as a sea breeze in early summer. Small, yet strong. He sensed the strength of trim muscles beneath the soft exterior. She wasn't just a hothouse flower, then. She exercised that elegantly curved little body of hers. He also sensed the fire within her. It had flashed like lightning in her smoky eyes when she'd glared at him from her hands and knees. It had sent the blood racing into his veins. It had aroused him. He wanted to taste that fire.

John was deeply annoyed at himself for this unexpected lapse in his usually impeccable self-control. He had obviously been without a woman in his bed for too damn long. That probably accounted for the problem. But he'd tired of flying down to Singapore to see his last mistress over two years ago. She had been happy enough to accept a money settlement, of course.

He watched Alyssa touch the water trickling through a piece of hollow bamboo, imagining what her fingertips would feel like on his skin. Hell, if he couldn't convince her to leave, maybe he'd proposition her instead. He'd work Alyssa Jones out of his system one way or another.

Alyssa turned and was momentarily startled by the expression she glimpsed on John Mori's face. He had been following her at a distance, watching in silence as she admired his elegant garden of stone and pine and falling water. The darkness in his eyes and the intentness of his gaze fastened on her made her want to turn and flee.

The naked look dissolved as he carefully masked his feelings from her view.

A short, thick-waisted woman in a dark blue *kimono* and white, coat-style, *mama-san* apron appeared at the opening of the house.

"Come eat!" she ordered. She turned and hurried away, paying no attention to whether they were following.

"Your housekeeper?" Alyssa inquired politely.

John laughed. The change in his features made Alyssa's heart skip a beat.

"More like the woman who has appointed herself the manager of the Mori family household, for which we are to be suitably respectful and appreciative."

When they reached the Western-style dining room, the gray-haired old lady was waiting impatiently. A timid young woman hovered a few feet behind her, holding an empty tray and obviously waiting for the older woman's next order.

John introduced Alyssa to the elderly housekeeper first.

"Alyssa, this is Etsu. Etsu, this is Alyssa Jones, our guest."

Etsu and Alyssa bowed. They each acknowledged the introduction. In Japanese.

John stared at Alyssa for a split second. Then he introduced the younger woman, who worked under Etsu's supervision. Alyssa and the young woman greeted one another.

They sat down. Food had already been placed on the table. It looked as if it had been painted by an artist. The aromas made Alyssa's mouth water.

"You need anything else right now, Johnny-chan?" Etsu asked, her wrinkled face a picture of serious concern.

"No, Etsu. Thanks."

"I go fix a room for missy, then," Etsu said, bustling off with a sly look in Alyssa's direction.

Alyssa thought she detected a mischievous light in old Etsu's watery eyes. *Just what I need,* Alyssa thought resignedly. *More mischief in my life.* She picked up the clear soup and sipped.

"Johnny-chan?" Alyssa asked innocently, when she was between the soup and another tasty appetizer.

John swallowed his tea in a gulp, barely avoiding choking. Looking at Alyssa from beneath lowering brows, he muttered, "I've known her a long time."

Alyssa nodded knowingly.

"I'll bet Etsu could tell me a lot about you, Mr. Mori," she said, warming to her subject.

John eyed her closely.

"She could, but she won't."

Alyssa took that as a challenge. She rather enjoyed a challenge.

"Are you sure?"

"Positive, Miss Jones. Etsu understands the meaning of personal loyalty and self-sacrifice."

"From the way you say that, I assume you believe most people don't."

"You assume right."

"Have you always had such a dark view of people, Mr. Mori?" she asked, growing a little more serious.

"I prefer to think of it as realistic," he said dryly.

"You sound like my brother," she said with a sigh.

"Oh?"

"Yes. He's always telling me to be more 'brutally realistic,'" she said.

She caught herself before she said any more, remembering her intention not to let him inside her mind any more than absolutely necessary. He was good at drawing her out when he wanted, she realized. Listening quietly, watching her with those intent blue eyes while they ate their broiled fish and vinegared salad and rice.

"You've decided not to talk about yourself anymore, I take it?" he guessed after a few minutes of deafening silence.

He looked somewhat amused, she thought. She lifted her chin stubbornly.

"I'd rather hear the story of your life, Mr. Mori," she said pointedly.

"Why?"

"Know thy enemy," she quoted.

"It seems you and I have the same goal," he said easily. "How about finding some common ground and seeing if we can both get what we want?"

"That sounds suspiciously reasonable," she pointed out.

He grinned.

"I'm known as an eminently reasonable man in many circles," he replied.

She looked doubtful.

"I can't say that's been my experience with you."

"Why don't we try a new experience, then?" he said softly.

He hadn't intended to look into her eyes so deeply, but for some reason, all of a sudden, he didn't want to look away.

"What kind of experience did you have in mind?" she asked weakly, unable to break free of his gaze, feeling as if she were falling into an abyss.

"Let's go back to the beginning. Tell me again why you want my father to loan your gallery a sword that means more to him than his life?"

Alyssa swallowed.

"Because it shouldn't be kept here, in the middle of nowhere, when it is one of the most famous swords ever made.

And because it should be reunited with the sword guard that was made for it. That I have in my possession.''

John poured her some green tea.

''Doesn't it matter to you at all, Miss Jones, that my eighty-year-old father has told you for several years now that he doesn't want to be parted from that sword? That he treasures it more than everything else he owns? Doesn't that count for anything with you?''

Alyssa leaned forward, pleading for him to understand.

''That sword is a link between us,'' she said softly. ''I have the other piece of the link...the sword guard. Ever since my mother died, I've dreamed of being able to reunite the *tsuba* and the *katana*. I have the *tsuba*. You have the *katana*. And up until last night,'' she added quietly, ''I was under the impression that I had your father's permission.''

John frowned and stared at her for a long time. She was good. It was easy to believe she was telling the truth. It had to be a lie, of course, but he had to admit, she was convincing. He sipped his tea and considered how to peel back another layer of her mask, how to get to the truth beneath.

He stood up abruptly.

''Since we've finished eating, perhaps you'd join me in a walk? There's something you should see, I think.''

Alyssa followed him into the house. When they reached a center room, she was surprised to see a man kneeling Zen-style outside the door. He was wearing a short sword and a walkie-talkie. A peculiar combination, she thought. Not to mention a little unnerving.

John motioned for her to go into the room.

There was a man lying on a *futon*-style bed on the floor. A nurse sat at his feet, monitoring his condition, apparently. He seemed to be having trouble breathing.

''Miss Jones, this is my father, Isamu Mori. He's been ill with pneumonia for the past two weeks.''

Alyssa turned and stared at John in shock.

''Now, tell me again how my father invited you here,'' he said. His voice was dangerously soft.

Alyssa was dismayed.

''But I saw the letter!'' she insisted. ''And the *hanko*.''

He went to a wall, slid back the *shoji* screen and opened a chest. Inside, he removed a small locked box. He dialed the combination and opened it. He withdrew a small cylindrical object with Isamu Mori's name carved in Japanese on one end.

"This *hanko?*" he asked, eyes narrowed. "It hasn't left the box. Only he and I have the combination."

"But...maybe someone made a duplicate," she said, saying the first thing that occurred to her.

John returned the cylindrical seal to its tiny safe and closed the *shoji.*

"That would invite my attention, Miss Jones," he said slowly. "No one on Onijima would do that, I can assure you."

Alyssa looked at the elderly man lying on the bed.

"How is he?" she whispered anxiously.

"Better."

He lightly touched her elbow and led her back outside.

"Do you always have an armed guard at his door?" Alyssa asked, perplexed as to why that was necessary.

"It's a habit my father has chosen not to break."

"He always has a guard at his bedroom door?" she asked, aghast.

"You aren't in Kansas anymore, Dorothy," he misquoted dryly.

"But you just told me no one on this island would raise a hand against you."

"True. But the same can't be said for those off the island. Not everyone wants to work for a living. Some prefer to take what someone else already has."

"Well, maybe those people had something to do with the *hanko* and the message," she said triumphantly.

"That was precisely why I suggested we talk about you, your brother and your business partner, Miss Jones."

Alyssa flushed.

"I'm an honest person. So is my brother. We all are."

She crossed her fingers. Her brother had been in a few jams, she knew, but nothing to hang a cloud over his head. It had just been silly stuff. Bad judgment. He was growing out of it. And working with George had been a godsend.

George Bodney was helping to polish the rough edges off her brother. After having almost the sole responsibility of doing so for so many years, Alyssa welcomed the interest. Besides, ever since he was a teenager, Alasdair had been trying to free himself from her influence. That was natural, of course. Still, she was glad that George had come along and offered to form a partnership with them when she'd been organizing the gallery.

Alyssa returned to her original point.

"Look, Mr. Mori, don't you and your father have any enemies? Someone who might want to do something like this?"

"Perhaps, but you're still way ahead of them on the list."

"Why me? I was nearly killed! No matter what you think of my sense of integrity, I can assure you that I wouldn't intentionally crash my own plane!" She was flabbergasted that he couldn't see that.

He seemed undecided whether to respond directly.

"Perhaps your accomplices betrayed you, Miss Jones," he said softly.

"I don't *have* any accomplices!" she said grittily. "I didn't plot anything. And if you're back to implying that my brother would try to kill me, I think you're losing your marbles, John Mori! Aside from the fact that he wouldn't do such a thing, why on earth would somebody try to kill me *before* I got here and obtained the sword?"

"I don't have an answer for that," he admitted.

"You see!"

"But there are some possibilities."

Alyssa groaned and rolled her eyes. "Why don't you take the simplest possibility," she suggested vehemently, "that someone on Onijima faxed me that letter, and you and I are both being victimized by that!"

"That's possible," he conceded. His face hardened. "But it's unlikely."

"So we've argued to a draw again," she said tiredly.

"It would appear so."

"Look, can I at least try to call my brother again? He should be home by now." *Surely.* Seeing the stony expression on his face, Alyssa decided to offer him an incentive.

"You can listen to everything I say. If you have a speaker phone, you're welcome to listen to both sides of the conversation. I have nothing to hide. Neither does my brother. I swear it."

She was good. Sincere. Earnest. Fresh and youthful. John found himself wanting to believe her. He recalled the conversation he had with Captain Waylon shortly before he was flown to Japan. The pilot didn't remember getting into his life vest. Couldn't remember getting out of his seat belt. Last thing he'd seen was the instrument panel; then he'd slammed chest first into the control wheel.

"You didn't have to get that pilot out of the plane," he said.

Alyssa blinked, disoriented by the unexpected shift in the conversation.

"What? Captain Waylon? Of course I did. I couldn't let the man drown."

"It could have cost you your life."

"It didn't."

"That plane sank fast. The water must have been rising up quickly while you got him out of his seat and into his life vest."

"Yes," she said in a thin voice. "We barely made it."

He saw the memories flood back into her eyes. Fear. Bleak terror as the cold water tried to swallow her alive. She was closing her eyes, as if closing a door in her mind and shutting the terror out.

He decided to give her the inch that she wanted. If it wasn't for her heroism, the pilot would be sleeping with the plankton. While he wasn't convinced she was completely trustworthy, it was possible that Alyssa hadn't planned whatever was going on. Maybe she was being used. Assuming that she was telling the truth about having received that letter, identifying the person who faxed it to her would undoubtedly go a long way to solving the mystery.

He hoped he wasn't making a mistake in giving her the slight benefit of the doubt. It could be that his primitive instincts were interfering with his intellect. He had to be careful not to let lust cloud his critical thinking skills where Alyssa Jones was concerned.

They had returned to the garden. Its tranquility had a soothing effect on Alyssa.

"This is truly beautiful," she told him with heartfelt sincerity. "I love *bonsai*. I have one at home."

"Oh?"

"A pine. About a hundred years old. It was a gift to my parents from one of my father's Japanese business associates." She looked at the carefully manicured and maintained trees, appreciating the wealth of human devotion that had brought each one to such rare perfection. "Each one must have a fascinating history," she murmured, glancing at John curiously, hoping he might tell her about them.

Alyssa was genuinely interested in such stories, but she also hoped it might open a channel of communication between them. After talking with him, she was becoming convinced that he could be persuaded to trust her, if only she persevered. He was simply an exceptionally wary man when it came to trust. She wasn't sure how much of that was the circumstances and how much was a generalized distrust of people he didn't know well. Or maybe it was women, she thought. Some men had a special distrust of women.

She had no doubt that the majority of women would easily overlook that small failing in him. John Mori projected a masculinity that appealed to a woman at a very basic level. And he was a handsome devil. There was no doubt about that, she thought uneasily.

Before he could respond to her invitation to talk about his *bonsai* collection, they were interrupted by Suzie and Henry Chan. Suzie hurried over and gave John a friendly hug. She was wreathed in smiles.

"Hey, Johnny-chan, there you are! We wondered where you'd got to!" She gave Alyssa a sly glance and a mischievous grin. "You showing Alyssa your etchings, huh?"

Alyssa blushed at the implication.

John looked irritated.

"It's just a little joke," Suzie protested, laughing. She gently punched John's arm. "Where's your sense of humor gone to, Johnny? Alyssa chased it away?"

"Did you want something?" John asked pointedly.

Henry stepped forward.

"We just wondered how Miss Jones was doing. We went by Mariko's and she told us that you brought her up here." Henry grinned at Alyssa and gave her a little bow. "We helped fish you out of the water," he informed her, just in case she was unaware of it. He gave John a sideways glance. "And we found the pilot."

"Oh. Thank you very much," Alyssa said sincerely. She shook hands with both of them. "If I can ever do anything in return, please tell me. I will do whatever I can for you."

"I'd be careful what I offered to Henry and Suzie," John said dryly. "They're a lot richer than they look. They didn't get that way by missing an opportunity when it knocks on their door."

Henry feigned a hurt look.

"Why, Johnny, you know we give to the temple. Suzie and me are very charitable people."

John laughed.

"Yeah, Henry. And I know where you got that loot, too. And just how hard you had to work for it."

Suzie giggled and drew Alyssa away. She looked at John with the eyes of a young girl begging for a favor.

Alyssa found that a little odd. Suzie had to be in her thirties. And Alyssa had the feeling that Suzie was nobody's fool.

"Johnny," Suzie said. "Why don't I show Alyssa the view of Onijima? I think Henry wants to talk business. I sure you don't want Alyssa around for that. And she probably want to see the famous rocks of Onijima before you kick her off the island. How about it, Johnny? Okay with you?"

"All right," he agreed. "But keep close together." He gave Alyssa a warning look. "I'd hate to have my houseguest get lost in the forest. She might be tempted to wander, Suzie. Keep an eye on her."

Suzie laughed and made a muscle with her right arm.

"Don't worry, Johnny. I still got my black belt. She won't get away from me!"

Alyssa stared at Suzie. Great. Suzie might be full of energy and bubbling like a fuzz-brain, but she was female

muscle. No doubt that was why John was letting them go for
a stroll out of his sight.

"You won't have any trouble from me," Alyssa assured
both John and Suzie, trying to retain her sense of humor.
"The only belts I have are leather."

Suzie laughed and led her out of the garden, into the pine-
covered woods of Onijima.

Alyssa felt John Mori's eyes on her until they were out of
sight. She had the eerie sensation that he was still watching
her, in his mind's eye.

She tried to shake off the sensation.

"Is this the first time you been around here?" Suzie asked
curiously.

"Yes. It's a beautiful island."

"Oh, yeah. Onijima great. Be a top tourist stop, don't
you think?"

"Somehow I don't think John Mori would go for tour-
ists," Alyssa said doubtfully.

"No." Suzie laughed. "John tries to keep people away.
Says our business is better kept small and private here. Says
times are changing, says we can't be hustlers like before.
John wants us to be respectable!" Her mirth rolled out like
the tinkling of temple bells.

Alyssa found Suzie's humor infectious and laughed a little herself.

"That's good," Suzie said encouragingly. "After all you
been through, you need to laugh. I know. I been a pearl
diver, you know. I know how scared you can be when the
sea tries to get you. Happened to my father long time ago.
My mother was saved, but Father went down with the
boat."

"I'm sorry," Alyssa murmured.

Suzie waved it off and grinned.

"But you got to go on, you know? You got to take care
of yourself in this life. Nobody else is gonna take care of
you. Well, Henry and me, we look out for each other, of
course, but when Henry gets married, I'll have to take care
of myself." She giggled again. "Or get a man to take care of
me. But Henry says no man tough enough to put up with

me. I tell him he full of it, that I'll find a man stronger than me.''

Alyssa didn't know what to say. Suzie was overwhelming her with all this personal candor. She didn't want to upset Suzie by saying something that might insult her. On the other hand, the idea of throwing yourself on the mercy of a man to care for you for all your days seemed a little risky to Alyssa. It wasn't as if Suzie was talking about marrying for love.

"Do they arrange marriages around here?" Alyssa ventured cautiously.

"Oh yeah. My brother's turned down a few offers for me over the years. There were a lot when I was young... you know, seventeen, eighteen, nineteen." Suzie shrugged philosophically. "They thought I'd get a big dowry from John, since Henry and me been his friend since he was little...."

"Is that so?" Alyssa's curiosity sharpened. "Where did you meet him?"

"Hong Kong."

"Really? Is that where you're all from?"

"Yeah. Henry and me went to the Buddhist school to learn meditation."

"You're kidding."

Suzie giggled.

"I have too much energy to sit still, so they kick me out. Henry lasted a little longer, but he got in trouble, and the monks kick him out, too. But we liked John, and he was so lonely. All alone, you know." Suzie lowered her voice conspiratorially. "His mother was a no-good woman, had a lot of men. I not telling secrets. Everybody on Onijima know that. Everybody in Hong Kong know it. Johnny, he spent all his time in a boys' school and in that Buddhist temple. When he went home, he always found her with a man. He almost killed one of them. Thought the man was trying to rape his mama." Suzie gave Alyssa a knowing look, shrugged and pushed out her lower lip philosophically. "It wasn't rape. He never trusted women after that, if you ask me."

Alyssa hadn't asked but she was grateful that Suzie had told her. It would explain a lot about him, she realized. Alyssa looked at Suzie curiously.

"Have you ever thought about marrying John? You seem to be good friends...."

Suzie shrugged. Her face became a little less cheerful. And Alyssa sensed Suzie's feelings ran deep on this subject. They were well masked, if that was true, however.

"Johnny and I are old friends. That doesn't make for red-hot lovers. Johnny not the type to get married. Unless he have a red-hot lover he can't stay away from. That might hook him." Suzie grinned. "Besides, I want a man I can manage. I don't think I'd do too good with Johnny that way."

"I don't know," Alyssa said dubiously. "You seemed to get your way very easily in the garden." She admired Suzie's skills, as a matter of fact.

Suzie looked the picture of innocence.

"That was easy. He wanted to talk to Henry alone. He let me talk him into it."

They had been wandering through the forest as they spoke, following a winding path that Suzie apparently was familiar with. Now they arrived at a cliff. Beyond lay the dark blue Pacific Ocean, as far as the eye could see. Below them was the magnificent, rugged coastline.

"It looks like a giant dropped huge clumps of wet clay and it dried," Alyssa said.

"Yeah. That's how one of the stories go."

"Stories?"

"You know...the legends about Onijima. They say giant ogres fought here and when they were through there was nothing but a pile of wet rubble. The mud fell off their huge bodies and it piled up and dried. That's where all that come from down there."

It reminded Alyssa of pictures of the coast of northern China. The legend was a more romantic explanation, of course. She smiled.

"Do you know other legends?" Alyssa asked, following Suzie down a narrow footpath that wound along the edge of the cliff. Nervously, Alyssa clung to the rugged wall of rock and the occasional pine tree root protruding out from it.

"I know a lot," Suzie said cheerfully. "The one about the *samurai* who became *ninja* and were banished to Onijima. That's where the Mori clan came from. You know that?"

"Yes."

"And then there's the one about the great battle when part of the Fujiwara clan sent armada to conquer Onijima. They got sunk. That's where the stories about *samurai* ghosts in the bay come from. I don't believe any that stuff," she said easily. "But it sure good to keep the *samurai* away for a couple hundred years! Now we tell it to the kids to keep them away from the water at night."

"How helpful," Alyssa murmured, gasping as her left foot slipped on loose sand and she imagined herself falling down the mountain to join the ghostly *samurai*. "Do you suppose we could go back? I'm a little out of practice as a mountain goat."

Suzie looked around in dismay.

"I'm so sorry, Alyssa! I didn't think how this would be for someone who doesn't come here often!" Her face was filled with contrition. "It's just a little way. Then we can sit down in the cave and admire the view. Here, let me hold you hand...."

Alyssa gave Suzie her hand, and after a few harrowing yards, she found herself standing in the mouth of a small cave.

The view was breathtaking.

"This is one of Johnny's favorite spots," Suzie confided conspiratorially. "He comes here and plays his flute sometimes. I can hear him all the way down in the bay when the sea is quiet and there's no wind."

"John Mori plays a flute?" Alyssa was fascinated.

"*Shakuhachi.* He learned it from the monks. Along with *kendo* and *karate*...."

"And meditation," Alyssa pointed out with a laugh.

"That, too."

The wind began to pick up and for a while, they sat and watched and listened. The pines moaned and the sea caressed the rocks below.

There was a sound of falling stones and they turned to look back up the trail. It was covered with loose rock and an upturned tree.

"Oh, no!" Suzie exclaimed, horrified. "We can't walk over that. Might fall down the mountain." She frowned and studied the mountain face above them. Then she put her hands on Alyssa's shoulders and spoke with great seriousness. "Look, Johnny'll kill me if anything happen to you. I promise him you be okay. You stay here. I'll climb up the rock face...."

Alyssa stared at the naked rock and looked back in horror at Suzie.

"You can't do that! You'd need mountain-climbing equipment to scale that!"

Suzie grinned. "I learn rock climbing from a boyfriend last year. I think I can do it. I got strong fingers...." She flexed them in demonstration.

Alyssa shook her head. "Absolutely not. We'll just sit here until someone comes looking for us."

Suzie shook her head. "I can get out. Then I bring one of the bodyguards, and we clear the path from above. Then you and I walk back up. No problem."

"But..." Alyssa was left with a protest in her mouth as Suzie, quick as a spider, began going up the wall of rock.

Toehold here. Fingerhold there. Alyssa watched with her heart in her mouth as Suzie agilely made her way up the fifteen-yard, nearly vertical climb.

When she reached a sturdy tree, she looked down and grinned at Alyssa.

"I be right back. Don't go anywhere!"

Alyssa couldn't see any likelihood that she would.

Time dragged by. Alyssa made a cautious attempt to climb over the rubble. When she felt herself sliding, she backed off. She explored the cave. Found a hand-hewn bench. A few rocks.

Then rubble began pouring down the mountainside.

She rushed to look but got covered with dirt for her effort.

The mouth of the cave was being obliterated, she realized, as she backed inside.

"Help! Stop! I'm inside the cave!" she screamed at the top of her lungs.

The rock and dirt kept sliding, till only a foot remained. A foot of daylight. Choking from the dust, Alyssa tried to push away the dirt. She heard it falling down the mountainside. If she attempted to climb through the hole, she would tumble down after it. The ledge was covered with dirt and rock. And the mass was too unstable for her to scramble across.

She was trapped.

Chapter 5

Fine dust permeated the air. Backing away until her shoulder blades hit the rocky wall of the back of the cave, Alyssa coughed until she nearly choked to death. There was no escape from the dirty haze. With just a narrow opening across the top and no cross ventilation, the dry silt had nowhere to go until gravity could drag it down.

Alyssa pulled her dress up over her mouth and nose and closed her eyes. She coughed until tears ran down her cheeks. Dry, hacking coughs.

Gradually the dust settled onto the cave floor. The smell of dirt clung to her nostrils. She felt as if she'd inhaled enough dust to fill her lungs a hundred times over. Grit coated her mouth, and her throat was so dry that she could barely swallow.

The fine silk dress hadn't been much of a filter, but it had probably saved her from suffocation.

She walked through the dust to the huge pile of rubble that blocked the mouth of the cave. When enough moisture returned to her tongue and throat to venture speaking, she cleared her throat a few times and tried calling for help again. Her shout was weak and hoarse.

She listened for any indication that her cry had been heard.

A bird flew by the front of the cave. Otherwise, there was nothing.

"Help! Suzie! Can you hear me? Help!"

Alyssa coughed over and over as her lungs cleared themselves of as much of the fine grit as possible.

"Help! Somebody! Help! I'm down here! In the cave...."

It didn't do any good. No one came.

Finally, exhausted and beginning to lose her voice, Alyssa sat down on the dusty bench and hugged herself for warmth. It was uncomfortably cool in the cave. She hadn't noticed being chilled when she and Suzie had walked through the woods. Of course, the sun had been overhead. The day had been a mild one for winter, and the long sleeves and knee-length skirt of her silk dress had kept her warm enough.

But now she was cold and rapidly getting colder. The temperature outside the cave was dropping as the sun sank below the other side of the mountain, leaving the cave in the cool shadow of its eastern mountain face.

"Why did I ever think I wanted to come to Onijima?" she muttered.

She was beginning to think the island might be cursed where she was concerned. So far, everything that *could* go wrong *had* gone wrong, and with a vengeance. Her vague fantasies about the legendary isle of demons were turning out to be far removed from its brutal reality.

She could only hope that Suzie had gone for help and someone would be here soon to get her out. Then she would live happily ever after, just like in the fairy tales, she promised herself ruefully.

But what if Suzie had been caught in the landslide? That awful thought struck her like a thunderbolt. Until that moment, she'd assumed that Suzie had already been long gone when the landslide occurred. But so much time had passed since Suzie had left. Alyssa felt sick. *Oh my God, Suzie...* What if the spry, talkative woman was buried beneath rubble farther up the mountain? Alyssa shivered in horror.

Alyssa recalled Suzie's easy banter and inviting gossip. It had been totally disarming, Alyssa thought wistfully. For the first time since the plane crash, Alyssa had felt relaxed. Suzie had accomplished that with her quick smile and openness. Poor Suzie, Alyssa thought, afraid for her. She desperately hoped that nothing had happened to her. What a horrible way to die.

Alyssa tried to stop imagining the awful scene. If Suzie were hurt, or…unable to go for help, well, that left her host to notice her absence. She wondered if John Mori would come and pull her out of this new catastrophe. She could just imagine how irritated he would be. Undoubtedly he'd assume her brother had been up on the cliff shoveling dirt, she thought. Well, if he were coming to dig her out, she preferred that he do it before she died from exposure.

"John Mori, I'm in your cave! Come dig me out!" she shouted before her sanded larynx temporarily gave up the ghost of speech.

Great! she croaked soundlessly. She curled into a ball near the dirt and tried to keep warm. When her larynx had rested a bit, maybe her voice would resurrect itself. Too bad John hadn't left his stupid flute here, she thought irritably.

Alyssa sat up and stared wide-eyed into the gloom. *His flute.*

She needed something to make noise besides her voice. She felt her way over to the bench and began yanking at the wood as hard as she could.

John Mori was standing on a salvage vessel in the middle of Onijima's harbor. He had dropped Henry Chan in town on his way to the docks and had come aboard alone. The vessel's captain, an old friend and sometime business associate, handed John a soggy leather briefcase. The captain was grinning broadly.

"It was like finding a needle in a haystack, John, but it was fun tryin' out the new equipment. Once we located the plane, we nosed around, and this was dangling on part of the door. Looks like it caught on it when somebody was getting out. What's in it, anyway? Gold coins? Stock certificates? Incriminating photographs of politicians?"

Mori took the brine-soaked object by its handle.

"I don't know yet. I've been told that the contents are ir-replaceable," he said dryly. "I'll let you know if that's an exaggeration. Have you had a chance to examine the condition of the plane?"

The bearded, middle-aged salvage captain nodded and popped a stick of gum into his mouth.

"Yep. Got some good photos. We're lifting her up tomorrow or the next day. The jet's basically intact. No evidence of explosion that I can see."

"Then you can't tell me why it went down?"

"Nope. I sure can't. It'll probably take an aviation expert with crash-analysis experience and labs at his disposal to answer that one."

John nodded. He was flying people in already. As soon as Henry told him the captain was in the harbor and had located the jet, he'd phoned the international authorities interested in such matters. When the investigators flew into Onijima in a day or two, he was planning on setting them up in a large hangar at the airfield. He and the charter company that owned the airplane would supply whatever they needed.

In the meantime, however, his gut instinct told him to treat this as some form of sabotage. That charter company that Alyssa had used had an impeccable safety record. He used them occasionally himself to fly in people. It was hard to believe that both engines would inexplicably fail. That's what the pilot had told him. They'd just stopped. As if the fuel simply ceased getting to the engine. But the gauges had all read that the fuel supply was adequate. Everything had been registering normal.

If it *was* some sort of sabotage, had the saboteur been trying to kill Alyssa? Or had she simply been in the wrong place at the wrong time? Or was it a trick to win his sympathy, or that of his father, so that they would soften their resistance to her relentless pursuit of the priceless sword that they had so long denied her?

That was the first thing that had occurred to him—that it was all some sort of twisted trick on Alyssa's part. She'd been hot to get her damned hands on the *katana* for years. She was a persevering witch. It was possible that this could simply be a dramatic effort to manipulate him. It could be intended to soften him, to deceive him into trusting her. After all, the sword was without peers. It was priceless. People had been known to go to extraordinary lengths for the priceless.

The fact that he found Alyssa attractive had made him focus on this possibility. His suspiciousness was a matter of self-defense. Over the years he had noticed that there was a direct relationship between the extent of a woman's beauty and the degree of her deviousness.

Alyssa was a very good-looking woman.

Well, now I have her damned briefcase, and the truth will out.

He was interested in seeing the expression on Alyssa's face when he showed her the briefcase. Would she be relieved? Or would she be shocked?

If it held items that could support what she'd told him, she'd be relieved.

But if it contained nothing, she would turn white with shock. Her game would be up.

He was annoyed to note that deep inside, a part of him wanted fiercely to believe her. He hadn't been this naively eager to believe in someone in a long, long while. There was something about Alyssa Jones that haunted him. She was a warm memory of happiness lost. He hungered for more even though he recognized that this was a potentially dangerous weakness. He detested this sudden, unexpected, unwelcome vulnerability in himself.

But he wasn't a fool. He had no intention of becoming one where Alyssa Jones was concerned, either. If it turned out that this was all some sort of elaborate ruse to allow her to gain access to his father's most precious possession, she would taste the full, bitter flavor of regret for as long as he cared to pour it down her pretty throat.

That sword was as much a part of Isamu Mori as the breath that the old man drew. John doubted the Alyssa would understand that. But he understood. Down to his bones.

The sun's rays slanted low in the west. John shook the salvager's leathery hand, eager to be on his way.

"Give your crew a trip into town at my expense," he suggested. "Mariko will see to it for you. I'll phone her on my way home."

The captain's black-and-gray beard was slashed by a white-toothed grin. He could hear the sounds of a celebration in town already. There was a local festival to honor the restless souls of the *samurai* who'd died in the seas around Onijima. There was a lot of fermented wine and good seafood consumed, along with some gifts to placate the envious ghosts of the long-departed. The rice wine and beer was already flowing among the happy inhabitants. People would be dancing in the streets before long, carrying revelers on their shoulders on simple wooden platforms while others sang and laughed and played a variety of traditional instruments. It was a vestige of medieval life that their ancestors had brought with them into exile when they had been banished from the mainland with the Mori clan centuries ago.

"You sure do know how to make a man feel appreciated, John!" the good captain exclaimed with a hearty laugh. "Lucky for us we were in the neighborhood when you radioed. Call us anytime you need a submersible to fish something out of the water for you. Anytime at all!"

"What do you mean she's not here?"

John Mori stood in the stone-paved entrance to his house and frowned at Etsu. Alyssa should have returned from her walk and been cooling her heels waiting for him for hours.

"She not back," Etsu repeated, looking worried because John was obviously surprised and displeased.

"What about Suzie?"

"She no come back, either."

"Did you send someone out to look for them?"

"No. There was a note. I thought everything okay. Thought Suzie left note."

Etsu removed a piece of paper from her *kimono* sleeve and handed it to John. It was written in Chinese, scrawled in a hurry in pencil on a scrap of plain paper that appeared to have been torn from the back of an envelope. John's first impression was that the paper had probably been snatched from a wastebasket in the front hall. The pencil was probably the one near the phone. He looked into the wastebasket next to it and saw another piece of envelope with a torn edge that looked as if it matched the scrap of paper he was holding in his hand. He read the note.

Honorable John,
We gone to west side mountain to watch sunset.

                                                                            Su

That was all.
"Hell," he muttered.
The sun had set fifteen minutes ago. The handwriting didn't quite look like Suzie's to him. And the grammar in the pencil-scrawled note was peculiar. It looked like something scribbled by a semiliterate foreigner. That described a lot of seamen who came through Onijima. It didn't describe Suzie Chan. She was semiliterate in English. But her grasp of Cantonese was impeccable.
He had a sick feeling in the pit of his stomach.
He handed the damp briefcase to Etsu.
"Put this in the safe behind my desk," he told her. "I'm going out."
She nodded and wrinkled her brow in worry. While old Etsu padded off, John picked up the phone and dialed Kojiro, his most trusted and senior bodyguard.
In Japanese, he asked, "Kojiro-san? I am sorry to bother you at the dinner hour. Please give my apologies to your honorable wife." Kojiro reassured him that was nothing to worry about. "I must ask a favor of you again, Kojiro-san. It appears that I have lost my honored guest."
"Ah? The honorable Miss Jones?"
"Yes. I'm not certain that she's missing. Suzie was with her. But they're both unaccounted for. It may be nothing, but..."
"I be right there, John-san. It is no problem. Should I bring others with me?"
"Yes. One or two. Men you can trust."
"And equipment?"
"The four-wheel drive, audio augmentors, visual scanners in infrared mode, ropes..."

"It is understood. Will be there quickly."

John peeled off his shirt and headed for his room. He would need to be inconspicuous until he was certain what was going on. It had been a while since he'd prowled around at night in black, but his training as a Mori clan member had been quite thorough. Tonight, it would come in handy, he thought grimly.

It was one of those things that, once learned, you never forgot.

Alyssa, her hands blistered from pulling one of the slats off the bench, her mind and body exhausted, was leaning against the wall, dozing.

Some stones trickled down the mountain face and spilled onto the pile of dirt blocking the cave entrance.

She opened her eyes and listened.

For a dreadful moment she wondered if there was some wild animal poking around. She had no idea what lived on Onijima besides birds, sailors and descendants of banished *ninja*.

Then she swallowed hard as another terrifying thought occurred to her. What if this landslide wasn't an accident of nature? What if Suzie had been attacked and killed, and *she* was the next target? Alyssa's blood ran cold in horror. For the first time, she hesitated to call for help.

Anyone searching for her should be calling her name. They should be making plenty of noise as they stomped around in their efforts to locate her. There was no reason for them to be stealthy and at least one good reason to make noise: so that she might hear them and call out to them. Since it was dark, Alyssa thought she should see flashlights or floodlights of some sort scanning the mountainside or trail in search of her.

But Alyssa heard nothing. And it was dark except for a smattering of starlight and a faint glow from the cloud-covered moon.

Her heart was pounding in spite of her best effort to remain calm and cool. She felt terribly vulnerable. She was alone and nearly defenseless.

The trickle of dirt came again. Then there was the faintest hint of a slithering sound, as if a large snake were coming down the side of the mountain.

Onijima had snakes? She shuddered. She absolutely *hated* snakes. Gripping the bench slat with both hands, Alyssa went over to the pile of rubble. She'd hit the thing, whatever it was, before it could get through the opening. Maybe it would go away, or fall down the mountainside. The way her luck had been running recently, she thought it too much to hope for that she might actually mortally wound it, whatever *it* was.

At first she thought there was an extra cloud passing in front of the moon. By the time she realized that the darkness was caused by something peering in at her, it was nearly too late to swing at it. With a flip of a long, coiled tail, it began to drop through the opening. The beast was big but remarkably fast. It filled the narrow aperture and sprayed dirt into the room as it passed through.

Alyssa's slat connected with John just as he slipped into the chamber. He had shimmied down a rope, which was still in front of his body and tailing around his ankles, when the hard wood connected with his left side.

He swore under his breath in Japanese. *Hell, I've found her.* His eyes were accustomed to the darkness. He would have recognized her silhouette anywhere, even in the poor light of the darkened cave.

Before she could take another swing at him, his arms closed around her like a steel vise.

"What the hell are you doing?" he whispered between clenched teeth. "Stop that!"

"John!"

"Very good. Now drop the board."

It slid from her fingers and thumped in the dust.

Alyssa tilted her head back to try to see his face. The terror of being grabbed by a man wrapped in close-fitting black clothing faded away and was replaced with a tremendous sense of relief.

"You scared me out of my skin!" she exclaimed.

He grinned slightly.

"It doesn't feel like it," he murmured, running his hand over her shoulder and hip. When she stiffened primly and would have protested, he covered her mouth with his hand

and whispered, "Keep your voice down. Until I know what happened, we're going to handle this the old-fashioned way."

Her eyes fastened on his. He was swathed in black cloth. She felt a little giddy. It must be hysteria, she thought. After all, how often was a woman rescued by a modern-day *ninja* outside of a Hollywood movie?

She put her arms around him and laid her head on his shoulder.

"Thank God you found me," she murmured. "I've been waiting and waiting. I didn't think anyone was coming, and then I thought maybe it was someone or something coming to get me...." She shivered, remembering the feeling of raw terror that had trickled through her heart. She knew she shouldn't hug him, but she needed to, badly.

"I'm here now," he said softly. "And Kojiro and a couple of our nearest and dearest friends are up top waiting for me to tell them I'm okay." He held her a little away. "You okay?"

She nodded. "Just dirty, scratched and scared as a rabbit."

He could feel her trembling. She was cold as ice but the shaking was as much from fear as it was from the cold, he thought. He rubbed her arms with his hands to warm her up. She molded herself to him, as if afraid to lose his heat. Deep inside his belly, a hot flame of desire flickered to life.

He gave the rope a quick series of tugs. It was his signal to Kojiro and the others that everything was under control.

"Why didn't you come sooner?" she murmured against his shoulder.

"I just learned you were missing less than an hour ago. Where the hell is Suzie?"

Alyssa shook her head but kept her face against his warm strength. Even the scent of his skin was comforting, she realized.

"I don't know. She scrambled up the cliff after the first slide on the trail. I thought she'd bring back help, but then the other slide covered up the cave. And then I called but no one answered."

She held her breath painfully.

"Do you suppose she's...under the rubble, or at the bottom of the mountain?"

John felt a stab of deep pain. He'd known Suzie Chan almost all his life. She and her brother were the closest things he had for family for a while when he was small, before Isamu Mori took him to be his son.

"I don't know," he said grimly. "You didn't hear anything? A scream or a cry of pain or anything?"

"Nothing."

Mori stood in silence, holding her. What the hell was going on? He frowned. It was a little hard to blame this accident on Alyssa. Or on her brother, for that matter. This "accident" was too convenient and too nearly lethal to be believable, as far as John was concerned. It had to involve someone familiar with Onijima's geography. Someone who knew where Alyssa was going to be this afternoon. But how could that be? Suzie had spontaneously invited her to go for a walk.

John was suddenly thunderstruck. What if Suzie's invitation wasn't spontaneous? His stomach clenched. He didn't want to believe that.

"Let's get you back to the house," he said quietly. "We can talk after you're cleaned up."

She leaned back then, her eyes open and pained and genuinely confused. She searched his face, but it was still partially covered with black cloth. Only his eyes were visible, but they were as hard and unrevealing as always.

"This visit isn't going the way I had planned it, you know," she said shakily. "I had planned to have a nice, civilized conversation with you and your father. Instead, I keep fighting for my life and keep being rescued by a man who transforms himself into whatever beast he needs to become." She felt the heat of his body through their clothing, warming her. In spite of herself, a small petal of desire unfolded inside her. *Oh, God, no...*

John removed the black cloth that covered his face and gently wrapped it around Alyssa's head like a kerchief. It wasn't much, but it would help keep her a little warmer.

He ran his lean fingers over her face and neck, hating the grime that had nearly suffocated her.

"You have elegant bones," he murmured.

Alyssa gave a soft, startled laugh.

"Thanks. I'm surprised you can appreciate them under all the Onijima dirt that's covering them."

He smiled slightly and his gaze traveled over her features with the intentness of a hunting sea eagle.

"After you get it washed off, we'll start all over again."

She looked at him in surprise.

"You mean . . . you'll believe me?"

"Let's just say that after two near-fatal accidents in two days, you've earned the right to get a fighting chance to make your case."

Her face lit up with delight.

"That almost makes it worth all the trouble!" She laughed softly and looked at her nails. "I tried to look neatly manicured, professionally elegant and smooth, you know."

"When you got on the plane to fly here?"

"Mmm-hmm. I wanted to impress you and your father as someone you would be pleased to work with." She grinned. "No one told me you had a soft spot in your heart for people who look like something the cat dragged in."

His eyes glinted dangerously.

"I don't. You're a first."

From the way he said it, Alyssa had the impression that he intended her to be the last, too.

"Tell me if anything hurts," he said, checking her over with his hands. "Before we climb back up, I need to know whether anything's cracked or broken."

His strong, muscular hands moved over her head, neck and shoulders. Down her slender, well-shaped arms. Around her ribs. She flinched when he brushed the undersides of her breasts.

"I said I was okay," she reminded him breathlessly.

"Hold still."

"But..."

"Sometimes a cracked bone isn't noticed right away. You've been too scared to think about how you feel, so maybe you've repressed the sensation."

"I would feel a broken bone. Believe me, I'm fine."

"Sometimes the pain doesn't kick in till later."

"I feel pain." When he looked at her face with sharp inquiry, she hurried to explain. "I mean, I can feel bruises all over me. Some left over from the plane crash. Others from coughing up dust till my throat's raw, and from blisters on my hand when I rubbed my skin raw trying to get that slat loose so I could make some noise."

His hands slid back down to her waist, her hips, her thighs. He knelt in front of her, wanting to do a lot more than run his hands over her to check for damned broken bones. *Hell.* He didn't usually find a woman he barely knew this arousing. Much less a woman he'd seen primarily half-buried in dust or half-drowned.

Maybe he'd been too isolated. His urges had been repressed so long that the first available female to come his way was enough temptation to make him crave satisfaction.

She was stepping away, trying to push his hands off of her.

John looked up and realized he'd stopped examining her and had been kneeling there with his hands on her hips, thinking. *Bloody hell!*

"I'd say you're all right," he muttered abruptly. He straightened and quietly pulled her close to the dirt-stuffed mouth of the cave. With businesslike, methodical thoroughness, he slipped the heavy rope around her. He then proceeded to tie it around himself.

"That raw hand of yours doesn't look like it can grasp a rope worth a tinker's dam," he pointed out.

Alyssa was trying not to touch him, but it wasn't easy. He'd intended them to be tied close. She stared up at him.

"I'll hold on if I have to," she promised. "Believe me, I don't relish spending the rest of my life trying to decorate and run plumbing into this cave."

He grinned.

"No. I guess you wouldn't. All right, so you're motivated. Have you ever done any mountain climbing? With pitons?"

"No," she said, shaking her head. "But I'll be happy to take the condensed course in the next five minutes."

He shook his head.

"It's too dark and too dangerous to coach you through it. I'm going to take you up with me. Hold on. Tight."

He waited while she put her arms around his neck.

Their bodies were plastered together. His cheek was warm and smooth against hers. She felt his heart beating. Slow, strong strokes. Felt the hard, round muscle of his thighs and belly.

"And your legs," he ordered tersely.

"Huh?"

"Wrap your legs around my waist. Link your feet behind my hips."

Alyssa did as he said, lifting herself with his help. She felt the blush rise in her stomach and slide all the way up to her hairline as the most intimate part of her body snuggled up against his hard waist. It wasn't easy to keep the *geta* on her feet. She curled her toes and hoped for the best.

"Relax, Alyssa," he said, grinning.

Which only made her tense up more.

"I'm not used to wrapping myself around a man I barely know," she pointed out primly.

He laughed and began hauling them up through the opening.

"Oh? Just those you know well?"

"That's not what I meant!"

He pulled them through the dirt and together they wriggled through the aperture.

"What did you mean?"

Their eyes connected in the moonlight. Warmth flooded Alyssa. Two people couldn't get any closer than they were, unless they were making love. Alyssa's heart beat faster. She swallowed hard, trying to disregard the intoxicating curiosity that was stealing through her. She found herself wondering what it would feel like to be in more comfortable surroundings with John Mori. With his mysterious gaze fixed on her with the intentions of a determined lover. With his hard mouth on hers. And his hands sliding . . .

She blinked and grabbed at her galloping thoughts before they carried her off into a third catastrophe. Two were more than enough.

"I meant that I don't do this at all, but especially not with a virtual stranger!" Her voice sounded strangely weak and hollow to her. God, was she that scared of the feelings that John Mori was mysteriously bringing to the surface in her?

"They say it only hurts the first time," he told her softly. Then he grinned and pulled them up into the air.

She tightened her legs and brought the heel of one foot against his muscular buttocks.

He grunted softly.

"Guess I'm taking it too fast for you," he whispered with feigned penitence. Whispering into her ear with husky sincerity, he added, "It gets better, baby. Be patient. We'll take it slow and easy."

He laughed as he felt her stiffen with indignation at the ambiguity of his words.

He grunted as he pulled them up again. The wind caught them and they twirled at the end of the rope. John let his shoulder slam against the hard rock, sparing her more delicate body, as the breeze blew them back.

Chilly, damp air kissed every inch of Alyssa's skin. Arms. Legs. Her fanny beneath the skirt hanging in tatters around her waist. She shivered.

"Keep your face against my neck," he murmured into her ear. "My heat will keep you warm." *Hell.* He was hot enough for both of them, he thought wryly. And if she kept snuggling against his belly, he'd also be hard enough for both of them.

Alyssa did as he suggested, soaking up his warmth, while John pulled them up the face of the mountain, grunting when the wind slammed him against the jagged rock, concentrating on the work instead of the soft, shapely woman clinging to him.

When they reached the top, eager hands pulled them over. She was quickly untied and someone threw a black cloth jacket over her. The first thing that Alyssa noticed about the rescuers was that they were all wearing the same black costumes that John was wearing. They were *all ninja?* She thought that was just a myth, or a hobby for people who'd seen too many *kung-fu* movies. Apparently not.

"No sign of Suzie?" John asked his men.

They were rapidly pulling up the ropes and looping them efficiently over their muscular shoulders. Within minutes, they were ready to go. There would be no trace of them left behind, except a few unidentifiable footprints.

"No, John-san. Suzie-chan not been here since you go down mountain for honorable Miss Jones."

So where was she? Alyssa wondered, worried. What had happened to her?

"Will you look for her?" Alyssa asked John anxiously. "She may be hurt."

"I'll send them back to keep looking," he said. He didn't think it would do much good, though. If she'd fallen off the mountain, it might be difficult to find her in broad daylight. And if she'd abandoned Alyssa, she was probably long gone and in hiding.

When they got back to the house, they entered through the back entrance, through the *bonsai* garden. They heard voices coming from the front of the house. Etsu. And a man with a rough manner about him. He had an accent that was a peculiar blend of English dialects—predominantly Australian, a dab of Hong Kong British and a hefty interweaving of Philippines American.

John halted and frowned ferociously.

"That sounds like Esau Holling. What the bloody hell is he doing here?"

It was a little late, even by Onijima's relaxed social standards. Besides, Esau never dropped by for just a friendly drink. With Esau, there was always an underlying motive. So what was the bastard's scheme tonight? John wondered irritably. He uttered a few guttural orders in Japanese. Kojiro and the other two men bowed and melted back into the darkness.

"Come on," he muttered, grabbing Alyssa's elbow and maneuvering her toward a small hidden gate at the back of the garden. "I'll sneak you in through my private entrance. Consider yourself honored. I rarely take anyone this way."

She opened her eyes wide.

"Thank you, Mr. Mori."

"After such an intimate evening, you might as well call me John," he said dryly.

Alyssa blushed and swore she'd stand her ground with the amoral pirate. The man was enjoying this! He obviously wasn't much of a gentleman.

"*John,*" she conceded tightly, forcing a smile. She followed him through a narrow doorway and watched him roll a lock until it released. When he took off his shoes and stepped inside, she removed hers and followed him. It was dark, and she couldn't see much at first. "Where are we?"

He slid the door closed behind her.

"Welcome to my private chambers."

He turned on a light.

Alyssa looked around and immediately realized that they were in his bedroom. When she glanced back to see what John planned to do next, she discovered that he was removing his clothes.

Chapter 6

He wasn't so much unfastening clothes as unwinding them.

The black covering that he'd worn over his head was now a strangely shaped cloth at his feet. The shirtlike jacket with unique fabric and seams that allowed it to cling to him and still stretch easily in any direction was being peeled off next. Alyssa assumed that the clever design permitted the wearer absolute freedom of movement, no doubt a crucial requirement in a fight.

That garment joined the first piece of clothing on the floor.

Which left Mori's elegantly muscled chest, arms and stomach as naked as an unsheathed blade.

He certainly didn't look like a man who spent his days behind a desk, she thought, momentarily hypnotized by his raw, male physique. Maybe George had been misinformed on that point, she thought faintly.

Mori glanced up and lifted an eyebrow in cynical amusement.

"Don't tell me that you've never seen a man's bare chest."

"Don't be silly! Of course I have!"

"I'm relieved to hear that. I thought for a moment that you might keel over in maidenly shock."

"Don't be ridiculous! I simply wasn't expecting a man who makes his money conducting stock transactions to look like the latest martial arts heartthrob." She could have kicked herself as soon as the giveaway words rolled off her tongue.

"Why, thank you." He grinned.

Alyssa blushed. The gleam in his eyes just made her feel worse.

"I didn't mean that you *were* a heartthrob," she hastened to amend, lest he get the wrong idea. She certainly didn't want him to think that *she* might view him like that! Even if she did.

"Why, Miss Jones, you wound my fragile male ego."

"Fragile?" She gave a short, disbelieving laugh. "I'll bet your ego is as tough as rhino hide! Besides," she argued, "you look more amused than wounded."

"Male pride. We're not permitted to show our tenderer feelings."

"Male *teasing*," she countered. Male pride, her Aunt Fanny!

He grinned and shrugged his magnificent, muscular shoulders.

"You're fun to tease," he said unapologetically.

"I'm so glad that you're having a good time!"

He laughed softly. He did enjoy teasing her, seeing the color rush to her cheeks. She'd been embarrassed to be caught admiring his body, and John found that strangely endearing. He hadn't been around women that easily embarrassed, he supposed. But there was something about Alyssa's reaction that touched him. She had a freshness, a naiveté about her, that he found fascinating.

And he liked arousing her interest in him as a man. He liked it more than he should, if he was thinking with his brains instead of his hormones.

He wondered if there was a man in her life. Or in her bed. John would have to kick him out, if there was. Normally, he avoided women who already had husbands, fiancés or boyfriends. He had great contempt for adultery. He'd seen enough of it when he was young. His mother hadn't cared what he thought when she brought home stray males from the bar. And she hadn't worried that some of the men had families, fiancées, girlfriends. Or children who would have been desolated to discover what their father had been up to.

He'd promised himself never to cause another child the kind of agony that he'd gone through with his mother.

He'd stuck to single women. Women who wanted to stay free.

He wondered how Alyssa could be classified. And for the first time, he wasn't absolutely certain he would keep away from her if she didn't fit the mold.

John slid back a wall panel, revealing a large closet filled with his clothes. At one end, fine wool suits, crisply pressed dress shirts and a row of highly polished designer shoes. At the other end, jeans, slacks and sweatpants, and the various shirts and sweaters that could be worn with them. Formal wear, business clothes and casual outfits. All neatly hung in their place. He'd come a long way from that dirty urchin wearing last year's cast-offs in the slums of Hong Kong.

There was one thing that Alyssa had said that bothered him. He decided to dig a little and see what he could find out.

As he selected some clothes to wear, he asked casually, "How did you know about my stock investing?"

"I don't remember exactly." She thought about it, relieved by the shift away from more personal topics. "I think George mentioned it last summer—no…maybe a couple of summers ago. He and Dair and I were trying to come up with a fresh angle to interest you in discussing a loan of the sword. So George did a little background check—nothing you'd find offensive, I promise. Just the usual kind of information that people in business can get about other business people."

"George . . . ?" He kept his naked back to her.

Alyssa watched in fascination as the muscles rippled as he lifted items from the closet. She fanned her face, feeling unaccountably warm. John Mori was having the strangest effect on her.

He turned to face her. Immediately she got herself under control. He'd been asking about George, she reminded herself, frantically trying to pick up the dropped thread of the conversation.

"George Bodney," she explained. "He's my business partner. And Alasdair's, of course."

"I see." And suddenly John did see.

Of course, she'd said. She thought of her brother as a damned appendage, and vice versa, John realized, thunderstruck at the implications. *Of course* they shared a business partner. *Of course.* What more natural for two kids who never developed their own completely separate lives as adults? He wondered if Alyssa ever resented it. Or if Alasdair did? And he wondered what had caused it.

Clothes slung over his shoulder, he closed the sliding panel door and turned to face Alyssa.

"I take it that you and your brother are quite close?"

"Like Siamese twins," Alyssa said with a rueful laugh. She sighed. Sometimes she thought they were too dependent on one another. She wouldn't admit it to anyone, though. It would seem like a terrible betrayal. Her brother deserved her loyalty.

"How did that come about? I thought siblings were supposed to engage in rivalry, not mutual self-support."

"We didn't have much choice."

"Oh?"

"We were orphaned at a young age. First my mother died. Then, within the year, my father."

"I'm sorry." And he truly was. He could see the veil of sadness in her eyes. It had hurt her. It still ached. He knew what that kind of pain felt like, and he could feel hers all the way across the room.

Their gazes met, and for a moment Alyssa felt the fire between them again. She wished she could step into it, be wrapped in its sizzling embrace. She ached to be burned in that flame. She swallowed hard and forced herself to resist the deepening temptation. She talked to fill the suddenly dangerous silence that had fallen between them.

"I guess I tried to be a mother to Alasdair, and a big sister at the same time. And he tried to comfort me, and encourage me when I couldn't see the light at the end of the tunnel.'' Alyssa didn't generally talk about those bleak years. If she were to be completely honest, the memories would begin to sound like a recitation of the trials of Job. And unfortunately, her brother, Alasdair, was often cast in the role of the plague. She tried to drop the subject. "Uh...could I get washed up now? It's not that I don't love your island, but I'd just as soon not wear it any longer than I have to.'' She looked down at the dirt still smudging her, feeling like Cinderella on the morning after the ball. "I don't suppose there's a secret passage to my room?'' She gave an uneasy laugh. For all she knew, there was.

"No secret passage. Just the hall. I doubt you'd be seen by anyone, but I'd prefer you stay here until I get back. You can use that bath," he suggested, nodding his head in the direction of a small door. "I'll use another one down the hall.''

He grinned at her obvious relief. He wondered if she'd been bracing herself for a suggestion that they bathe together. Not a bad idea, in his opinion. A bit premature, unfortunately. And inopportune at the moment, regrettably.

"I'll send Etsu back here to help you,'' he went on. "Put on the cotton bathrobe that you'll find folded on the table inside the bathroom door. It's fresh and clean.'' He let his gaze slide over her in leisurely inspection. Beneath the grime, she had one hell of a good-looking body, he thought. Damn Esau for showing up. "The bathrobe's probably three sizes too big for you, but better too big than too small.''

"True,'' she replied.

"Stay here unless Etsu tells you otherwise. I'll go see what Esau wants, and I'd prefer that he not know that you're here and in perfect working condition.''

John had never completely trusted Esau. Henry and Suzie had liked him well enough. Even Mariko and Kojiro seemed to get along well with the trader. But John had never warmed to the man. He'd always had the feeling that part of Esau Holling was a fraud. And then there was the night of the plane crash, when Esau had somehow managed not to see the pilot floating in the ocean, even though Esau's boat had been close enough for Esau to spit on the good captain.

"If you insist," she agreed tiredly. In exchange for a bath and a clean robe, Alyssa was ready to agree to nearly anything. "But frankly, I think you need to develop a little more trust in life." And in people, she added silently.

"That could be," he said evenly. "Or perhaps it is you who needs to develop a little more skepticism."

She felt a cool chill, as if the hand of danger had passed over them just then. She hugged the black cotton jacket that she still had draped over her shoulders, thanks to one of her rescuers.

"What's the matter? Chills?" He frowned in concern.

"No. Just a mouse running over my grave," she murmured. "John?"

"What?"

"Be careful." Her large gray eyes found his cool, dark blue ones.

He was momentarily surprised. Their gazes held for a long moment. He fought the idiotic urge to put his arms around her and kiss her until the worry faded from her elegant face.

"Don't worry," he said dryly. "If I can't take care of myself, there are several people on this island who will personally beat my brains in as punishment. You see, they expect their students to do them proud."

"Now that's comforting to hear!" she said in dismay.

He grinned.

"It would be if you know how determined I am not to tangle with them."

"I'm having a hard time imagining you backing down from a fight," Alyssa said dubiously.

"I'm glad you're exercising that skepticism that I was urging you to develop," he said dryly. "Now try redirecting it to someone besides me. And take my word for it when I say that I have no intention of disappointing the men who've been like fathers to me."

Alyssa stared at him. There was an underlying intensity in those last words that reached out and wrapped itself around her innermost feelings. He meant it. To the core of his soul. And he wanted her to know it. For a man who had been cold, distrustful and unrevealing, it was sort of an olive branch, she decided. Maybe he *was* willing to give her a second chance.

John turned and left the room, leaving Alyssa, at a loss for a reply, staring after him. When he was out of her sight she suddenly realized that John Mori hadn't made a single sound as he departed.

He moved as quietly as a ghost.

Alyssa shivered and tugged the black cotton jacket around her. But the shiver wasn't just from the cool temperature of Mori's bedroom. So the jacket didn't help much.

"What say, John! What have ye to say for yourself, eh, mate?"

"Not much. How about you, Esau?"

Esau Holling threw back his graying black hair with one swipe of a darkly tanned hand. He laughed, showing a partly chipped front tooth.

"The same. D'you realize that's the same way ye always greet me? Never give anything away, do ye, Johnny?"

"A man of few words gets into few conflicts."

"You sound like that crazy old monk up on the hill, Johnny," Esau said with a crooked grin. "I never could follow him, ye know."

"I know."

"D'you realize, Johnny, that in the nearly twenty years that we've known each other, we've never had to really trust each other?"

"We've collaborated on a couple of deals. That involved a certain amount of trust." A certain, miniscule amount, to be precise.

"Bah! That was just enough to exchange some guns for money, or some bullion for oil, or some such. That was simple economics. It was in our best interest to come through for each other. We each stood to lose big money if we didn't."

"True. But isn't this a late hour for philosophical reflections on our long acquaintance, Esau?"

"That wasn't why I come up here."

"I didn't think so. I assume you're here on business?"

"In a manner of speakin'. I was down at Mariko's, havin' a last *sake* with some of the boys before we up anchor tomorrow, and I asked where the hell that scamp Suzie Chan went to. She owes me fifty quid, and I intend to collect it before I sail for Hong Kong tomorrow morning. Somebody said that Suzie had come up here earlier today with her brother, but nobody remembered seeing her come back into town. I thought maybe you might know where she is."

"Why didn't you call?"

Esau's ingratiating smile hardened a little, and his black eyes beaded into a hard stare.

"Why, Johnny, I was afraid you might be tempted to tell me she wasn't here, even if she was," he said slyly.

"Now why would I do that?" John's eyes frosted over. He didn't care for the slur on his integrity. Especially coming from the likes of Esau Holling.

Esau lowered his voice to a conspiratorial whisper.

"Well, man to man, you and I both know that Suzie's been angling to get into your bed for a long, long time now." He shrugged philosophically. "I just figured she might have succeeded. And if she was warmin' your sheets, I figured it wasn't likely that you'd roll off her long enough to let her pay me my money, now. Suzie's got a hot spot that needs cooling, I hear, and considerin' how long she's burned for you, I couldn't see her letting you go, not for all the pearls in the Orient."

His years of training at the monastery had taught John how to kill his emotions, and decades of surviving in a sea of human sharks had honed his skill at concealing the feelings that he didn't kill outright. Out of habit, his face was smooth and empty, devoid of anything revealing, but inside, what he most wanted to do was reach out and wring Esau Holling's dirty neck.

"I see. Tell me, Esau, does your description of Suzie's charms come from personal experience?" John asked lazily.

Esau blinked and measured John's meaning.

"Bloody hell, no, mate! I've offered, of course, but she's a mite proud for a she-cat with a shady past. It's others that have said it. I've just heard the talk. That's all."

"Maybe the rumors are just the jeers from disappointed men," John suggested, managing a credible air of disinterest.

"Could be," Esau conceded. He looked around the room, then back at John. "So, uh, has she been by here? Is she still around? I surely would like my damn money 'for I leave."

"She's not here."

"Ah, double damn. That surely is a pity." Esau eyed John narrowly. "You're certain she couldn't be about somewhere?"

"Positive."

"And, uh, Henry?"

"He's not here, either."

Esau nodded and paced around the room. There was a hint of the larcenous carnivore in his cautious tread. Esau was well-known for spending hours patiently tracking his target until the perfect opportunity presented itself. Then he went for the jugular.

He was limping slightly, John noticed. And there was a long, red scratch down his jaw and throat.

"Hurt yourself, Esau?"

"What?" Esau looked at him sharply.

"You're limping…and I don't remember your front tooth being chipped…." Or that angry-looking scratch.

Esau rubbed a weather-worn hand along the telltale scratch. A peculiar flatness slid over his black eyes.

"I had a bit of a fall," Esau said with a shrug. "Scratched myself up on some rocks."

"Around here?"

"Yeah."

"Today?"

Esau nodded. His eyes narrowed.

"You better see a dentist about that tooth."

Esau grinned and touched the rough corner experimentally, as if enjoying his ability to withstand the pain. John wondered how anyone could trust Esau farther than they could spit. The man made his stomach turn.

"Yeah, well, mate, when I get to Melbourne, I'll look one up. Till then I'll use a little gin on it. Keeps a fella right warm and relaxed."

"Be there long?" John asked casually.

"In Melbourne? Oh, mebbe a month or two, I imagine. I figure I earned myself a mite of a vacation, and it's damn cold up here this time o' year." Esau strolled around the room and stopped to admire the formal flower arrangement in its low, black ceramic vase. "I never could get the hang of this stuff," he said with a snort. "Just give me a big bunch of flowers. That's easy to admire." He touched one of the long white petals, but he seemed to be seeing something else. "I bet that girl's skin's as soft as this."

"What girl is that?"

"You know, the one that we fished out of the water." Esau kept examining the flower arrangement. He was a little too casual when he asked, "Say, where's that little she-bird? I haven't seen hide nor hair of her all day down in the village."

"I thought you were falling down the rocks."

"Not all day, mate," Esau snorted. He eyed John narrowly. "I'd like to meet that little chick, if she's still about. Don't see many of her kind out here."

"What kind is that?" Again John felt the urge to throttle Esau.

"Oh, you know the kind. Rich. Pretty. Talks fine. Dresses fine. Walks fine. Soft and polite. The kind that never had a bad thing happen to 'em, and never will."

John didn't think that described Alyssa, from what little he knew about her. And he was certain that he didn't care for the speculation about her that he saw in Esau's hungry eyes.

"So's I don't waste the visit, maybe you could introduce me to the little lady," Esau suggested softly. His eyes were fixed on John, like a snake's.

"Sorry, Esau. I can't help you there, either," John said, hoping that the ambiguity would lead Esau to believe Alyssa wasn't there. He walked toward the door and held it open.

"Now, if you'll excuse me, I've got a few things to take care of this evening. Since I can't help you, maybe you should go back into town and get a good night's rest. It's a long voyage to Melbourne."

Esau's face hardened. He didn't like the dismissal. And he wasn't satisfied with the brush-off he was getting. That was obvious.

"All right, Mori," he said dangerously. "But I've heard there was some sort of accident up here today, and I don't like being kept in the dark. If Suzie or that other bird were hurt, I'd like to know about it. After all, I've been a resident of Onijima for a long time. It's island business when something bad happens. Everybody needs to know about it. Just in case the bad stuff spreads and they're next."

He pinched his fingers together and the blossom broke off, falling in shattered petals onto the polished ebony table. Esau feigned regret.

"Bloody hell! Look at that, will ye? Ain't I the clumsy one? Like I said, I'm not used to fine things." He brushed off his fingers and ambled over to the door. Just before he left, he turned to look at John and added, "You're more like me than you care to admit, Mori. Don't think you're a gentleman, just because you went to a big university and know how to dress fancy. Scratch the surface and you crush flowers, just like me. It's in your blood, mate. All this pretty crap can't cover it up. So if you hear anything about Suzie, or that other one, ring me up. You and me, we have a lot in common. You'll see that, someday." A knowing light filled his eyes. "Someday pretty soon, mebbe."

Esau turned and limped toward the door. John's hand curled into a fist and he nearly went after him. For a long, cold moment, all John could think of was wrapping his hands around Esau's neck.

But he stopped himself.

And flexed his hand until the fury receded.

Esau knew how to needle him. But why the hell was he doing it? Had Esau wanted him to go after him? That made no sense to John at all. Unless . . . John frowned.

He went to the door and stood in the shadows as Esau limped down the drive. He'd left his car about twenty yards from the front door. Quite a distance from the house. An unnecessary one, at that. Unless Esau had intended to draw him down the drive after him.

Much as he disliked Esau, John found it hard to believe that Esau would bait him in order to lead him into some sort of prearranged ambush. If it had been someone he barely knew, John would have suspected exactly that. But Esau did a lot of business here on Onijima. It made no sense for him to draw John out into danger. What could Esau gain from such a dangerous undertaking?

And yet…John had the intuitive impression that he'd just narrowly missed being jumped.

He stepped back inside, locked the door and checked the alarm system. Everything was in working order.

He lifted the phone and dialed the guard at the back of the house.

"Have someone keep an eye on Esau Holling till he leaves the island."

"Yes, sir!"

John hung up and went back toward his rooms. He had one last task to perform. Alyssa had better still be awake, he thought. Because he had no intention of waiting till tomorrow to show her the briefcase. There were too many peculiar things happening. He needed to find out what was going on before anything else happened.

Alyssa was wrapping the belt around the pajamas and struggling to keep the pants up high enough not to trip on the hems.

Etsu frowned like a prune and shook her gray old head.

"I thought you fit. But Mariko-san must be taller."

"These are Mariko's?" Alyssa asked, stopping dead still. Etsu nodded.

"Uh … does Mariko-san, uh, come here often?"

"Mmm."

"Is she, uh, a very close friend of John-san?"

Etsu looked slightly outraged and bustled about the bathroom gathering the remnants of Alyssa's clothing.

"I not know what you mean," the old woman said primly. "Mariko-san and Johnny-chan are old friends. Is that same as close friends?'' She eyes Alyssa shrewdly, daring her to voice her suspicion aloud.

Alyssa sighed and extended her hands in a silent request for help.

''I'm very sorry if I've offended you in any way, Etsu-sama,'' Alyssa said earnestly, ''but I'm lost here on this island. I know no one. I'm not really welcome, since Mr. Mori wasn't expecting me, although I certainly thought he was.''

Etsu stood with the armful of clothes and watched Alyssa in silence.

''When I was at Mariko's last night,'' Alyssa explained, ''I was under the impression that John and Mariko were very close. I just don't want to put myself in an awkward position here. Could you help me? Please?''

Etsu lowered her eyes.

''They old friends,'' she muttered. ''But Mariko-san would be happy to give you her clothes. She no be jealous.'' Etsu looked at Alyssa sharply. ''And Johnny-chan honorable. He no bother you. Don't worry.''

The old woman waddled out of the room.

''Etsu! Where's my room?'' Alyssa called out, realizing she was being abandoned.

''I come back in little bit. You wait.''

Alyssa stood in the large dressing room connected to the bathroom and counted to ten. She was so tired of being left in places and picked up again, she could have screamed.

She opened the door that Etsu had passed through, thinking she'd simply follow the old woman around until she took her to a bed. But Alyssa stopped in her tracks.

She had entered an office. There was a large desk. A desktop computer. A large console telephone with a fax attached.

A telephone! Alyssa rushed over to it and wondered if she could call her brother. Surely John wouldn't have a cow, she told herself. He'd relented enough to let her phone when he was standing beside her. Besides, she was a free woman! She intended to check in with her brother and tell him about the disaster she was in, whether John Mori liked it or not.

That was when she saw the metal safe. And on top of it, her briefcase. Still damp from the sea.

She forgot about the phone. She forgot about everything.

"You lied," she murmured in shock. "John Mori, you have my briefcase!"

And he'd told her that he didn't.

She didn't hear him enter the room behind her.

"Yes. I have it," he said tightly. "But it was just given to me. When I told you before that I didn't have it, that was the truth."

She turned to face him. She was furious. He was as shuttered as a house preparing for a hurricane.

"And how can I know whether to believe that?" she asked distrustfully, backing toward the phone.

He approached, treading like a cat.

"That's one of the difficulties about life," he said softly. "You never know for sure. You always have to make an educated guess."

Her hand closed over the phone and she whirled, desperately punching out the numbers of her home phone.

He closed his hand over hers and pinned her against the desk. When she fought, he caught her in his arms and held her fast.

She looked at him with a mixture of fear and defiance.

"I don't know what's going on around here," she said breathlessly, "but I think I'd just as soon go home. Either you let me call my brother so I can get off this island, or..."

"Or?" he said softly.

She stared into his eyes and felt herself falling. It was the most peculiar, most intoxicating sensation. As if she had been in his arms before. As if she would be in them again. As if it was where she belonged.

And he seemed to be feeling something, too, she thought. His eyes were a little unfocused, as if he were seeing her through his thoughts as much as through his vision. Their hearts were beating and their bodies seemed to meld together.

"Do you believe in fate?" he asked softly, sliding his hand up until her hair fell through his fingers.

A shiver of desire coursed through Alyssa's back and dove down into her center.

"Fate?" she murmured. "I don't know."

He hadn't known, either. Until that moment. But now he had the distinct feeling that their lives were entwining, not for the first time. That this was meant to be.

He just wasn't certain what "this" was going to turn out to be.

Reluctantly, he stepped back and went over to retrieve the briefcase. Etsu must have been called out of the room before she could open the safe and lock it inside, he thought, frowning. Not that anyone would be foolish enough as to trespass on his private quarters any more than they'd dare break into his safe. Still...

He turned his attention back to Alyssa. "Before you call your brother, I want you to open this and show me the proof you spoke of."

He held it out to her.

Alyssa sat down on the couch across from the desk and placed the briefcase on her knees. She opened the case and pulled out a damp paper.

"This proves my case," she said.

She handed him the paper.

She looked very confident, he thought. He took the paper from her and read it.

Part of the puzzle fell into place.

Chapter 7

"So you *did* receive a written invitation," John said thoughtfully.

Alyssa hugged the briefcase and bowed her head. She had thought she wouldn't ever see it again, or the precious item still inside it. When she had told John that she had lost something virtually unreplaceable, she hadn't meant the letter. There was something else inside, infinitely more precious than anything she owned. Her eyes and throat felt hot and swollen and she fought back the humiliating urge to cry. She didn't want him to see her that nakedly vulnerable. Alyssa never cried, not in front of other people. She swallowed hard and hung on.

The note was brief.

Dear Miss Alyssa Jones,
Please come to Onijima within the next week. I would see the *tsuba* and the *katana* together again, one last time, before my days are ended here. Make arrangements quickly. I await your arrival. Do not write or telephone, for your own safety and that of the *tsuba*.

Sincerely,
Isamu Mori

And there was the round *hanko,* Isamu Mori's name carved into a seal and pressed down onto the paper.

John examined the *hanko* carefully. The seawater hadn't helped matters. The paper was soft and the ink had spread along with the dampened fibers. Still, he could make out enough of the seal to tell that it was either authentic or an extremely professional forgery. Since he was certain Isamu had not sent this note, that meant it had to be a forgery.

"Someone went to a lot of trouble to be convincing," he muttered, frowning.

"I hope that 'someone' doesn't refer to me," Alyssa said, stiffening in self-defense.

He glanced at her. His eyes were opaque, his face carved of stone.

It was still too soon to be absolutely certain about Alyssa's role in all this, but he was more and more inclined to believe that she was more of a victim than a perpetrator. "For the time being, no," he said. "I don't think you forged this. But someone did." His mouth softened ever so slightly.

Alyssa took the hint of a smile as a reprieve. She'd take what she could get, considering how parsimonious John Mori was with his trust.

"Thanks," she said, relaxing a little. "So, how about showing the letter to your father and asking him if he knows anything about it? Is he well enough to talk yet?"

"Perhaps. The worst should be behind him."

"Why did you let Dr. Alsop leave with your father still sick?" Alyssa asked softly. She was sure John wouldn't have allowed it if he didn't think it was safe.

John sighed.

"My father avoids Western medicine."

"I see."

It was nothing short of a miracle that they'd convinced the old man to permit Derrick to examine him, X-ray his chest and start him on antibiotics and intravenous fluids.

"I wanted to fly him to Japan and have him admitted to a hospital, just to be safe, but he wouldn't go."

"You must have been very worried...."

Worried? More like scared sweatless, John thought. He'd never realized how hard it was going to be to lose that old man until now. No. Isamu had insisted on sleeping in his own bed. *Life. Death. It is all the same,* Isamu had whispered. He would take what fate had in store for him, but in his own bed, in his own room, on Onijima.

"My father can be as determined as a migrating whale when he puts his mind to it," John muttered darkly.

"Is he well enough to talk? Could we speak with him tomorrow?" Alyssa asked hesitantly. She didn't want Isamu to have a relapse. On the other hand, only he could convince John that the letter was legitimate. "Perhaps he knows something that would shed some light on what's happened."

"I doubt that he knows a damn thing, but he might be strong enough to talk about that forged letter tomorrow. We'll see in the morning."

"John?"

He looked at her. She felt his gaze pierce her heart, and she softened toward him a little more.

"Did it ever occur to you that your father might have sent that letter but not mentioned it to you?" She swallowed hard. She didn't want to add to their problems by suggesting that Isamu had cut John out. Still, that was a distinct possibility in her opinion.

To her surprise, John laughed. He didn't appear to be the least bit concerned about her suggestion.

"No. It never occurred to me. And it's about as likely as a blizzard in July in the Philippines."

Alyssa lowered her eyes and thought about the priceless object inside the briefcase.

"Did your father ever say anything to you about wanting the sword guard that I have?"

"No. That's the one thing that is peculiar about the letter. There is a request for you to bring the *tsuba* with you, so that you and he can both see the sword and its *tsuba* together. That sounds completely out of character. Whenever you wrote requesting we meet with you or loan you the sword, he said he'd parted with a piece of soul and it was dead to him. What was dead, should not be brought back."

"A piece of his soul? The *tsuba?*"

"Yes. The *katana* has the rest of his soul. It's an ancient tradition among the *samurai* . . . and their black-sheep cousins, the *ninja.*"

Alyssa nodded.

"I've heard the sword referred to as 'the soul of the samurai,' but I didn't realize that the attachment, the honor, could extend to the sword's *tsuba,* as well. Besides, since he gave it to my mother, I never dreamed—" Alyssa stopped, realizing she would be giving away family secrets. Until she discovered how much John knew about the relationship between her mother and Isamu Mori, she thought it would be wise to be careful what she said.

John's eyes narrowed.

"Do you know why he gave the *tsuba* to your mother?"

Alyssa hesitated.

"Tell me."

"I think you'd better ask your father that."

"Are you being evasive? Or are you unsure of the truth?"

"Look, just ask your father," she repeated nervously. John's relentless stare was unnerving. Besides, the truth about Isamu and her mother hadn't been easy for her to accept. She had no idea how John would take it. "I don't want to get in the middle of old family secrets."

"So . . . our family secrets are shared?" He looked at her thoughtfully. Then he remembered the instruction in the letter that Alyssa bring the sword guard to Onijima. "Did you bring the *tsuba* with you?"

She reached inside the leather bag, smiling triumphantly. "Yes."

Alyssa removed it from the airtight, padded metal container that she had made for it years ago. The guard was as clean and elegant as when she and Dair had taken it out of the safe-deposit box at the bank before she left. For a long, aching moment she held it tight in her hands, pressed against her cheek. *I thought I'd lost you. . . . Don't worry, Mom, I didn't.*

"I thought I'd have to hire a treasure hunter to bring it up," she said at last. She managed a broken laugh and brushed away a tear that had broken through her defenses.

Then she offered the *tsuba* to John. Silently he took it. "By the way, how *did* you find it?"

"Good karma."

Alyssa stared at him. "Karma?" she said dubiously.

"In the form of an old business associate with a salvage operation who happened to be fairly close by." He glanced at her, amused. "I'd call that good karma. Wouldn't you?"

"I'd call it a minor miracle," she muttered.

He grinned and turned his attention back to the *tsuba* in his hands.

It was circular, and made of iron and iron mixed with gold or copper and silver. There was a fragment of a Buddhist meditation, called a warrior koan, inscribed along its outer rim. The Japanese characters were so small that it was hard to imagine anyone being able to carve them into the hard metal. Beneath the koan inscription, the *tsuba* maker had cut away a piece of metal, leaving an elegant space shaped like a crane in flight. Across from the crane had been carved an arrow. Was it in flight to slay the beautiful crane? The answer had died with the swordsmith, centuries ago.

A stylized scene from an old story had been etched on the inner metal. There was a vigorous *samurai* nimbly wielding his fine, curved sword against a ferocious, attacking demon.

Finally, in the center of the *tsuba,* was the distinctive slot through which the sword blade was passed.

The *tsuba* was very old and was much simpler than many which had been made more recently. But it had seen hundreds of years of history. As had its mate, the sword that the *tsuba* had been made for.

John held it in his hand and turned it over, examining it carefully from every angle. He found the mark of its maker engraved on the back of the sword slit. Takehira. One of the most famous sword makers of Japan.

Takehira had been one of the three great smiths of the Ko-Bizen school, but his name had never been found on a single sword or *tsuba*.

Except for Isamu Mori's sword.

And Alyssa Jones's *tsuba*.

"It takes half a lifetime to be expert enough to authenticate swords and their fittings," John murmured, his fingers sliding reverently over the hard, cool metal. "But this looks authentic to me."

"Of course it is! Your father gave it to my mother! And he had inherited it from his father's father's father, or whatever."

John didn't say anything.

"Thank you for retrieving it from Mother Ocean's watery arms," she said sincerely. "I can never repay you for returning it to me." *Or for saving my life. Twice.*

"The pleasure is mine."

Alyssa leaned forward and laid her hand over his. Their eyes met.

"*Now* can I call my brother?" she asked, feeling like a fool for having to ask this simple question.

He lifted the phone off the hook and handed it to her.

"Go ahead," he told her.

"At last!" Alyssa sighed, fiercely relieved and feeling as if she'd just won a boxing match round with him.

"Dial direct. The call's on me."

"Thanks."

"You're welcome. However, I'd like to listen in," John added, pushing the intercom button. He wanted to see what kind of a reaction Alyssa got from her brother and her business partner when they realized she was alive, just in case they weren't the loving friends that Alyssa believed them to be.

"Go right ahead. We've got nothing to hide from you, I assure you," Alyssa said blithely. If she hadn't been so happy to finally get a chance to call home, she would have been annoyed by John's demand. However, if allowing him to listen to her conversation with Dair was the price she had to pay to use a phone around here or gain a little trust from John, she'd just have to pay it.

She punched in the number of the apartment. It was early morning in San Francisco. Alasdair would still be in bed. After a few rings, someone picked up the receiver. She tried to control her elation.

"Dair?" she asked breathlessly.

"Alyssa?" There was a muzzy sound to his voice, as if he were still groggy from sleep. "Alyssa, is that you?"

"Yes! I'm on Onijima. Can you hear me okay? I can barely hear you."

There was a sound like covers being tossed about, feet hitting the floor, a groan as a man tried to shake his head awake.

"Lyssa? Oh, God..."

Alyssa frowned and wet her lips nervously. He sounded awful.

"Dair? Are you sick?"

"Uh...no. No, I'm...I'm not sick. Jeez...I just wasn't expecting... God, what time is it?"

Alyssa heard a crash—like glass shattering on tiled floor. He must be on the balcony, she thought. Covers on the balcony, though? Then she realized the sound was more like paper. Newspaper. He'd fallen asleep on the patio with a drink on the table next to him and the newspaper spread over his chest. She turned back to Mori so she didn't have to endure his cynical regard. She twirled the telephone cord around her forefinger nervously.

She heard Alasdair muttering the correct time. No doubt he'd finally located his wristwatch in its usual place on his arm, she thought, depressed.

"Dair, uh, have you been drinking?"

"Jeez, Lyssa, you called me from hell to nag me about drinking, again?"

"I didn't mean..."

"If it matters, yes! I had a couple of drinks last night. And I fell asleep on the patio. Now why are you calling? What's going on? I thought...I thought you were supposed to have gotten there... When the hell was it? Yesterday? The day before? I never could keep the days straight once you cross the date line."

"Never mind about that, Alasdair. Look, did you hear about the plane crashing?"

There was a heartbeat's worth of silence but it felt as big as the Grand Canyon to Alyssa. He was planning how to answer her. He was going to lie. Her heart froze. Oh, God, no... What was going on? What was Alasdair involved in?

"Uh...yeah. Yeah, I heard about it. But, uh, George said that, uh, that everyone was all right. So, we've been waiting to hear from you. Uh... you okay?"

She lowered her head. She felt slightly nauseated.

"Yes. I'm all right, thanks to Mr. Mori."

"That son of a bitch? You're lucky he didn't run you through with one of those damned swords of his," Dair muttered sourly.

Alyssa turned to face John and tried to make apologetic gestures toward him. He looked unaffected by Alasdair's nastiness, but rather amused by her efforts to soothe him. He waved her off and pointed to the phone. He mouthed, *Ask your brother when he heard about the crash.*

"Alasdair? When did you hear about the plane going down?"

"I don't know... Uh, about the time you were supposed to get there, I suppose."

"I tried to call you yesterday, but I couldn't reach you." She smiled wanly. "Were you out on a hot date?" she teased, hoping to ease the tension.

"None of your business!" Dair said, laughing. The laughter subsided into a groan. "Hell, I've got a gold-plated hangover. George and I were out celebrating...."

"Celebrating?" she prompted him.

There was another pause, just long enough for Alasdair to reconsider his words and plan what to say. Alyssa had seen him do it many times over the years. She didn't have to be in the same room to see it now. She closed her eyes, knowing something was wrong with her brother, and wishing she didn't have to admit it to herself. Or to John Mori.

"Uh, you know... celebrating your getting to the Moris' and finally having a shot at getting that old sword out from that dying old man's hand."

"Alasdair!" Alyssa exclaimed, shocked.

"Don't be such a sweet little thing, sister mine." Alasdair's voice hardened. "Everyone gets old someday. It's important to make sure you're well taken care of when that day comes. This little deal is taking us a step in that direction. Why shouldn't I say so?"

"Look, Dair, I just wanted to let you know that I was all right, in case you'd heard about the crash."

"Alyssa..." There was a boyish ache in his voice that always softened Alyssa toward him. "I'm glad you're okay. I'm really, really glad."

Alyssa gave John an I-told-you-so look. He remained unpersuaded. He mouthed, *Ask him when and where they received the facsimile transmission.*

"Oh, by the way, Dair...uh, could you tell me exactly when and where George got that fax?"

"Why?" There was a slight edge to the question.

"It's not terribly important, but apparently the younger Mori is not convinced the letter was sent by his father."

"Yeah? Well, tell the SOB to read the damn thing. It's even got old Mori's seal on it. How much more authentic can something get? Next he's gonna say we forged it!"

Alasdair laughed and made what sounded like swallowing sounds. He was drinking something, Alyssa thought, shocked. He must really be feeling stressed out. He'd cut back on his drinking in the past few months. And he hadn't had a drink before noon since his undergraduate days.

"Dair, is everything all right?"

"Hunky-dory, sister. Hunky-dory."

"Well, uh, maybe I'd better call George."

"Yeah. You do that. George'll be blown out of the water to hear your voice. I guarantee it."

"Take care of yourself, Alasdair," she said softly. "Please. For me?"

"I always do," he said tiredly.

After she'd hung up, she mustered her courage to look into John's face.

"He may be weak, but it isn't completely his fault," she said defensively. John's eyes never left her face. She felt heat turn her cheeks red. "My brother was just a baby when our mother killed herself. It hasn't been easy for him." She looked away. "I don't know why I should try to explain to you," she murmured. "It's not really something that concerns you."

He watched her fiddle with the telephone and try to avoid her own sense of humiliation.

"Your brother just let you down," John pointed out. "He had been partying while you were drowning. He knew about the crash and made no effort to call. And he was as nervous as hell. He was lying to you about something. You know it. I know it. And you'd stand there and defend him. Why?"

"Because he's my brother and I love him!" Alyssa cried. "Is that so impossibly difficult to grasp? Didn't you ever love anybody who had problems?"

"Oh, yes." His smile was bitter. "But I got over it. I learned to let go. And not to repeat that particular mistake."

Alyssa was still angry at him but she couldn't help but feel embarrassed for attacking him and forcing him to dredge up his own skeletons.

"Your mother." She stated it as a fact. She was sure that's what he meant.

His eyes narrowed.

"How would you know?"

"Suzie told me. Not much. This afternoon, when we went for our walk."

John paced across the room and looked out of the window. In the distance, he could see lights in the town.

What the hell had happened to Suzie? he wondered.

"Why don't you go to bed," he said abruptly. He walked to the door, taking her by the elbow. "I'll show you to your room."

"But I was going to call George...."

"Call him tomorrow. We've lost the element of surprise."

Element of surprise? Who cared about that?

When he left her at the door to her room a few minutes later, Alyssa felt like she'd been through an old-fashioned clothes wringer.

"Tomorrow has *got* to be a better day," she murmured as she closed her eyes.

And she dreamed of a black dragon that swam through the sea and wrapped her in burning fire and had blue eyes and the hard heart of a man who would not be betrayed by a woman ever again.

* * *

"Johnny! I think we find Suzie Chan!"

John and Alyssa looked up from their respective breakfasts and turned to stare at black-swathed Kojiro, who had just rushed into the dining room.

John was out of his seat and heading to the door before Alyssa had swallowed her melon. Dabbing her mouth and frantically gulping some coffee, she jumped up from her chair and trotted along behind them.

"Stay here," John ordered sternly.

"Women have been emancipated in my country for a long time," Alyssa pointed out feistily, running to keep up with their quickened pace.

Fortunately, her clothes fit today. Mariko had called in a favor from one of the local boutiques overnight, and Etsu had laid the clothes inside Alyssa's room before dawn.

"I don't recall inquiring about emancipation," John muttered. He swung into the Jeep that was waiting for them, motor running.

"Suzie was with me until she disappeared. I have a right to know what happened to her. Maybe it will explain what happened to me!"

John looked as if he could have picked her up and tied her to the nearest tree.

"I won't interfere," she promised, holding up her palm and trying to look as innocuous as possible. She hopped into the seat beside him before he could order them to pull away without her.

He sighed and reached across her to lock the door.

"Where is she?" John asked Kojiro.

"In the Witch's Cauldron."

John swore in Chinese.

"What's the Witch's Cauldron?" Alyssa asked as they careened down the mountain.

"A whirlpool. If you fall in, it sucks you down. Even strong swimmers can't get out of it. You just get dragged to the bottom."

Alyssa paled.

"Then, she's...dead?" Alyssa whispered.

"Not necessarily," John said grimly.

They turned a corner and, even with her seat belt fastened, Alyssa was thrown against John. He turned his head and their lips were inches apart. He looked into her eyes, as if he would see into her soul. The heat from his body warmed her. In spite of everything, part of her instinctively wanted to trust him.

Alyssa remembered what Mariko had told her. *John is a man I would trust with my life.*

"This may not be very pretty," he said softly, looking at her gentle face with concern. "Are you sure you want to come along?"

Alyssa swallowed hard. She nodded.

"I'm sure. I want to know what's going on," she explained. "I was always the responsible one, I'm afraid," she added, somewhat apologetically.

"Ah, yes," he said softly. "Big sister will take care of everything. Superwoman."

She laughed.

"I wish I had her stamina!" she exclaimed ruefully. "It's just that I've never considered ignorance the slightest bit blissful."

"All right. Down with ignorance. Full speed ahead."

John leaned back in the seat and tried to remember the last time that he and Suzie had bet each other they could outswim the other in the Witch's Cauldron. And how they'd managed to escape it. Alive.

When the Jeep screeched to a halt at the edge of a cliff, the men jumped out, so Alyssa did, too. The minute she reached the edge, she looked down.

"Oh, no!" she whispered, aghast at what she saw.

"Oh, yes," John said grimly.

There, twenty feet below them, swirled the slow, watery cyclone called the Witch's Cauldron. And at the bottom, caught in the fast-circling heart, was the limp body of Suzie Chan. She was ensnared in the needles of a large pine tree branch, but she was too far away from Alyssa to see if she was alive or dead. From this distance, Alyssa couldn't even see if Suzie's eyes were open.

"Surely she can't have been there all night?" Alyssa said, appalled.

"Probably not. But I'll bet someone tried to throw her into that hellhole and didn't realize she was strong enough to swim under it," John said grimly. He pointed to a small pine tree clinging precariously to the lower rocks. "I'll bet she made it as far as the lower branches, but they broke off when she tried to pull herself up. Then, when she fell in the second time, she wasn't strong enough to swim under the Cauldron."

Alyssa could see a man and two women, swathed in white, swimming into the eye of the watery hurricane. They wore black face masks and life jackets. And each was carrying a spare.

"That's Henry..." John murmured.

"Her brother?"

"Yeah. And two of Henry's best pearl divers."

Holding her breath, Alyssa watched as the three swimmers swam courageously into the brutal strength of nature. When they reached Suzie, Alyssa felt both elated and terrified. Suzie's chances had improved. But what about the odds for her rescuers' safe return? Surely they had just taken a slow nosedive.

John and the others were making their way down the cliff face to help at the beach. Alyssa, following, saw several fishing boats hovering at a safe distance, anxious faces lining the decks. If the prayers of others on one's behalf helped mold one's fate, Alyssa thought that Suzie would definitely have a fighting chance.

When she reached the sand-and-rock beach, she saw something that she hadn't noticed from farther away.

Tether lines ran from the sturdiest trees out through the waves to the rescuers. And John and the others gathering on the beach were preparing to haul the rescuers in. Hand over hand, if necessary.

"Horizontal mountain climbing," Alyssa exclaimed.

Startled, John looked over his shoulder at her.

"That's as good a description as any, I guess," he agreed.

Alyssa found an empty spot on a rope and helped pull.

It was a struggle, but the sea was outnumbered this time. After what seemed like an hour or horrendous physical exertion, Alyssa saw the three swimmers emerging from the outer edges of the swirling cauldron of water. And cradled in their arms in the dark sea was Suzie.

They had her wrapped in thermal blankets and were carrying her up the cliff face within minutes. Suzie's eyes were closed. Her face was ashen. She appeared to be just barely hanging on to the last faint thread of her life.

When she was laid in one of the vehicles, the medical evacuation helicopter came in for a landing to take Suzie to the airport. She was too badly hurt to keep on Onijima with no doctor.

Suzie's eyelids fluttered open just as she was being placed on the helicopter's stretcher. She saw John and caught his eye through sheerest luck.

John bent low.

"Hang on, Suzie," he said encouragingly. He squeezed her cold hand. "Damn it, Suzie, you hang on, you hear?"

"Yeah…boss…Johnny…" She swallowed and shut her eyes. "Sorry…Esau…tricked… He trick. I thought…get rid her…"

"Esau did this to you?" John said, whispering close to her ear.

"And to her…" Suzie's eyes found Alyssa behind John.

Then she closed her eyes, and the air went out of her lungs in a long, painful sigh.

Henry, who was helping lift her into the aircraft, screamed.

"Suzie! Suzie! No! No!" And then it turned into a rapid stream of Chinese, drowning in a sea of grief.

The paramedic began working on her feverishly. Henry slammed shut the copter door and it lifted off, heading for the airport.

"Good luck, Suzie," Alyssa whispered, as the prop wash from the helicopter rotor whipped her hair about her face and plastered her slacks and sweater against her body.

Kojiro was talking urgently with several of his men. His face uncharacteristically angry, Kojiro hurried over to John.

"Where the hell is Esau?" John asked tightly.

"Good thing you had him followed," Kojiro said. "He not dare come back to make sure Suzie dead. The man who followed Esau say he left little after dawn, sailing to Australia.''

John swore softly.

Alyssa felt the cold caress of fear. No wonder Mariko had warned her to tell John the absolute truth. He *would* be a very dangerous man to cross.

And Esau Holling had just crossed him.

''Call our friends in Melbourne,'' John told Kojiro. ''Have them keep a look out for Esau. And while you're at it, pass the word around the Pacific Rim that we're interested in finding Holling. Just in case he decides to alter his plans and hide out somewhere else.''

Kojiro grunted the monosyllabic Japanese word for yes. *''Hai!''*

Alyssa touched John's arm sympathetically.

''I'm sorry about Suzie,'' she murmured. ''If there's anything I can do to help...''

His face was hard and his eyes narrowed. Alyssa was very thankful his fury wasn't directed at her.

Finally he turned his attention to her. His fathomless blue eyes revealed nothing of himself.

''Hold the thought,'' he suggested curtly. ''There may come a time when you'll hold a key to whatever's going on here. You'll know when that time comes. You can help Suzie then.''

He turned back to the car. Alyssa walked alongside him.

''I need to conduct a little business, Alyssa. I'll take you back to the house first. Think you can keep yourself occupied today?'' He held the door open for her as she got in the back seat. Sliding in after her, he added, ''I can have someone take you on a tour of Onijima's port city, if you like. Last time you were there, I believe you passed through in too much of a hurry to see much.''

That was an understatement!

''Since I can't do what I intended to, I might as well play shameless tourist,'' she said agreeably. ''But... I still want to talk to your father when he's strong enough....''

''Agreed.''

''And I still need to call George.''

''When I'm with you.'' Blue steel pinned her instantly.

"All right! All right!"

So he was still touchy about phones, she thought. At least they were making some progress in developing a more reasonable relationship. Rome wasn't built in a day, she reminded herself. And neither was John Mori's view of life.

He got out at the foot of the drive and said something to the driver. Then he leaned in the back window to speak to her before leaving.

"Your driver's name is Daichi. Stick close to him. You've had more 'accidents' in less time than any visitor Onijima's ever had."

"So Daichi's my good-luck charm?" she teased, breaking into a soft laugh.

John's expression altered slightly. The danger in his eyes was of a different kind altogether. It made Alyssa feel both very vulnerable and incredibly strong. As his gaze traveled over her with obvious male interest, her blood beat in her veins. No man had ever looked at her like that. With such honest, open appreciation. With such earthy interest. And she had never responded the way she was responding to his frank look.

"Daichi's with you because I can't be," he said softly. "Everyone on this island will know that."

"So *you're* my good-luck charm?" She had meant to say it teasingly, but as she stared into his eyes, she felt as if the breath had been stolen from her lungs.

A slow smile spread across his lips. His eyes never wavered from her face.

"That's a rather quaint way of putting it, but it captures the essence, I suppose. Anyone who harms you does so at the risk of crossing me. No one on Onijima will touch a hair on your head. Or stand by and watch someone else do you harm. I guarantee it."

"John, that didn't stop Esau," she pointed out gently.

"Esau was a different matter. He's never been part of our clan here. He's always been an outsider." John's expression hardened. "He knows he can't step foot on Onijima now. One of my men will nail his butt. I'll take care of Esau in my own way."

"Don't get mad, get even?" she said, frowning in worry. "Don't you think you should contact authorities somewhere? If he's being accused of attempted murder, shouldn't the law get involved?"

"On Onijima, we have our own law," John said.

"You?"

He didn't bother to defend himself, although something flickered in his eyes, as if she had touched on a sensitive subject, something he hadn't quite resolved to his own satisfaction.

"Be careful," he said curtly.

"You, too," she murmured.

She didn't want anything happening to her good-luck charm, after all. With such a lot of "bad karma" going around lately, she'd take whatever good luck came her way.

"Daichi-san, what time do things open up down in the village? I seem to have lost my luggage and need just about everything...."

Chapter 8

The salvagers had lifted the plane out of the water almost intact. John stood on the sheltered strip of beachfront where the aircraft lay like a drowned bird and he contemplated the work that was underway.

The two crash investigators had flown in that morning and were already crouching under the wings and crawling around the wreck, taking photos and making notes and consulting with one another in quiet, scientific shorthand.

John had assigned half a dozen of the island's police force to guard the wreck. They were dressed in Mori clan black *ninja* clothing. And they were armed.

John leaned on his car and watched as the local air-traffic-control safety experts exchanged observations over one particular gauge. The crash investigators took note of the item and jotted down something in their notebooks.

When Onijima's safety chief came over to brief John, he looked perplexed.

"It seems the fuel gauges and both engines' fuel lines were tampered with," he said, scratching his head. "There wasn't enough fuel for the plane to reach Onijima. But the gauges were giving faulty readings."

"You mean the pilot and the ground crew would have believed that there was adequate fuel in the tanks, but in reality, he was running on fumes."

"Basically. Yeah."

John straightened up.

"I suppose it couldn't be accidental?" John said, just for the record. "Equipment malfunction? Poor maintenance? Stupidity? Carelessness?"

His safety chief shook his head.

"No, sir. Somebody who knew what they were doing tampered with that plane. I guess they assumed it would ditch in the ocean and no one would bother trying to bring up the evidence. It's not going to be that hard to make a strong case."

"Thanks, Julian."

"Yes, sir."

John's eyes glittered in anger. Who would cold-bloodedly try to murder two people? He no longer seriously entertained the possibility that Alyssa was involved. Her personality was basically too honest, too open for that kind of behavior. Besides, he couldn't see her hurting a fly.

One of the things he'd learned in the monastery with the Buddhists was how to use all his senses in evaluating imminent danger. When he was with Alyssa, he felt no threat at all, just newly awakened desire. That was a danger of a different sort.

John returned to his office to wrap up some business transactions that could not be delayed any longer.

When Alyssa came back, he'd ask her about anything unusual she'd noticed before takeoff in that plane. He'd ask for a discreet inquiry by the airline company, also. They didn't want to scare off the perpetrator if he or she was still around.

Alyssa was standing in the garden after dinner, watching the *koi* swim in their pond, appreciating the infinite tranquillity that bathed this peaceful spot.

"Henry just called from the hospital. Suzie's still hanging on. By a thread."

She whirled and grabbed her throat with one hand. John! The cat-footed man just took six months off her life, she thought in exasperation.

"That's wonderful news," Alyssa exclaimed, trying to recover. "I hope they're right about that golden hour people are supposed to have to get to a doctor after a trauma." If they were, Suzie just made it.

"Her odds improve every hour that passes and she's still with us."

He could remember other times when the odds hadn't been good enough for the victim. Like his old man. And his mother. Of course, they'd brought their problems on themselves, to a certain extent. He wasn't certain whether Suzie had or not. Her last words to him had been ambiguous. It sounded as if she'd willingly helped trap Alyssa at Esau's request, and then things had gotten out of hand. He resisted believing that Suzie had known that either Alyssa or herself were to have been murdered. Suzie was wild and greedy, but she wasn't a murderess.

"You know, John," Alyssa said, trying to cheer him up by changing the subject a little, "you scared me to death when you came into the garden. You don't make a sound! Either you've got to learn to make more noise, or I have to start wearing a hearing aid when you're around!"

His eyes softened with amusement. As he walked toward her, he watched her strain to hear his shoes against the pebbles. *Too bad, honey. You can't hear me unless I want you to.* He watched her face fall and then cloud up with a frustrated frown.

"I still can't hear you," she pointed out, shaking her head to underscore her mystification. "How can you walk that quietly on loose pebbles for heaven's sake?"

"I spent years perfecting silence," he pointed out reasonably. "Why should I undo all that hard work now?"

"So you don't give urban guests like me heart failure?" she suggested hopefully. "You see, we're accustomed to high-volume traffic and yelling pedestrians. We've become totally insensitive to low levels of noise."

He stood in front of her.

"Shut your eyes." When her eyes widened and she looked somewhat alarmed he donned his most innocent expression and held up his palms to show his harmlessness. "Shut them. I'll teach you how to hear better."

Alyssa rolled her eyes and muttered, "Sure you will." But she closed her eyes agreeably and waited to see what would happen next.

"Listening is just concentration focused on sound. I want you to focus your entire body, every cell from the marrow of your bones to the ends of your hair, on picking up the sensation of movement. That's what sound is. Movement. One air molecule against the other. Air molecule against leaf. Shoe against pebble. Shirt against skin. For example, can you hear the *koi* blowing bubbles and snapping at the leaf floating on the water?"

Alyssa, absorbed in the low rhythm of his voice, listened. In her mind she heard the small fish's mouth open and smack the surface.

"Yes. I hear it."

"And can you hear the wind running through the bamboo?"

Not enough to make them rattle like chimes, she thought, then, deeper, deeper, into her mind she followed the wind, and...

"Yes. I hear it," she whispered. God, he *was* making her hear things, she realized. There was a whole world of sensation, and she had been unaware of it until now.

"Now listen for me," he said softly.

She heard the softest scrape of leather against stone. Just one tiny hint of sound. Then nothing. She stood in the darkness of her mind, eyes closed, willing her body to sense the motion of his, somewhere in the vicinity. The air behind her felt warmer. Was that a hint of trouser fabric, rustling against his thigh as he moved closer?

On a burst of intuition, Alyssa put her hands behind her and touched his chest. The cotton of his shirt, the buttons down the front, the hard bone and compact muscle beneath. She withdrew her hand, feeling she had crossed a barrier of intimacy that she shouldn't have, but he caught her hand with his and held it. Heat surged through her palm and burned every inch of her skin.

Alyssa opened her eyes and pulled free, turning and backing away from him a step at the same time.

"Your hearing is better than you think," he said softly.

She smiled, although she didn't feel like smiling at all.

"Maybe you're just a very good instructor," she murmured uneasily. "Is this the kind of thing you used to practice in the monastery?"

"Suzie told you?" he guessed. He didn't look angry, just lazily curious.

"Yes. She said you studied meditation and karate and *kendo.*"

"Suzie always did talk a lot."

"So did you learn to walk like a cat there?" she asked, trying to find her nerves. They were around here someplace, she was sure. If he'd just stop looking at her, as if he'd like to do something ... forbidden.

"I walk like a *ninja,*" he said bluntly. "How much do you know about me? Exactly."

"Oh, not that much," she said, backing up until her thighs hit the edge of the brick wall that encased the *koi* pond. "Since I was interested in the sword, I tried to learn about Onijima, but there hasn't been much written about the island. Or about you."

He stood where he was, effectively trapping her in the corner of the garden. She couldn't get past him without brushing against his body, something she obviously would prefer not to do. He could smell the scent of perfume. Something light and intoxicating. Like the woman wearing it.

"Go on," he said in a low voice.

"Well, I suppose everyone knows that the Mori family runs the island like a medieval barony. And the people are free to come and go, but those who stay are fiercely loyal to you...."

"And?" He looked at the shape of her shoulder and arm. Noticed the tension in her. She was shaking, he realized. Was she frightened of him? No. There was no fear in those clear gray eyes. Wariness. But no outright fear. Repressed desire, perhaps? Heat pulsed through his body. So he wasn't the only one feeling the dull tug of attraction between them. "What else, Alyssa?" he asked softly.

"George says that you make money by trading in commodities and stocks and bonds and precious metals and currencies...."

"George...your business partner?"

"Yes. And he says..."

"Since you're blushing, he must have said something very interesting indeed," John observed. He lifted a dark brow and came a step closer. "What did George say?"

She glanced at the *koi*, then to her left and a little behind her in the pond. She hadn't wanted to get this personal with him. They were, after all, completely alone for all intents and purposes. Etsu was tending to a personal matter, the guards were at their posts at the perimeter of the house and Isamu Mori was in his room with his nurse. And there was this strange attraction between them. She felt it more strongly every time they were together. That was very dangerous. She knew it.

She felt John's gaze and knew she couldn't lie to him. She'd never been very good at evasions, and with John, she was certain any effort to evade the truth would only invite more attention. She swallowed and told herself she was a big girl and that talking about a man's mistress to his face wasn't something to blush about.

She blushed anyway.

"Well, George said you had the best-looking women in the Orient for mistresses."

Defiantly, Alyssa lifted her chin and turned to stare straight into his eyes. To her surprise, he looked shocked. Instinctively she reached out to soothe him. She touched his arm lightly with hers and her face reflected her remorse.

"I'm sorry. I shouldn't have repeated that. It was really something that I never should have heard in the first place...."

John stared at her, not knowing exactly what he thought. At first, he was simply stunned. It never occurred to him that she would have heard about his damned love life.

Bloody hell, he didn't know a single thing about hers. Besides, he'd always been reasonably discreet. He frowned.

"How the devil does this George of yours come to know about my mistresses?"

She dropped her hand and looked at him, surprised and a little hurt that he would admit to having mistresses in this day and age. Maybe he lived a more baronial, medieval life than she had thought. Maybe some of the wilder tales she'd heard weren't the exaggerations she'd assumed. Maybe they were true.

"I repeat, how does George know—or think he knows—about the women I involve myself with?"

"Why don't you tell me the truth, and I'll tell you if it matches what George said?" she suggested. From the darkening expression on his face, she knew he wouldn't go for that. She hastened to cooperate in the interest of peace. "He said there was a woman in Singapore that you kept like a courtesan. After you parted with her, she got involved with some oil sheikh's nephew and they're talking marriage. Before her there was a flight attendant in Hong Kong, and before her there was a wealthy widow in Thailand, or someplace..."

"Bloody hell!" he muttered.

"I'm sorry! That's what George said."

John frowned ferociously.

"Has he been having me followed?"

"I think he just gossips a lot." She sighed. "You see, George prides himself on being a successful day trader in stocks and other financial investments worldwide. He gets on the phone and talks with people in Taiwan or Hong Kong or Tokyo and keeps tabs on people who interest him."

"And I interest him?" John asked, controlling his anger and struggling with the renewed suspicion that Alyssa was too honest to be real. Maybe he had been too hasty in exonerating her from all complicity. Maybe she *was* a plant or a spy of some sort. With a partner like this George, he had to wonder about her character.

Alyssa bit her lip and wished they hadn't ever gotten onto this embarrassing subject.

"George Bodney has one of the finest collections of Japanese art that I've ever seen. He concentrates on metalworks, especially armor, swords and related pieces. I met him when I was just beginning my business. He's very private about his collection. Very secretive about where he gets his pieces, but of course that's understandable. Most collectors who can afford masterpieces prefer anonymity. They don't want to attract thieves, for one thing."

"What does that have to do with me?" John asked darkly.

The idea that the man had spied on him made him angrier than he'd been in a long time. And under the circumstances, it was highly suspicious. For some reason, Alyssa didn't seem to see the connection. That further fed his old suspicions about her. But he fought them. He'd been ready to trust her. His instincts had been that she was honest.

"When he heard about the Asian art gallery that my brother and I were opening, he introduced himself. He became a friend of ours and also a business partner. He loans us some of his pieces for special display from time to time. And when someone he knows is interested in selling a piece, he steers them into the gallery."

"What the hell does that have to do with my personal life?" John demanded, thoroughly tired of wading through Alyssa's long explanation.

"When he saw the *tsuba* and realized how valuable it was, he became interested in the sword, just as I had. He tried to find out about you so that we could decide how to approach you. It wasn't possible to know what he'd find out. He just put out feelers, and some of the information that came back wasn't just...financial." She felt awful. Still blushing, and looking rather bewildered, she said, "I'm really sorry that he delved too deeply. I know I would be very angry if someone talked about me the way I've just talked about you."

He felt the anger unknot inside his heart. No one could lie and look like such an angel, he thought. He wanted to pull her into his arms and kiss her until he could forget about all the peculiar things that were happening. He wanted to bury himself in her soft, gentle warmth. When she looked at him like this, he found it nearly impossible to remember what he'd ever doubted her.

He got an iron grip on himself and fiercely ignored the craving for her that was consuming his better sense.

"Did he tell you that I only take a mistress if she's willing to walk into the arrangement with her eyes wide open, knowing it's not going to last forever, willing to accept the relationship on those terms?" he asked, intentionally being as tough-sounding as he knew how to be.

He saw her flinch, realized the idea of such ruthless love-making bothered her.

"No," she said. "He didn't mention that."

"Does that offend your sensibilities, *Miss Jones?*" he asked cynically.

"I . . . don't know."

She pondered what he'd said. He was still afraid of love, she thought. After all these years. Having been bitterly disappointed early on, he never learned to believe that love truly existed. Or that it could last. She herself had a certain amount of sympathy with that point of view. She'd certainly seen little enough love, and much of it evaporated apparently, in a matter of years. Even after a torrid weekend, if some of her friends were to be believed.

"You look shocked," he said coolly. "I take it you've never been made such an offer."

She smiled and shook her head.

"No. I guess I don't look like mistress material."

"I wouldn't say that."

Alyssa thought she'd forgotten how to breathe. They stared at one another across a gulf of time and space, cynical experience and bitter memories. She'd never believed in love at first sight, but at the moment, she was sorely tempted to give it some credence.

Because she felt as if she were falling.

If it wasn't love, it was a close cousin. Alasdair would call it lust, no doubt.

She knew it was insane, but she had the almost irresistible urge to step into John Mori's arms and tell him he was wrong about everything. That if he'd just unshackle himself from the past, he would be able to see the truth about love, and he would stop wasting himself on temporary mistresses whose affections were bought by money.

"Johnny-chan! Johnny-chan? You out here?"

It was Etsu. She was charging into the garden like a woman possessed of an important assignment.

John stepped away and turned to face the housekeeper.

Alyssa tried to remember how to breathe.

Etsu had a fistful of photos and wore a determined expression.

"Spring come before you know. Very auspicious time for wedding, early spring. I talk to fortune-teller. He say March good time for you this year. Marry pretty woman with heart of gold and make good babies. Now. To find woman, we got to look at pictures. How about now?" Noticing Alyssa, she added politely, "Hi, missy. Please excuse. This very important. We be done soon. Won't take long to look at pictures." She smiled cajolingly at John. "They very pretty girls, Johnny. You like one, we arrange a meeting. You talk. You like each other..." Etsu shrugged and grinned.

Life was uncomplicated to her. She liked to get right to the point. At nearly eighty, she never wasted time if she could avoid it.

Alyssa felt her mouth drop in shock. A giggle threatened to overpower her. She couldn't imagine old Etsu running a bride-selection operation for John Mori. As a matter of fact, she couldn't imagine John picking a bride at all. He seemed determined to be an iron man, living alone.

"Not now, Etsu." Leave it to Etsu to keep harping on his need to move on in life, he thought, bracing for resistance. Etsu was very determined on the matter of selecting a wife for him. *Bloody hell.*

"You not so young anymore," Etsu said uncharitably. "And your father need grandchildren to carry on family name. So when you get started? We been through lots of pictures. I wait. I come back every year. But you always say, 'Not now.' What you want? Perfect woman?"

"I'll pick my own wife, Etsu."

"You always say that. I no see any wife around here."

"Etsu!" John glared at her.

Alyssa smothered a laugh as a miffed Etsu waddled back into the house, photos of John's marital prospects in her hand.

"She's not shy, is she?" Alyssa teased.

"Marriage isn't personal to her. It's a practical arrangement."

"I hear that arranged marriages are often happy," she murmured, trying to smooth over some of John's lingering ire as she edged away from him.

"Sometimes." he conceded. "Etsu's been a go-between for seventy-five marriages. She's very proud of her track record."

"And she intends you to be number seventy-six?"

"Yes." He turned his attention back to Alyssa. "Have you been married?"

"No."

"Engaged?"

"No."

"Live with a man?"

"Now, just a minute!"

"Hell, George told you about my mistresses. Why shouldn't I know about your lovers?"

Alyssa blushed furiously.

"Because it's none of your business!" she said, laughing with outrage.

He pulled her into his arms and trapped her hands behind her back when she would have fought free and slapped him in the face.

She knew he was going to kiss her and she turned her head, but he found her mouth with his and captured her before she could escape.

Red fire consumed her from out of nowhere. She felt the heat from his body, the muscles binding her to him, the faint taste of his lips and the intoxicating scent of his skin.

He ground his mouth against hers and pushed her back until she was trapped between him and the bricks.

Sweet, hot temptation. That was what the kiss was like. A delicate flame that burned with a delicious heat across her mouth, down her breasts, into her belly and thighs.

He was moving against her and the sensation made the glorious heat spread.

Then he lifted his head and looked into her eyes.

She looked as if she'd been struck by lightning.

That was exactly how he felt.

He released her as if he'd been burned.

He stepped back, trying to erase the arousing memory of her body pressed tightly against his, of her warm mouth softening beneath his, of her sweet taste and delicate scent and the hypnotic sensation of falling into a whirlpool of fierce desire.

"You don't kiss like an experienced mistress," he conceded after giving it some thought. "But in your case, I don't think there's a man on the planet who'd utter the slightest complaint."

She watched him walk away, and she touched her lips with the back of her hand. That had sounded suspiciously like a compliment from a man who had been startled to discover that he enjoyed kissing her, she thought. Against her better judgment, she smiled. At least she wasn't the only one in that kiss who'd been stunned by the impact.

Alyssa leaned against the bricks, grateful for their solid support.

Good God, how could John Mori's mistresses have let him go? she wondered in amazement. The man kissed like Lucifer on a rampage. And he took no prisoners. She was still tingling. Right down to her singed little toes.

The steel blade arced through the air so quickly that the eye did not see it, only its deadly trail, a sliver of shimmering death in the pale moonlight.

John moved, feet gliding with such quickness that he, too, was a blur of black in the skeletal white light of moon and stars. Starlight glinted off the tempered steel with each graceful cut and slice. Around him fell ghostly bodies of imaginary attackers laid low forever by the mortal bite of his ruthless sword.

To most observers, the fluid yet brutal motions would have seemed like perfection. To the aged *kendo* master who had silently come to stand and watch, John's struggle with himself was soon apparent. Stepping out from beneath a low-hanging pine branch, the old teacher stood, waiting to be discovered. He was amazed that his star pupil still did not realize that he had arrived.

When John finished assassinating the last imaginary attacker, he stood in the center of the small clearing. The curved sword, held firmly in both hands, was in front of him in a position of ready defense. The words that came from the edge of the pines startled him.

"Your mind is troubled tonight." He spoke in Japanese.

John whirled. Realizing who it was, he immediately lowered the sword and bowed deeply out of profound respect and affection for the man who had taught him so much over the years.

"*Sensei*," he said, greeting his mentor by invoking his honored title, which meant "teacher" in Japanese.

He had been unaware of the *sensei*'s arrival. John frowned. He knew he'd been preoccupied, but to have his concentration slip this badly was disconcerting. He had sought this training ground to sharpen his mind and focus his thoughts. It appeared he was having little success.

"I didn't hear you," he admitted ruefully, bowing again but this time in apology. "Excuse your humble pupil's miserable performance. It isn't worthy of his teacher's many hours of patient instruction."

"Hmm." The old man accepted the apology with equanimity. "Your mind is not emptied of human diversions," he observed. "The ego interferes perhaps?" John's ego had been a major burden for the monks to whittle into shape. It was still rather large for their taste, but they'd grown used to it and decided that it must be John's karma to have more ego than was usually tolerated.

John slid the razor-sharp tip of the tempered steel blade into the opening of the scabbard tied at his hip. In one smooth motion, he sheathed the *katana* and walked over to his old *kendo* master.

"Not the ego this time, *Sensei*. I regret to say it is the id that keeps my mind from emptying as it should," John said, grimacing.

The old man laughed and laid a hand on his favorite student's shoulder.

"You are a young man," he said comfortingly. "It is natural."

"Thirty-seven isn't that young," John noted somewhat skeptically.

"The blood doesn't run as hot as seventeen, perhaps," the old master agreed. "But when the woman fits your soul, the body tells you. Perhaps that is the problem?"

"Perhaps."

"And I have heard there are other problems, as well. The students have talked at lessons. Will there be more of these so-called accidents?"

"Possibly."

"Then it is important for you to eliminate this...problem of the id that you mention. A warrior whose mind is not empty of distractions may not live to enjoy them."

"Yes. So you have told your humble student many times, *Sensei.* That was why I came here tonight to practice."

"Hmm." The old monk nodded.

"But this particular distraction is...difficult to put out of my thoughts."

"Embrace it, then," the old man said with a shrug. "Make it part of you. Then it will cease to distract."

That was easier said than done, John thought. Although he himself had been entertaining thoughts along those lines.

"Perhaps you could bring the 'distraction' to the *kendo* school someday? I would like to meet the woman who has so captured Iron Man's thoughts that he cannot rid her from his mind for even a few minutes." The old man's eyes reflected his amusement.

John sighed and lapsed into English.

"I'll never hear the end of this, will I?"

The old man laughed.

"Probably not. But that is a compliment to you, Iron Man. You give us little to tease you about. I must thank your distraction for reminding us all that you too are only human."

They walked together through the grove.

"Come to the teahouse," the old man suggested, his vigorous stride and balanced carriage belying his age. "I'll make you a cup of tea, and we'll empty our minds of all but oneness with the Mind that contains us all."

John left the sword at the door of the hut and followed his old mentor inside.

John knelt in the place reserved for guests in the teahouse, while the *sensei* knelt in front of him, heated the black iron pot of water and assembled the necessary utensils.

"I was coming here to enjoy a cup of tea in the moonlight when I happened upon you," the monk said. "Fate brought you to be my guest."

When the hissing sound of boiling water filled the still air, the ancient ritual began.

The monk executed the simple steps of making a formal cup of tea with a smooth effortlessness born of many years of practice. His confident, flowing motions eased inner conflicts and soothed the heart. A light touch of carefully folded red silk on black *raku* tea bowl...the scooping of the bitter green powder from its black lacquer container...the hollow sound of the delicate bamboo scoop being tapped against the rim of the bowl. Pure simplicity.

"It is said that the art of taking tea is as important to the warrior's training as the handling of the sword," the *kendo* master observed. "Many of the motions are the same. Destruction and creation, two faces of the same force. Always they are one."

With a bamboo ladle, the old master poured hot water into the bowl, leaving a bit in the ladle so it could be returned to the heavy black pot. He laid the ladle on the open mouth of the pot, easing the handle onto the back of his hand between thumb and forefinger. He hesitated for a moment, then slid his hand away, leaving the ladle balanced on the black iron.

It was the motion of an archer, letting loose his arrow.

After vigorously whisking the tea into a light green froth, he withdrew the bamboo whisk, just as a man might draw his sword.

He placed the whisk upright in front of him and slightly to right of center. Then he placed the bowl of tea on the *tatami* in front of John. He rested his hands on his thighs. The honored guest had been served.

John bowed, placing his hands on the floor. Then he put the bowl on the palm of his hand and made two quarter turns, in order to drink from the back, as was considered polite.

The bitter green tea was warm and familiar to John's tongue.

It brought back memories of his life with the monks, both as a boy in Hong Kong and as a young man on Onijima.

They had conquered the raw, visceral anger that had embittered him as a youth. Only a small, stubborn residue remained. They had healed many wounds over the years. Physical ones. Mental ones. Even spiritual wounds that he hadn't been aware of until many years after they had mended.

But they'd never completely resolved the void created by his aversion to letting himself truly know the face of love. He was aware of that, but it had never concerned him. Until now.

He wiped the edge of the cup with a small piece of white paper the master had thoughtfully supplied, since John hadn't come prepared to be a guest for tea. Then he turned the bowl two quarter turns back and replaced it for the *sensei* to remove.

As the elderly man took the bowl and rinsed it with cool water he noted John's renewed preoccupation.

"You thought practicing *kendo* would clear your mind?"

"Yes."

"But it did not."

"No."

The hot water hissed as cool water was added and the lid replaced on the simmering cauldron.

"Perhaps you chose the wrong sword to ease the pain," the old man noted shrewdly, a smile forming.

John grinned. He'd long ago become accustomed to the monk's frankness and earthy sense of humor, but it never ceased to startle him. It always came in stark contrast to the ascetic atmosphere of the monk's solitary life.

"You're probably right, *sensei*. But I need a willing sheath for that one."

"Ah! Now I truly understand your problem!" The old man chuckled.

They sat together in tranquil harmony in the moonlit hut, meditating on the oneness of the universe. Of life, which could not exist without death. Of creation, which was the same as destruction. Of woman and of man, two distinct halves of one seamless and timeless whole.

Of a mind that ached for the peace of emptiness. And of the tranquil solitude found in a mind filled to overflowing with earthly joy.

Chapter 9

John had already left the house when Alyssa arrived at the dining room the following morning.

"He go see airplane," Etsu announced with a toothy grin as she shuffled into the room.

She was wearing a white *mama-san* smock, the standard uniform of the Japanese housewife, and bearing a tray of Onijima-style breakfast: broiled fish, a bowl of steamed white rice, some pickled vegetables and a pot of hot green tea.

Alyssa, accustomed to a thin slice of California melon and a cup of coffee with no-calorie sweetener, wondered how to politely turn away all this food.

"Uh...I rarely each much for breakfast," she murmured apologetically. "I hope I won't upset the cook if I can't finish everything...."

Etsu wasn't phased. She plopped the tray down on the table and proceeded to take critical stock of Alyssa's slender build.

"Maybe you get more offers if you have more than bones for man to hug."

"Offers?" Alyssa asked with trepidation.

"Offers for marriage." Etsu eyed her shrewdly. "You have a go-between?"

"No..."

"Ever married?"

"Uh, no."

Alyssa sat down and gingerly wiped her hands on the rolled, steaming towelette that sat on a small dish near the chopsticks. It was a little early in the morning to have her future plotted, she thought, but apparently Etsu never missed an opportunity to put a single person on the road to marital bliss.

Etsu shook her head. Her face was smooth and placid, but her eyes clearly registered her disapproval.

Alyssa picked at her broiled fish and forced a small bite down her throat. It was tasty enough. It's just that it was at least ten hours before dinner, and in Alyssa's book, the food staring back at her belonged at the dinner table.

Etsu didn't appear to be in any hurry to attend to her chores.

"How old you, missy?"

"Uh...thirty-two."

Looking quite shocked, Etsu pondered Alyssa's advanced age and sorry marital prospects.

Alyssa wondered in horror if the old lady was beginning to view her as a challenge to her matchmaking skills. By Etsu's standards, Alyssa had obviously passed marriageable prime quite a long time ago. Alyssa tried to withstand the professional assessment with her ego intact. After all, Etsu was obviously from the old school. Make that old, *old* school, she amended. Alyssa certainly had never thought of thirty-two as being over the hill, marriage-wise.

"Thirty-two is not considered old where I come from," Alyssa pointed out optimistically. "Lots of women don't marry until their careers are underway nowadays. Why, it's common to find people tying the knot for the first time when they're thirty-five, thirty-six, even into their forties."

Etsu made a disrespectful smacking sound with her lips.

"They crazy. Can't make good baby that old. Need baby to carry on family, to take care of you when old."

"I wouldn't want to be a burden on a child," Alyssa pointed out uncomfortably. "And people in my country rely on Social Security and retirement plans to keep a roof over their head in old age."

"Caring for parent not a burden! That honorable obligation. Duty!"

"Yes. But still I think it better to marry for love than for the sake of family procreation...uh, but then I come from San Francisco and I guess we think a little differently there." Obviously on Onijima the populace had one foot in a medieval past and was a little slow to catch on.

"Marry for love okay," Etsu conceded with a bored shrug. "But someone have to check him out before ceremony. Make sure he okay."

"I certainly wouldn't argue with that."

She recalled a friend in college who'd married at nineteen. The man had conducted a passionate courtship and her friend had fallen wildly in love, falling into his skillful hands like a ripened plum. Unfortunately, the Romeo had perfected his technique by seducing women from Tijuana to Toronto. He already had several wives. Her friend's annulment on grounds of bigamy had been approved in record time. Her broken heart had taken much longer to mend.

If someone like Etsu had checked his references before he'd crawled between her friend's sheets, Alyssa had no doubt that her friend would have been spared a great deal of agony and embarrassment.

"Maybe you don't like babies?" Etsu suggested bluntly.

"Well, of course I like babies! Everybody likes babies, don't they? They're soft and warm, and they smell like all your childhood memories, and they laugh like angels and sleep like beautiful rag dolls, and they cling to you with such total trust and hope. I mean, who wouldn't love a baby?" Alyssa frowned. "How did we get to the subject of babies?"

Alyssa's nerves stretched taut. Babies were a sensitive subject with her, and she sincerely wished that Etsu hadn't brought it up. The one problem with marrying late was figuring out how to have a child before nature gave up on you and eliminated the possibility forever. Not that Alyssa was quite in that situation yet. She had time. Lots of time. More than enough time. She kept telling herself that.

Betsy De Laguna, one of her best friends, had begged her to let her help out at the gallery while Alyssa was gone; she wanted to take a break from the nerve-racking efforts she and her husband were going through, trying to conceive.

Betsy had blithely planned her life for years. After getting her M.B.A., she'd methodically hunted for a husband and had found the perfect man. They had so many things in common it was incredible. Alyssa was amazed at Betsy's phenomenal luck. Betsy and her husband had chosen career paths that would keep them in the San Francisco area. They'd been politically active, like all rising young professionals. They'd given to the proper charities, built a house and selected the best month and year in which their first child should be born. They'd even calculated the tax implications in coming up with the suitable dates.

To their surprise, the designated year came and went without success in the baby department. It was the first bump on an otherwise smooth highway to the top for them. They'd been perplexed at first, then concerned. They'd had themselves evaluated inside and out and counseled to a fare-thee-well.

Now Betsy's birthday was coming up. She'd be forty-two. They were *way* behind on the baby-making schedule and were becoming increasingly frantic. Every time Betsy dropped by for lunch, Alyssa braced herself for a recitation on the latest dreadful woes. Betsy unloaded everything on Alyssa. She seemed refreshed by the end of the lunch, but Alyssa slunk out of the establishment utterly exhausted.

Sex had lost its glow. The marriage was a strained battleground where fertilizing a ripening egg had become the all-consuming obsession. Each suspected the other was somehow the culprit. Communication was strained. The marital bed had become an office where each slammed away at their duty, doing their damnedest to release the baby that was stuck somewhere in limbo.

Every time Betsy passed a pregnant teenager, she broke into tears. Alyssa had feared she'd have a nervous breakdown. She wouldn't be surprised to hear they were heading for divorce. It was just awful.

Alyssa dearly hoped that the distraction of handling the gallery for a few weeks would help Betsy get a grip on herself again. Give her and her husband a little space, a breather from their anxieties and disappointments.

The De Lagunas' problem had forced Alyssa to confront the biological facts of her own life that she'd been putting off facing. She hadn't been dating much and she had difficulty viewing the men she had dated as potential suitors.

If she didn't make progress soon, she'd be too old to have a child. After all, it took a while to get to know the man. Then there was planning for the wedding. And a year or so to adjust to marriage. That added up to a lot of time.

And she did long for a child. Someone to love and nurture and watch grow. Someone to fill her heart with the laughter of childhood.

"You sure you want baby but don't want man?" Etsu poked into Alyssa's wandering thoughts with her usual disregard for delicacy.

Alyssa blushed. Actually, that hadn't been too far off the mark. It had been easier for her to envision a child than a husband. Somehow, he'd always been a blur. A vague, unthreatening, sexless shadow. Maybe that was the problem. She dated colorless men that aroused absolutely no sexual interest whatsoever.

John Mori's thoroughly masculine image burst out of nowhere and consumed her. Her mouth suddenly tingled again from the memory of his kiss. Heat flashed through her body like wildfire as she recalled his hard belly and chest pressed against her as he hauled them to safety up the side of the mountain.

She blushed. No one would ever describe John Mori as colorless. Or sexless. She fanned her hot face and told herself her fascination with John Mori was an aberration born of being on this strange island with danger all around.

Under normal circumstances she wouldn't react this way. Surely she wouldn't.

"Uh . . ." Alyssa struggled to regain the thread of the conversation. "I think children should be raised by both their parents if it's possible for that to happen. Of course I'd like a man to go with the child. I'm not *opposed* to it, for heaven's sake! Why are you asking me all these things, anyway?''

Etsu shrugged.

"Your mama very unhappy woman. I thought you decide not to marry, so you not have unhappiness like your mama had."

"Don't be silly...." Alyssa immediately brushed off the insinuation, but then she blinked. Alyssa's head came up and her eyes widened. "Etsu? You knew my mother?"

"Yes. I know. Your mama and papa died."

"How did you know that?"

"Mori-sama. He was told. I here when he receive the news. Both times. First time, for your mother. Second time, for your father."

"I barely can remember her. I was so young when she died. I tried to take care of my brother the way I thought she would want me to. I suppose in a childish way I was trying to bring her back. You know...if you're a good child, your parent will magically come back to you? All evil can be undone if only you are good enough."

"Not silly. Good karma help control bad karma," Etsu said philosophically.

"Well, perhaps... As a small child I thought that way. Then you get older and realize life is more complicated than that." Alyssa sighed. "I always told myself that Mother couldn't have abandoned us like that unless she was in horrendous pain."

She pushed a small pickled vegetable a few millimeters this way and that. Tears welled up in her eyes. She blinked them back as fast as she could.

"Um...where did you meet Mother and Father?" Alyssa asked, clearing her throat and trying to maintain her composure.

"They come here. Father come once. Mother come alone many times."

"Really?" Alyssa said, scarcely able to breathe the words.

"You were baby. Nanny take care of you at home where you live. You no come to Onijima. But I see your mama.

She come here on boat. Husband always gone." Etsu's face was artfully smooth.

"My father traveled a great deal. He had lots of business dealings that required personal attention." So she'd been told often enough, Alyssa thought. "Mother was lonely much of the time."

"Yes. She ache with emptiness."

Alyssa knew that her mother had been agonizingly lonely for much of her marriage. That's what Alyssa's great-aunt had said, when Alyssa was in her twenties and deemed old enough to be told some of the darker family secrets. Her aunt had wanted Alyssa to know the truth about her parents, at least, as much of the truth as the aunt knew. Or thought she knew.

It had been a depressing revelation to Alyssa. But so little had been said about her mother's suicide, she had always suspected bad things had been happening. Alyssa wondered if Etsu might help her understand what had led her mother to kill herself. The aunt's explanation had never completely satisfied Alyssa, but, since her aunt had been living in Boston at the time of her mother's death, Alyssa doubted that she had all the facts. Her aunt had only known what Alyssa's mother had told her in letters. That was a one-sided view of the problem.

Before she died, her aunt gave Alyssa the letters and, with a certain amount of trepidation, Alyssa read them. They had been written with a very circumspect hand. Her mother hadn't felt free to be completely candid in the correspondence. Alyssa could understand that. It would have been terribly embarrassing to lay out in black and white precisely what was happening in the marriage. So, interspersed with happy descriptions of travel and art and culture were oblique mentions of conflict, neglect and what might have been abuse.

It had all happened long ago, though, and Alyssa had never had the opportunity to speak to someone who might have known her mother during the years just prior to her taking her own life.

"How often did Mother come to Onijima?" she asked, trying not to show how important this was to her. Alyssa feared that Etsu might be reluctant to talk if she knew how intensely Alyssa wanted to know.

"Many times. Her husband say it okay to come, but she must stay on boat."

"Wasn't he...jealous?" Alyssa asked, feeling very strange talking about her parents like this with Etsu.

"No. Maybe not really love her." Etsu shrugged as if she didn't really know about that. "He trust her, though. And he trust Mori-sama to protect her. Mori-sama is a very honorable man. And he much older. Husband think wife wouldn't feel anything for 'old man,'" Etsu explained, shaking her head. "Her husband a fool. He no take care of wife. Woman does not care how old a man is sometimes." Her face crinkled in a smile.

"What happened?" Alyssa watched Etsu's earthy smile turn sad.

"Her husband say she must always stay on boat when she come. He not all dumb. He not want her to have all her freedom. He give her just enough to keep her. She always did as he say. She know crew tell him if she does not. And she wanted to come back, walk on the beach, see the art, talk to her new friends she make here on Onijima, so she do what husband ask. Only one time, she not stay on boat."

"Oh?" Alyssa's mouth went dry. "Where did she spend that night?"

"She come here. And stay. Last time. After that, she never come again." Etsu watched Alyssa closely, as if trying to assess what Alyssa might know. "Your mama love art. Mori-sama has beautiful art. He show her."

"And she stayed?"

Etsu nodded.

There was another message in those old eyes, Alyssa realized. Etsu wasn't free to say any more, but she was testing Alyssa, to see what she knew about her mother and Isamu Mori. Alyssa decided now wasn't the time or place to share any deeper secrets. After all, she barely knew Etsu. And this was a house of strangers. She felt an obligation to guard her mother's privacy, as much as she could.

Etsu seemed pleased that Alyssa had refused to comment further. Filial loyalty was considered a virtue, apparently, Alyssa thought.

"Your mama dead. You are alive," Etsu said, in a rare show of genuine tenderness. "She would want you to be happy."

Alyssa thought Etsu was probably right about that.

"You afraid marry. Afraid suffer same pain. Afraid love."

"That could be said of a lot of people, don't you think, Etsu-sama? Besides, in my case there's a certain logic to it. Besides, I've had boyfriends," she pointed out defensively. "I *like* men. I'm not phobic about them or anything like that. Up until now it simply hasn't been the right time for me. And I never met the man for me...."

Etsu looked unimpressed.

"Time past right. You like overripe fruit. You need man. You have warm heart. Need someone share it." She looked at Alyssa with great seriousness and lowered her voice to a whisper. "Your mama happy here. She and Mori-sama gave each other much happiness. She no afraid to take happiness when it given by a good and noble man. You her daughter. Do not be less a woman than mama."

"But...that killed her," Alyssa murmured in dismay. "She felt so guilty about their relationship that, she used the knife that he'd given her on herself...."

Obviously, Etsu knew everything. There was no point in being protective of her mother's honor.

Alyssa shuddered, as she always did imagining what that must have been like. Her mother, alone on the yacht. Desperate to escape her marriage. Tied to a domineering and powerful man who refused to let her go, who'd forced a pregnancy on her in an effort to keep her dependent on him. Terrified that the man she loved would murder her husband to set her free, her mother had decided the only way out had been to immolate herself. And she'd used the old *samurai* knife that Mori Isamu had given her. She'd slit her wrists.

Alyssa felt sick.

She laid the chopsticks down and got up from the table.

"I'm sorry. I can't eat any more, Etsu-sama."

She turned to go to the garden but saw a familiar form standing in the doorway. He'd been listening to them talk. He'd come with the characteristic silence that made him impossible for her to hear. Old Etsu, with her back to him and her hearing dulled by the years, had not been aware of him, either.

Etsu, seeing Alyssa's shock, turned to see who had arrived.

"Johnny-chan!" She bowed and color pinkened her wrinkled parchment cheeks.

"Somebody's got to tie a bell around your neck," Alyssa muttered. Her heart was pounding, but she knew it wasn't simply because he had startled her.

"It takes courage to bell the cat." His expression lightened to one of amusement.

"I'll buy the bell if you'll hang it around your neck," she offered.

Etsu looked from John to Alyssa. Her old eyes narrowed and she seemed to be contemplating an intriguing possibility.

"I thought you were looking at an airplane," Alyssa said, remembering what Etsu had told her when she had come to the dining room for breakfast.

"I was."

"The one I was flying in until it turned into a submarine?"

"The very one."

"How's it doing? Out of intensive care yet?"

"Yes. We're crating it up and arranging to have it hauled up to the airport. The company that owns the plane sent their chief mechanic over this morning to decide whether to repair it or cannibalize it for parts—or simply junk it."

"Well, if they repair it, I certainly don't want to *ever* fly anywhere in it again!" she exclaimed.

"I'll make sure they understand that," he said dryly. "I had to come back to take care of some morning business, and I thought you might like to try to call your partner, George."

"Yes!" She flashed him a smile and impulsively rushed over to his side.

She looked as if he'd just handed her a Christmas present, he thought. Funny what it did to the region of his heart to see her smile with such enthusiasm, such spontaneity.

He also felt slightly irritated that calling old George would provide such a lift in her day. He told himself that was simply because he had serious doubts about George. Especially since he'd started gathering a little business information about the man himself.

"Come on, then," John said brusquely. He took her elbow lightly and walked with her toward his private suite and its large, well-equipped office.

Alyssa thought she'd stepped through an invisible net of electricity as soon as he touched her. Her heart skipped a beat. Her breathing caught in her throat. And something warm flooded her skin.

"I'll be very interested in hearing what George has to say for himself," John muttered.

"You'll like George," Alyssa assured him earnestly. "He's a man of the world, like you...."

John certainly hoped not.

"He spent a year at Cambridge..."

Figures, he thought, recalling the university's endless rivalry with his alma mater, Oxford.

"And he's an expert on swords. He's even studied *kendo.*"

"Is that so? How good is he?"

"Well...I don't know enough to say. I've never actually seen him practice."

"I see."

"Do you still...practice?"

"I wouldn't call it practice. It's simply part of my existence."

"But don't you need to practice with a person?"

"We have a *kendo* school here. As a matter of fact, the master has invited you to come observe."

"Oh, I'd love that! I rarely have the opportunity back home, and I don't get to Japan often enough to see school demonstrations there."

John opened the door to his office and ushered her into his private domain.

"I'm surprised you never studied *kendo,* since you're so interested in swords."

Alyssa bit her lip and shook her head.

"I tried once. I got through a half-dozen basic lessons. Of course, you use those bamboo-slatted poles in the beginning, but I kept imagining the razor-sharp edge of a real sword, and I just didn't have the stomach to go through with it."

"That's hard to believe," he said, sitting on the edge of his desk and motioning for her to sit in the chair near him. After she was seated, he noted softly, "You're a lady with the guts to put an unconscious pilot into his life vest in a drowning plane in the middle of the ocean at night. You aren't a coward."

She swallowed and looked into his searching eyes.

"It's the idea of cutting someone.... It..."

"Reminds you of your mother's suicide?"

She nodded.

John wondered if that was part of her fascination with the swords, and with Mori's sword in particular. Was she trying to exorcise ghosts from her past by spending a career on objects that reminded her of her greatest loss?

"You're a determined lady, I'll say that for you," he muttered. "And someday, if you want to exorcise those ghosts completely, maybe you should master the art of the sword. Women did, you know."

"I know," she said, smiling. "The *samurai* women had to be able to defend themselves and their homes. But they usually learned to handle the *naginata,* that long-poled halberd, didn't they?"

"True. A skilled lady could take down an armed man on horseback with that long pole and its curved steel blade."

"Can you teach me that?" she asked curiously.

"I can teach you anything you want."

His gaze was steady. Alyssa couldn't look away. A current of awareness shot through her like a high-voltage charge. She was very glad that she was sitting down.

He held out the phone to her.

She took it.

For a moment, her mind was wiped clean of phone numbers. That high-voltage shock wave had apparently erased her memory. She closed her eyes and forced herself to stop feeling the vibrance that John had stirred to life. The numbers came back, thankfully, and she bent over the phone to punch them in. Naturally, John put the call on the intercom so he could listen.

"Hello?"

"George! I was beginning to think I'd never get you!"

"Alyssa? Alyssa, is that you?"

"Yes!"

"My God, Dair said you'd called. You have no idea how we felt when we heard about the plane! It was the longest night of my life. Dair took it very hard, but he's doing all right now."

John thought the man sounded vaguely familiar. Had he met him? He frowned. He knew he didn't recognize the name. The business search had turned up no significant common investments or business associates. Still, there was something about the man's voice that had a ring of familiarity about it. Damn. What the hell was it?

He listened to them exchange reassurances. Every time Alyssa soothed him with that honeyed voice of hers, he found himself becoming annoyed that she wasted it on George. Impatiently, he mouthed, *Ask him what you should do.*

"Oh, George...what should I do? I mean, things haven't gone exactly as we planned..." Alyssa thought that was a whale of an understatement. "Uh...you see, Mr. Mori apparently didn't send the letter that arrived at the gallery..."

"My God! How can that be? He specifically stated that he wanted to reconsider his longstanding opposition to letting the sword go. He knew about the gallery. Naturally, he knew you and your brother." There was a modest pause. "I imagine some of my contacts helped him look at the matter in a new light. I've asked everyone I know to put in a good word for us with his friends in Japan and the rest of the Pacific."

"Yes, George," Alyssa sighed.

"So how could anyone say he didn't write?"

"Right at the moment, George, I don't have an answer for you."

"That would put you in an awkward position," he said cautiously. "You're all right, aren't you?" he asked worriedly. "They aren't threatening to throw you off the island or anything, are they? I've heard the Mori clan, especially the young heir, John, can be quite ruthless."

John looked at her in some amusement.

Alyssa blushed.

"I'm perfectly all right, George! I'm not being thrown off. They've been very gracious. Heavens, they've even saved my life...." Alyssa looked at John and her mouth went dry. "I owe John Mori my life," she said softly, never taking her eyes of him.

"Be careful of that one," George warned. "Alyssa...can I speak openly? Or..."

The implication was clear. He wanted to know if anyone was listening. Alyssa felt torn. She didn't like misleading people. She didn't want to lie to George. Yet, she couldn't bring herself to betray John's silent monitoring, either. She looked at him helplessly.

Speak openly, he mouthed. He grinned and shrugged. That wasn't an admission, one way or the other.

"Speak openly," she said, crossing her fingers and hoping nothing was said that she'd later regret.

"John Mori is a dangerous man. He was questioned regarding a slaying years ago. And there was something about his mother and a boyfriend of hers that he attacked. He was quite young then, you know."

Alyssa could see the coldness in John's eyes. Well, George had definitely said the wrong thing, she thought.

"How do you know all this is true? Maybe it's just gossip, George. You know, some of the people you talk to may simply be repeating wild tales they've heard. And you know how stories get embellished with every repetition...."

"Believe me, it's all true. And he wants that sword. It's worth a fortune. When the senior Mori passes on, John Mori intends to sell it to pay for business losses he's suffered. You know, the market in Japan plunged not so long ago. He lost a great deal. His margin accounts were called in and he had to liquidate some holdings to come up with the cash he needed. That sword would nicely replenish his reserves, if he sold it to a wealthy buyer.''

"I'll keep that in mind," Alyssa murmured.

"Stay. Try to get through to the old man. I think he'll come around if he just meets you."

"Why do you say that?" she asked, perplexed. She glanced at John. Unfortunately, his face was a portrait of inscrutability.

"Darling, what man could resist you?" George asked teasingly. "You know you have me at your feet."

"Nonsense!" She laughed nervously. She didn't want John to believe any of that. George just talked like that.

"Your friend Betsy seems to be happy in her work. Everything at the gallery is running smoothly, so don't hurry back on account of us. Keep on your secret mission, and we'll hope for your complete success."

"Is that a pep talk?"

George laughed. "I suppose it is."

"I'll let you know when there's something to report," she said.

"Fine. By the way, where are you staying? I tried the hotel by the airport on Onijima. Good God, there's only one, so it was bloody easy. But they didn't have you registered."

"I'm staying at the Mori residence."

There was a moment of silence. Alyssa had the strangest feeling that George didn't like that answer at all.

"George?"

"That's wonderful," he said with sudden enthusiasm. "You'll be able to unravel a lot of mysteries, being that close to all the clues," he said.

Alyssa hesitated. Mysteries? Clues? This didn't sound like George. They'd always focused on the sword itself when they'd discussed her coming to Onijima. What did George know about any mysteries?

"Terribly sorry, Alyssa, but I've got a long-distance call coming in on another line, and I've got to take it."

"Of course. Take care, George."

"I think you're the one needing those good wishes, my dear. Take care, yourself. We don't want any more unexpected problems, now, do we?"

"I certainly don't," she murmured.

After she'd hung up the phone, she turned toward John.

"Well? Are you still suspicious about my partner?" she asked bravely, hating to admit that she herself was getting bad vibrations about George.

John was frowning.

"I'd swear that I've heard his voice before," he muttered. He formed a fist and hit his thigh once with it. "But I'll be damned if I can remember where or when." He looked at Alyssa sharply. "Has he ever said anything about meeting me?"

"No. I always had the impression that all he knows about you came from research over the phone."

There was an urgent knock at the door.

"Come in," John said, standing.

It was the young woman who served as a nurse to Isamu Mori during the day. She bowed and lifted an anxious face.

"Mr. Mori is calling for you, sir. And he asked that you bring the young lady with you."

Now how did he know she was here? Alyssa wondered. She glanced at John. She'd bet her new pair of shoes that he was wondering exactly the same thing.

He lifted a brow and motioned for her to precede him.

"Let's start unraveling mysteries," he murmured dryly. "For starters, we'll ask my father how he knew there was a young lady around the house."

And then we'll ask him what happened the last night my mother was here, Alyssa added silently.

Chapter 10

Isamu Mori was sitting on the pallet in his room when they arrived. He was no longer hooked up to any intravenous lines, but he still looked very frail. The faded black-and-brown *kimono* that he wore was starched and clean, however. He'd even put on black *tabi,* so that his feet were covered, too.

The old man had dressed for them, Alyssa thought, humbled by the effort he had made. His light gray hair was neatly combed back. And his facial hair, while slight, had been shaved.

His skin was pale and shrunken on his bone; no doubt he had lost weight from his battle with pneumonia. His dark brown eyes were tired, but he was alert and lucid. And the moment he saw Alyssa, he looked as if he'd been struck by an unseen hand.

"You look very much like your mother," he murmured.

His words contained both great pain and deep tenderness. He motioned for them to come close, to sit near him on the *tatami* floor.

Alyssa felt the warmth and strength of John's body as they knelt side by side, their hips a few inches apart. With a wave of his hand, Isamu dismissed the nurse from the room, leaving them alone.

"How did you know that Alyssa was here, Father? I've tried to keep you as undisturbed as possible, so that you would regain your strength and be well again."

Isamu smiled indulgently at his adopted son.

"You protect me well, my son. I thank you for your filial loyalty, for your diligent protection of my life and our honor over many years. But my old ears are not deaf yet. I heard Kojiro-san say something to the guard last night...about the honorable Miss Jones who was resting in my humble home and was to be protected. Kojiro said you gave the order."

"Yes."

Alyssa glanced at John. His face was hard to read.

She had never been protected by a man before. It felt strange, but a peculiarly pleasant strange. She couldn't help wondering exactly what it was about John Mori that made her glad that he was looking out for her. She knew that there were plenty of men whose efforts to protect her wouldn't have been so warmly received. Was it the tantalizing myths surrounding Onijima that made John so attractive to her? It was a land of dark and moody enchantment, and John was the embodiment of mystery and danger. He was a man without a country, banished to this rugged pile of rocks. A man who lived by his wits, yet bound by ancient codes of chivalry, of which she was now a beneficiary. He'd passed the word around to all his men that she was under his protection. That was a little more specific than he'd led her to believe. He had said everyone would know she was under his protection. She hadn't realized he would issue explicit orders to that effect, ensuring that his intentions were clear.

Alyssa turned back to Isamu only to find him studying her with sad fascination.

"Why have you come, if I may ask?" Isamu inquired politely.

"She received a letter faxed from Japan. It was an invitation to come here. The letter held your signature and your *hanko*," John explained carefully.

The old man looked quite surprised.

"I know nothing of any letter. I did not have it sent."

Alyssa felt terrible.

"I'm so sorry," she murmured. "I would never have come if I'd known how you felt."

Isamu coughed. When he recovered he waved off her concern and smiled wanly.

"I am sure you would not," he said. He turned to John, becoming quite serious. "Have you an explanation?"

"Not yet, Father. There are several possibilities...."

"Yes?"

"Someone on Onijima may have been involved."

"Who?"

"Esau Holling. And Suzie Chan. She's hospitalized. It appears the Esau may have tried to kill her. He tricked her into leading Alyssa into danger. He may have tried to kill Alyssa."

Isamu had heard many sordid and deadly tales over the many decades of his life. In spite of the shocking nature of John's news, he took it calmly.

"Why would someone wish to harm Alyssa?"

John looked at her, his face as inscrutable as his father's. "We are not certain. But other people may be involved."

"Oh?" The senior Mori waited patiently for John to elaborate.

John didn't.

Alyssa realized that he was not going to mention his doubts about her brother and her business partner. She wondered if it were out of some sense of empathy for her. Somehow, she wanted all the ideas out in the open among them. If she were to win their trust, she had to extend it herself. Even if it was embarrassing.

"John suspects that my brother, Alasdair, and my business partner, George Bodney are involved. They were the ones who actually received the letter. Of course, my brother and I recognized the *hanko* and your signature."

Isamu thought about that.

"You have the letters that I sent to your mother, then."

"Yes," she said softly. "She treasured them very much. They were carefully wrapped and hidden among her things. My father never saw them. I'm sure he would have destroyed them if he'd found them."

Isamu nodded.

"Yes. He would have."

John looked at Alyssa.

"So that's how you recognized his seal," he said softly. She'd seen it before. On letters his father had sent years ago. He frowned and said, "Then perhaps that's where the seal on your faxed letter came from. And the signature."

Alyssa blinked.

"You mean someone forged it? Copying it off my letters?"

"Why not?"

"Well, for one thing, they're never out of my control. I've kept them in a safe-deposit box, along with the *tsuba*. They were just too precious to be kept at home."

"When did you take them out last?"

Alyssa thought.

"Well . . . about three months ago or so, Alasdair and I went to the bank and took out the *tsuba*. We brought it into town and took it to an expert to be appraised for insurance purposes. But I stayed in the shop while it was there. And we took it back that afternoon."

"Did your brother look at the letters?"

"No . . ."

"Did you leave him alone with the box at any time?"

"No . . ." She stopped suddenly. "Well, as a matter of fact, I did leave him in the booth with the safe-deposit box for a few minutes. George had come along. He had to put some things into his safe-deposit box. He has an account at the same bank . . . ."

"Interesting," John said grimly. "Go on."

"Well, he knocked on our door and asked me to come out for a minute. He wanted to show me an old Chinese dagger that he'd had for years. He kept it in the box because he hadn't had time to authenticate it yet and get it insured. He said it probably wasn't valuable enough to bother with, but he liked the piece, so he kept it. It was an interesting piece. The blade was slightly twisted . . . like a corkscrew."

"Like a corkscrew?" John's eyes went blank and a distant memory surfaced. "George Bodney," he muttered coolly. "Well, well, well. So that's where I remember you from. I'll be damned!"

"You know George?" she exclaimed in surprise.

"In a way. We've never been introduced. You could say that our paths crossed once at an unfortunate moment."

John stared hard at Alyssa.

"This is very important. Tell me what happened just before you got onto that airplane in Japan." He'd been meaning to ask her that but never seemed to get around to it.

"What?" She was still mentally at the bank with George and his Chinese dagger. "Well, we were getting loaded. My bag was stuffed under the plane in the storage compartment. There was a ground crew working on the plane, doing last-minute checks, when the captain was called over to a small vehicle that had come out onto the runway. The cabin attendant was too ill to fly with us. We'd have to go alone." She shrugged. "And we took off."

"Was anyone alone around the engine or the instrument panel?"

"Well, there were only two mechanics, and one helped load the luggage. The other one seemed to be left to do the work."

"So he could have tampered with the fuel and the gauges. I'll bet the cabin attendant was intentionally given food poisoning. Either to save her, because whoever sabotaged the plane wanted her alive, or because she was part of the plot. Maybe a distraction... Without her there, the pilot had to do his job and hers, basically. And that may have been enough to allow him to overlook the fact that his fuel gauge wasn't reading properly when they fueled the jet."

Alyssa was shocked.

"How much of this is theory and how much is fact?" she asked, feeling sick at the implications.

"Fact and theory are not so far apart," Isamu said quietly. "Trust John's instincts," he suggested. "His karma has brought him out of darkness many times."

"The accident investigators and the company detectives will be able to serve up some hard evidence as proof in short order," John said. "Some of the facts are already established. I think the rest will be falling into place before too long." He frowned. "But why is someone doing this now?"

Isamu sighed and spread his hands.

"I am dying. If not this time, then the next. One day an illness will take my breath forever. Then you will inherit all I own. When the old stag dies, jackals may come to attack his young."

"But why bother with me?" Alyssa asked, shocked and thoroughly perplexed. "I just wanted to borrow the *katana* and put it on exhibit. That's hardly something to get killed for!"

"Your partner George might feel differently," John said grimly.

"George said as much about you," she pointed out.

John looked at her. "Did you believe him?" he asked softly.

That strange sensation curled over her. Like a storm rolling in from the sea.

"I hardly know you," she said, her voice becoming strangely unsteady. "It isn't fair to ask me that."

"Many things in life are unfair," he said quietly. "And knowing someone isn't always a matter of time."

Alyssa couldn't bear the intensity of his gaze and she looked away, fleeing from the riot of feelings he was igniting deep inside her. She focused on Isamu, who had been listening with sober interest.

"I've always wanted to meet you, Mr. Mori," she said shyly. "I'm terribly sorry that we finally have met under such dreadful circumstances. You're one of the last links to my mother, you know. I hope you'll forgive me for arriving here under such a cloud."

His eyes softened, and he seemed to be thinking of another time.

"You are like your mother. I see her honesty in your eyes."

Alyssa was confused. "But I thought she had . . ."

"Deceived your father? With me?"

Alyssa blushed.

"It's not precisely my business," she murmured uncomfortably. "What happens between a man and a woman belongs just to them."

Isamu nodded.

"Yes. But in this case, I think you should know the whole truth. You have read old letters. Heard old tales. I didn't want you here, not because I haven't wondered about you, but in honor of your mother's memory. I wanted no gossip about her after her death. It seemed wise to prevent you from having any contact with me. Then her soul would rest in peace."

Alyssa had never seen such sadness in a man's eyes as she beheld in Isamu Mori's then. She leaned forward and touched his hands with hers.

"You don't have to tell me anything," she assured him.

"I had a wife as a young man," Isamu began, smiling sadly. "She was beautiful. I loved her very dearly. We had a son. He grew healthy and strong, and he began to learn the sword as a boy. Then the war came. It burned through the Pacific. My trading routes were destroyed. We had to struggle to keep Onijima out of harm and maintain our livelihood on the black markets of the Orient. Unfortunately, the *yakuza* were interested in using this island as a hiding place for their own business. We fought. My wife and son were killed. My heart died. And it remained dead until I met your mother. She was not happy with your father. But he didn't care, so long as she obeyed him. You were a joy to her, but a child cannot fill the life of a woman. She came here often. We talked of many things. She was learning Japanese, so we practiced. She was curious about art, so we walked through the Mori collections. We gave each other pleasures for which there are no words. Pleasures of the mind," he said, so Alyssa would not mistake him. "I was in my fifties. She was younger than you. She could have been my daughter, and I let her think I felt that way. But I did not think of her as a daughter after a while."

Alyssa looked at John. He seemed surprised, she thought, in spite of his lack of expression. He'd never heard this story, she realized. Isamu must have kept it to himself all these years. Only Etsu, who was old enough to remember and close enough to have seen the truth, knew what had happened.

"She had never thought of me as a father figure." He sighed, shaking his head. He gave a soft, bitter laugh. "I was a fool not to have seen it. So noble, so determined to treat her honorably, I was blind to her need, to her feelings."

"Would you tell me what happened the last time she came here?" Alyssa asked hesitantly. Much as she was reluctant to ask, she knew she would always regret it, if she didn't. And Isamu Mori was apparently willing to tell them the truth, even though it brought him great pain.

"I showed her the Takehira sword, the one that you have wanted to see for so long. She admired it more than anything in my possession. I told her the story of how my ancestor was given the sword and the many tales associated with it. She was fascinated. I took the *tsuba* from the scabbard and showed her the intricacies of the piece. Our bodies were close together. We were alone. We had wanted each other for a very long time. The effort to hide it was unbearable. Our fingers touched and she looked at me. I saw the fire in her gentle eyes, and I could not hold back the truth from her any more."

He fell silent. Neither Alyssa nor John spoke a word. It somehow seemed like a sacrilege to intrude on Isamu's bittersweet memory.

"Afterward, I pleaded with her to stay with me. I swore that I would protect her with my life. She was crying. I can still taste the salt of her tears on my lips. Her husband had raped her repeatedly, she said. He was trying to make her pregnant again. She wanted to escape the marriage and desperately wished to avoid more children. She did not want them to suffer for her mistakes. I could not convince her to stay with me. Part of me raged. Part of me was old enough to see the problem. To destroy a child's faith in mother and father is a very bad thing. We didn't want our passion to be visited on you as a punishment. But I could not just let her go. I gave her the *tsuba* and told her we were two parts of the same soul. I had the *katana* and she had the *tsuba*. They would never be together again, unless we could be united."

John stared at the familiar face of his father, wondering how he could have heard that phrase and not realized what it meant. *Part of my soul. Lost to me forever.* I must have been blind, he thought bitterly. How could I have not realized the truth until now?

"But why wouldn't you let me bring them back together, Mori-sama?" Alyssa asked with the greatest gentleness.

"I gave her the knife that killed her," he said painfully. "I told her to plunge it in her husband's heart if he ever threatened to hurt her. I swore to her that I'd bring her to Onijima, beyond the reach of the law if that happened. When she left, I was wild with worry. Months went by and I did not hear from her. I sent spies to find out what was happening, fearing her husband had discovered what had happened. She was giving birth to Alasdair when my informants finally found her. You cannot imagine my feelings. She was his wife. I have no doubt that he raped her. She may have told him of us, and his rape may have been an act of vengeance. And I was helpless to protect her. I considered murdering the man myself, but I knew your gentle mother would never look at me the same way, so I had to stay and suffer. But I arranged to have a young woman sent to be a servant in your mother's house, so that I would know if the situation worsened. Unfortunately, your mother needed me when I was beyond her reach and could not help her."

"What do you mean?" Alyssa said, a sickly feeling sliding over her. There was a sense of doom about Isamu's tale. And she already knew that it ended tragically. But she sensed there was something more. Some truth she hadn't learned about until now.

"Your father threatened to divorce your mother for adultery. He intended to take you and your brother back to the United States and abandon her somewhere in Singapore. But his rage overcame him, and they fought. She must have carried the dagger I gave her, because she tried to use it to protect herself."

"To protect herself?" Alyssa exclaimed in astonishment. "How can you know?"

"Because the girl I sent was on the boat, and she heard the struggle. She also saw the dagger cut on your father when he staggered out of your mother's cabin and onto the deck. When he told the crew your mother had slit her wrists, they accepted it, no matter what they thought. They were paid to think what he told them. He was a powerful man. No one would dare challenge his word. The girl could do nothing, but she was with your mother when she died. Her last words were to take care of her children and to explain to Isamu Mori what had happened."

There were tears in Alyssa's eyes. She brushed them away and saw the suspicious glimmer of pain in Isamu's.

"She didn't kill herself?" Alyssa whispered incredulously.

"No. I am sure she did not. And I regret very deeply that you have had to wait this long to know. I could not prove it. And until your father died, I was concerned that he might use you and your brother to protect himself from my vengeance."

Alyssa was afraid to ask Isamu if her father's death at sea had really been an accident. From the hardness she saw in the old man's eyes every time he mentioned her father, she could believe that he had seen to it that primitive justice was served. A death for a death. She hesitated pressing their fragile acquaintance to that level of candor.

Isamu did not elaborate.

"I wrote a letter, long ago, detailing the facts about your mother, but when you seemed to be all right, healthy and happy and cared for by your family in the United States, I was undecided about sending it. I kept the letter, thinking to give it to you eventually, or if the burden of your mother's death appeared to be causing terrible problems for you."

"How did you know about us?" Alyssa asked curiously. He smiled.

"I have done business in many places. There are times when one accepts the promise of a favor instead of money. I asked a favor from time to time. Someone I knew would be traveling near you. They inquired, discreetly, about your family."

Alyssa had never known she had a guardian angel hovering in the background. She wished she had. Then again, if she'd known, she might not have developed her own ability to transcend challenges and disappointments.

"Thank you for telling me all this now, Mori-sama," she murmured sincerely. "It means a great deal. And I think it will mean a great deal to my brother. He was just a baby when she died. He's never understood how she could abandon him like that."

Isamu nodded. "I would be cautious about what he is told. Hearing that you were born out of rape is not necessarily a happy tiding."

Alyssa nodded. "I'll wait awhile. And . . . I'll be careful what I say at first."

"She loved both of her children more than anything in life," he reminded her with great compassion. "More than she loved me, if that helps Alasdair to accept the truth someday."

"Would you like to see the *tsuba* again?" Alyssa asked gently.

"Is it here?" he asked.

"Yes."

After a moment, he sighed and bowed his head. "I think it is my karma to see it again." He lifted his head and smiled tiredly. "Bring it to me, daughter of my soul."

John stayed with his father while Alyssa went to her room to fetch the *tsuba*.

"You never told me," he said quietly.

"It was my sin," the old man said. "I did not want to burden you with it. You had suffered enough. I wished to free you from suffering, not add to it."

John nodded. "I understand." Isamu was like that. In a way, he wasn't surprised.

"Take care of Alyssa, my son. Her mother was pure of heart. You know the saying, *If you would see the daughter, look at the mother.* I have seen the mother, and she was beyond compare."

Alyssa returned and held out the *tsuba*. Now that she looked at it, though, it somehow didn't seem quite right. When she'd showed it to John, she'd been too exhausted and the room had been too dark to notice much. But here, in Isamu's room, the *tsuba* looked . . . different somehow. The weight wasn't quite right either.

She thought she was imagining things again. Her mind was really getting warped by all the unexpected events, she told herself sternly.

Isamu took the *tsuba* from her and laid it on his palm. After a long, long time, he raised his head and stared at her.

"There is something wrong with it, isn't there?" she murmured worriedly.

He nodded and handed it back to her.

"That is not the *tsuba* I gave to your mother. It's a copy." John and Alyssa looked at one another.

"How the hell did that happen?" John asked grimly.

"I don't know, but I'm sure it's been recent. I would have noticed. It's the small file mark . . . it's missing," she said, pointing to the spot that had bothered her. "And it doesn't feel like it weighs enough. It's just a little off. The shape and details are otherwise perfect. It's as if someone took a mold and rebuilt one to replicate the original, but the file marks are too small to be picked up. They have to be done by hand."

"So the forger was in a hurry." Like trying to get the switch done in an appraiser's office, John thought. And getting the fake on a plane in time to have it deep-sixed forever.

John frowned. Could someone have switched it while it was in his room in the briefcase? Somehow, that seemed unlikely. Not many people could know about the forgery. Or that the *tsuba* was in the briefcase. Or that it was sitting near his safe unattended briefly. Besides, a stranger would have great difficulty slipping in undetected. And he trusted Etsu and the guards. That meant the switch had to have been made just before Alyssa last had the time to examine the *tsuba* in a leisurely, unhurried fashion. Which was before she left on this trip.

And who would want a one-of-a-kind *tsuba* that could not be displayed in honest company?

John could come up with one candidate immediately: that well-known sword collector, George Bodney. Or perhaps some wealthy crook willing to pay Bodney money for a priceless piece of history.

Which meant the Takehira sword might also be on the shopping list, he thought.

He glanced at his father.

"I think I'd better check on the sword, Father."

Exhausted, Isamu lay back on his bed.

"Yes, yes," Mori senior murmured faintly. "I think you are right, my son. And remember, see to it no harm comes to Alyssa."

"I will." John looked into Alyssa's eyes. He didn't need any urging. "Would you like to see the sword?"

"Oh, yes!" she said breathlessly. Her eyes sparkled with excitement. "I've wanted that for so long."

He smiled slightly and drew her toward the door.

"We'll see you later, Father. Rest. Get well."

The old man waved them off weakly.

The nurse came back into the room.

"Let's go to the *kendo* school," John said. "There's a special demonstration today. Some of the students are graduating to higher levels."

"That's where the sword is?"

"Where else would we keep a sword?" he teased.

"I thought it would have a place of honor in a corner of a main room," she said.

"It does. But it's a room that's the least accessible on Onijima and least likely to be thought of as a hiding place for something irreplaceable."

"Do you always talk in riddles or do you do this just for me?" she asked, laughing.

"People who cannot see the truth claim they are surrounded by riddles."

Alyssa laughed again. He was enjoying teasing her, she realized. But beneath that deadpan expression he'd donned, she sensed a restless tension. He was worried.

Well, so was she.

Chapter 11

They drove John's silver sports car up into the mountains until they arrived at the monastery. People had already been watching displays of swordsmanship and there was a quiet milling around as onlookers expressed their admiration for the determination and ferocity of each student's performance.

After they parked and got out of the car, Alyssa saw Mariko. She was standing with a youth who looked about fifteen. He was grinning. And he was dressed in the black clothing worn by the students.

"That's Mariko's son," John explained.

Alyssa glanced at him in surprise.

"She's married to an American submariner. He's out at sea and won't be back for several months."

"She's married!"

He heard the surprise and faint relief in her voice and glanced down at her.

"I thought you two seemed very close," she murmured.

"We are. Close friends. But just friends."

The old *kendo* master emerged from the main building and caught sight of them. When they met on the grounds a few moments later, he gave Alyssa a penetrating once-over.

"I can see the problem, John," the old monk said with a sage smile.

"What did he mean by that?" Alyssa asked under her breath when the monk's attention was absorbed by some visiting swordsmiths.

"I'll explain it later." He put a hand against the small of her back and steered her through the thick of the crowd. "Let me give you a tour first. Have you ever seen a *tatara?*"

"The old-style Japanese smelter that the swordsmiths used to make their steel? No. Do you have one? In operation?"

"Over here," he told her. "And you can meet one of the finest swordsmiths keeping alive the ancient craft."

It was an unusual day, filled with fascinating experiences. Alyssa thought she'd been treated to a walk in some other lifetime. She watched the sword maker fold steel, demonstrating the art of creating the various forms of sword used by *samurai* for centuries.

"The sword presents a difficult dilemma. It must be able to bend so that it doesn't break. Yet it must be hard enough to cut through the toughest resistance. Bending too easily defeats that. The smiths eventually discovered the solution to that dilemma. Have an inner core of softer steel and an outer covering of harder, tempered steel."

"So it bends when it has to, but cuts down anything in its way?" Alyssa admired one of the swords on display. "That sounds like the same strengths needed by the man wielding the sword."

"Maybe. But you rarely hear a warrior praised for his inner softness," he said dryly.

"Maybe that's just a matter of habit. Or shyness?"

John looked as if he were making an effort not to laugh. Firmly, he turned her toward the main performance area.

"After you've seen the two stars duel, tell me how important softness is in a swordsman," he challenged her.

"*Inner* softness is important," she argued. "You have to know when to stand and when to give way, don't you? Well, that inner softness helps a hardheaded warrior have the sense to know when to step aside."

He stared at her with increasing respect.

"You should have stayed with your *kendo*," he said. "You could have done well. I don't suppose you ever studied *aikido?*"

"No."

"Their philosophy might appeal to you. The magic circle of movements allows you to defeat your enemy by going with the force of his attack."

"The ultimate in inner softness!" she exclaimed triumphantly. "I knew we could find respect for that somewhere around here!"

"I have plenty of respect for inner softness," John murmured.

She caught the expression in his eyes and felt a slow burn crawl over her skin. They weren't talking about swordplay anymore. And the inner softness that was melting inside her beneath the intensity of his gaze was the worst kind of danger for a woman. But she wanted to embrace the danger! She knew she was out of her mind; it had to be some sort of insanity, and hopefully it would pass, but...that aching, melting sensation was intoxicating. It drew her in and made her want more. No matter what her common sense was trying to tell her.

John reluctantly turned away to answer an earnest young man's questions and Alyssa sat absolutely still, trying to focus her attention on the magnificent *kendo* being performed in the old-fashioned arena in front of her.

All the time she was intensely aware of John Mori beside her.

Finally, the performance concluded. The last visitors closed their car doors and drove back down the mountain. The monks retired for a simple dinner and meditation.

John led her down a narrow footpath to a small house nestled along a wall of rock. He pressed his thumb against the low metal gate and an electronic lock released, having scanned his thumbprint.

"That looks like a fancy alarm system for a simple mountain cabin," Alyssa said, impressed.

"This is officially the building where a monk goes when he has a contagious disease, and no one is permitted near him except medical personnel."

"A quarantine?" Alyssa gave him a worried look, but she followed gamely as he led her into the house. At the front door, he used a key, however. And he turned off an electronic burglar alarm.

"Uh . . . have they been sick a lot?" she asked in growing trepidation. They'd all looked healthy to her.

"They're healthy as horses," he said, grinning. "But a few years ago, we let the rumor get around that there was a contagious death here, agonizing and slow. We don't get many local people showing any curiosity about the place. And outsiders don't know about it."

He took her into the inner room, releasing hidden alarms as he went. Until they reached the room in the center. The sword was sheathed and resting on its black wooden stand.

John knelt and removed the blade from its scabbard with one smooth motion. He held it out for her to examine.

Alyssa was momentarily unable to speak.

"It's really beautiful," she murmured at last. "It makes you wish that he'd made many swords."

"And signed them."

"Yes."

For that was what gave this blade its unique place in the world of *katana*. It was the only sword known to have been made by the renowned Takehira. The blade gleamed like polished silver. When it was held at just the right angle, you could see the fine waves of black and gray embedded in the steel. Takehira's signature was restrained but clearly visible. And the blade as a whole had an elegant, pleasing feel to the touch.

"Have you heard the story of how it was given to the Moris of Onijima?" John asked softly.

He was watching her with the unwavering interest that he had shown for most of the day. Alyssa felt the tug of desire between them strengthen.

"No," she said huskily, as she handed the sword back to him.

"The first Onijima Mori was a free-lance *samurai,* a *ronin* who hired his services out to any lord who needed an extra sword. He was with the lord when an earthquake struck and fire broke out in the town. Everything was burning and the lord saw his wife and son trapped in their home about to be burned alive. None of the family retainers were willing to go through the fire to save them. Neither was the lord, in spite of his screams of agony. The lord shouted that he would give his sword, the priceless O Takehira, to any man who would save his wife and child. Mori jumped into the horse trough, wrapped himself in wet straw armor and ran into the burning house. He brought them out."

"So they gave him the sword?" Alyssa breathed, raptly listening to the tale.

John smiled cynically and slid the sword back into its scabbard of black lacquer.

"Have you ever known a politician to come through with what he originally promised?"

"Well, then, how did you end up with the sword?" she asked curiously.

"The lord told the *ronin* he'd present him the sword in a special ceremony befitting the occasion. But when the time came, the Mori *ronin* found himself surrounded by the lord's most loyal retainers with their swords drawn. Unfortunately, they weren't as good with a sword as he was. He killed them all. Including the lord. Then he took the sword from the lord's house and left."

"The poor man. He must have felt awful... being betrayed like that, I mean," Alyssa said thoughtfully.

John shrugged.

"Word got back to the higher level *daimyos,*" John went on. "They couldn't very well let their lord be slaughtered by some no account. So they called him an outlaw and offered rewards for his capture. They were also intensely interested in getting back that sword. It was worth a lot of rice, the old-fashioned measure of wealth, even back then. The lord's family was persuaded to offer the sword as a reward for Mori's capture."

"Did they capture him?" she asked with bated breath, envisioning the desperate escape, the lonely period of hide-

and-seek and the constant threat of death that the man must have suffered.

"Hell, no," John said, grinning. "My clever ancestor kept a charming courtesan, a lovely *geisha* who was madly in love with him, and she kept him well-informed of the various efforts to hunt him down. He probably spent half his time in hiding in her bed. Then, one night, fate handed him the key to his freedom. There was an assassination attempt on a vice-*shogun* who was dallying at the *geisha* house. Mori jumped in on the side of the vice-*shogun,* saving his life. The vice-*shogun,* being an honorable man, wanted to show his appreciation. When he heard the story of the dishonorable behavior of the *samurai* who'd welched on his offer to hand Mori the sword for rescuing his family, the vice-*shogun* decided he had grounds to lift the virtual death sentence that had been issued. However, he couldn't persuade everyone to his point of view, so a compromise was reached. They'd banish Mori forever. The dead lord's family was forbidden to pursue him. They had to accept Mori's banishment as punishment for the lord's murder. But since the lord had promised Mori the sword, Mori was allowed to take the sword with him."

"That sounds like a decision worthy of Solomon," Alyssa murmured. "But it certainly makes for a lonely victory."

"You don't have to live on a desolate island to feel lonely," he said slowly.

"That's true," she agreed.

Suddenly the air was thick with something that shouldn't be. Alyssa's heart beat faster and she knew what would happen if they stayed here. She told herself she should leave right now, but she couldn't seem to move at all.

"I can see why your father wouldn't want the sword to leave the island," she said, her voice trembling.

"Yes." He closed his eyes and tried not to feel the burning inside. He'd never felt lonely before. Why did he feel it so intensely now? Here? With her?

"You're still worrying about your father, aren't you?" she asked gently, laying her hand on his.

He opened his eyes and looked at her. He knew that placing her hand on his had been a spontaneous offer of comfort. He should have felt only kindness or appreciation for the gesture. But what he felt was desire—pure, fierce desire.

"Yes. But that's not all I'm worried about."

She saw the hunger in his eyes and was terrified to feel an answering hunger deep inside her soul.

He reached out and touched her hair, letting the soft strands spill between his fingers. Slowly his gaze traveled across her face, as if drinking in every aspect of her beauty.

"Do you know what real loneliness is, Alyssa?" he asked huskily.

"What is it?" she whispered. Her soft gray eyes were wide with guileless concern.

"Loneliness is having nowhere to go when you're in trouble. It's being unwanted in your own home. It's trusting the kindness of a stranger when you have no one to turn to."

Alyssa swallowed hard.

"Is that what it was like for you growing up?" she asked unsteadily.

He smiled bitterly, but his hand wandered down her jaw, across her lips. "I was just thinking out loud."

She looked at him doubtfully.

"But you've stayed, John. You could have left years ago if you wanted to. Has becoming a Mori made up for the loneliness?"

He traced a slow trail of fire across her shoulder with his hand.

"People are resilient," he said. "Look at you. You've made quite a success of your life, in spite of a tough start."

He lifted her hand and looked at it, sliding his fingers over the palm. Goose bumps ran up Alyssa's arm and rioted all over her skin.

He hadn't felt the ache of loneliness for years, he thought. He had been lonely. He simply hadn't felt it.

"I think we'd better go," she whispered.

He looked into her eyes.

"Not just yet," he murmured. His gaze dropped to her mouth, and the dark blue of his eyes deepened into the color of winter twilight.

Alyssa's mouth went dry. Her whole body ached for him. She knew it was crazy, but knowing that didn't seem to have the slightest effect on her reactions to him.

She swallowed and made a last heroic effort to marshal her common sense and get out of this small, intimate room before something irrevocable happened between them.

She stood up, but he was too quick for her. Before she could turn to find her way out of the maze of doors, he was standing in front of her, blocking her way, reaching out to grasp her shoulders gently in his hands.

"You're trembling," he said softly. His eyes glittered in the darkening room.

"I'm frightened of you," she said, trying to pull away.

"Frightened? Are you sure that what you feel is fear?"

"I'm shaking like a leaf," she said breathlessly. "My knees are knocking together. I can barely catch my breath. What would you call it?"

"I doubt you're ready to hear the word I'd use."

She pushed against his strong chest, but he easily caught her in his arms and held her fast.

Alyssa tilted her head back to look at him. She knew the trembling wasn't fear. She knew exactly what it was. And she had little doubt that John knew, as well.

"So let's neither of us say it," she suggested breathlessly.

"That won't change the fact that something's happening. Even if you don't name it, it's there."

He pulled her close, holding her until their bodies were so tightly pressed together that she could feel the beat of his heart against her, feel his chest expand and contract with each breath that he took, feel the warmth of his hard body spreading over her like a seductive caress.

"Do you feel that, Alyssa?" he whispered against her ear.

Electricity danced through her earlobe, skipped into her breasts and skittled down to her thighs.

"You aren't the only one feeling strange," he murmured. "And I know damn well that I'm not experiencing fear."

Alyssa felt her soft inner core melt like molten steel. There was something heady and intoxicating about hearing him admit that he wanted her.

"Do you think it could be something we ate?" she asked weakly.

"Broiled fish? I doubt it." His lips traced a tender path along her jaw. She gasped softly in surprise when he slid his hand down to the small of her back and pressed her closer still.

"This is crazy...."

"Agreed."

"We can't do this...."

"Speak for yourself."

"I don't do this kind of thing!"

"Then this will be a first."

"John...."

"Hmm?"

"I don't..."

"Neither do I."

"You liar!"

"It's the truth."

He caressed her in long slow strokes. Alyssa's legs weakened. The warm lethargy that he'd been skillfully arousing with feathery-light kisses was spreading fast. His mouth was like cool velvet against her hot face, his breath sweet, his voice low and soothing.

Then he cupped her face between his hands and fastened his mouth on hers, igniting a sweet, hot fire of longing. Alyssa couldn't help herself. She tightened her arms around his neck and opened her mouth to him.

He immediately deepened the kiss. His tongue touched her inner mouth, scattering the sultry delights that Alyssa had always hungered for but never tasted.

John felt the change in her. A subtle yielding in her body, a softening in her mouth. The heavy pounding in his veins concentrated suddenly in his loins. He slid his hands down her back and grasped her hips, pulling her close to his hardening flesh. He sensed her shyness when she felt him hard and ready. He knew enough about women to recognize the shyness born of inexperience. She wasn't just being coy.

He made an effort to control the pace, but this was different from what he was used to. He touched her and his body hungered as he had never hungered for a woman before.

He felt her tongue in his mouth and he groaned.

"Wait a minute," he murmured against her soft, sweet lips.

She looked dazed. Gray eyes opened slowly, disoriented.

"Alyssa?" She was staring at him through a glaze of warm desire. Suddenly John felt an unexpected sense of guilt. He wanted her all right, but he didn't want to seduce her and have her feel taken advantage of afterward. "Alyssa, have you ever had a lover?" he asked softly.

She blinked rapidly. Red roses of color filled her cheeks and she pushed him away.

"Now, why would you ask me something like that at a time like this?" she asked in disbelief. "Was I doing something wrong?"

"Damn it, no! I want to know what I'm getting into."

"Well, thank you!" She tried to pull away. "You didn't seem to be in much doubt a few minutes ago!"

He refused to let her go.

"We can't go back to the house like this."

"Why not, for heaven's sake?" Alyssa's humiliation was rapidly overtaking her libido.

"Because we're both as aroused as hell!"

"I'm sure the feeling fades." She glared at him.

He laughed.

She glared more.

"I wouldn't bet on that."

"Maybe we've just got incredibly compatible pheromones," she suggested in desperation, as she tried to shake off the irritating frustration that was needling every part of her body.

"Pheromones?" Every generation had a name for it, he supposed. If Alyssa wanted to call mutual lust a case of pheromonally stimulated biological attraction, she could go right ahead. "Lust is a lot easier to pronounce," he pointed out with a slow grin.

She looked uncertain. Lust. So that's what it felt like. Well, at least now she knew, she thought, trying to find some silver lining to this dismal cloud.

"Do you often lust after a woman you've just met?" she asked in a small voice.

"No," he said seriously. "As a matter of fact, you're the first."

"Isn't that the kind of thing a man would say to a woman he was trying to seduce?" She lowered her eyes and realized in horror she felt like bursting into tears. And she'd been trying so hard to be calm, to take this disaster in stride! She was *good* at disasters. She had lots of practice. So why now was her self-control failing her now?

John lifted her chin and saw the telltale silver glitter on her lashes.

"Bloody hell. You're crying."

"Don't be silly. I never cry. Alasdair says I'm the only girl he knows who never sheds a tear." She sniffed and brushed the evidence away. Then she lifted her gaze and smiled at him bravely. "See? No tears. It must have been some sort of optical illusion."

Like hell, he thought, his eyebrows rising skeptically in the darkened room. He didn't say anything, however. Giving them both relief from their "pheromonal attraction" obviously was going to require a little more time. Alyssa's body was way ahead of her mind. He'd just have to help her mind catch up. That was a delicate matter, courting a woman's mind.

"It may be the kind of thing a man would say to a woman he wanted to take to bed," he conceded calmly. "And I think it's perfectly obvious that I want to take you to mine."

Alyssa blushed but she was shocked to realize it wasn't out of embarrassment at his straightforward admission. She enjoyed hearing him say it. She was flattered that he was attracted to her. Deep inside, a primitive part of her was positively thrilled.

"However," he continued patiently, "it's also the simple truth. You *are* the first. Maybe it *is* our damned pheromones. Whatever it is, it's unique. Believe me."

He stepped away from her, his body throbbing with regret. The dull heat in his groin refused to subside. He fiercely wanted to make love to her. Knowing she wanted him, physically at least, made his withdrawal doubly painful. He knew that he could force the issue. He thought he probably could overcome her reluctance with some serious foreplay and a prolonged, concerted effort to arouse her. She'd get to the point that her rational thinking simply shut down. And they'd have nothing but hot, sweet ecstasy from then on.

But he wanted no regrets from her in the morning. No shadow in those soft gray eyes. No sense of betrayal in her pretty face when their clothes were on again.

Alyssa wasn't like the other women he'd wanted in his bed. There was something sheltered and delicate about her inner feelings, in spite of her guts and determination and her unwavering sense of responsibility.

He had an overwhelming urge to protect her. Even if it was from himself.

"I'll take you home," he said quietly. "We'll pick up this conversation later. Depend on it." Alyssa stood shivering in the dark and realized he was walking away from her. She hadn't heard him move, but somehow she'd sensed that he was no longer close. It was as if a part of herself had moved away, she realized in surprise. That was silly and melodramatic, of course. Still . . . that's what it had felt like. A tearing away of a piece of her soul.

"Wait a minute! I can't see a thing," she protested, anxiously reaching out with both hands to see if she could find his body in the darkness. "John? Where are you?"

A warm, strong hand closed over hers, and all her fears went away. Alyssa breathed a sigh of relief. She knew he heard it, because he laced their fingers together and squeezed comfortingly.

"We need to improve your seeing as well as your hearing," he teased. "Hang on to me," he said huskily. "I have eyes like a cat."

"Naturally," she murmured, rolling her eyes. "Well, they say if you can't bell them, join them."

John laughed softly.

"You've got pluck, Alyssa Jones. I like that. Almost as much as I like your sexy pheromones."

Alyssa was contemplating her imminent demise.

On the playing board in front of her, her stones occupied

a shrinking amount of space. And John was poised to swallow up several more segments.

"*Atari,*" he said. He was about to capture more land.

"I don't suppose you ever considered going into land development for a living?" she asked, ruefully looking over his conquests.

"No."

John rarely smiled when he played Go. He gave away nothing by his expression. And he watched her like a wolf. Of course, he also watched her like a wolf when they *weren't* playing Go, she had noticed. Ever since that night near the monastery.

Alyssa put a playing stone on an intersection that she thought John might covet in a couple of plays. Then she watched in resignation as he consumed her space and removed her occupying stones from the board. She picked up another smooth, flat stone and rubbed it absentmindedly between her thumb and forefinger. She hadn't enjoyed playing Go this much in years, even though she was losing.

She usually beat Alasdair. She even gave George a good run for his money playing Go. But John was a different story. Even with a handicap, he outmaneuvered her. John was a challenge. Alyssa frowned and contemplated the mess in front of her. It appeared he was about to defeat her again.

"Rats!" she muttered. She wondered what it would feel like to beat him. Someday she was determined to find out. Just once. Even with a handicap. She'd take what she could get!

She laid the stone down and shrugged her shoulders. There wasn't much to do under the circumstances except surrender gracefully.

John leaned back and lazily poured more warm *sake* into her small porcelain cup. Alyssa took the small bottle from him and poured a measure of the heated rice wine into his. They lifted their tiny cups and looked at one another across the low *go-ban* table.

"*Kampai!*" John said softly, toasting her with the traditional phrase, his gaze never wavering from her face.

"Kampai!" she returned, feeling warm from his regard, and from the wine, and from the many hours they had spent together getting better acquainted.

She knew he was doing it intentionally. It was a preliminary courtship before beginning a full-blown love affair. He'd made it fairly clear what he wanted. He had also been straightforward about what he wasn't offering: marriage. And he somehow had managed not to make that seem hurtful. She didn't know why she wasn't offended. She kept telling herself she should have been. But the truth was, she wasn't offended. She was tempted. Very, very tempted.

And John was biding his time. Watching her. Soothing her. Waiting for her to agree.

She looked down at the tiny bowl in her hands, mainly to escape the heated look in his eyes. It was melting her insides in the most alarming way. As it always did.

"I've stayed longer than I should, you know," she pointed out hesitantly.

He poured more wine in their cups and waited to hear the rest.

"Your father is much better. I've enjoyed getting to know him more than I can ever tell you. And seeing the island has been an education beyond my wildest dreams. I mean, I thought you just had an airstrip and a little fishing village!" She laughed at her own naiveté.

He'd taken her up to the huge airport complex and the buildings that were being built around it. Within a few years there would be a modern town. He had business headquarters there already. He only used the office in his home as a convenience, or for exceptionally private matters.

"Even the Isle of Demons has to move into the next century," he said, studying her, wondering what she was going to do now. Run like a little rabbit, he was willing to bet. She was weakening and she knew it. If they spent much more time together, she would yield to her feelings and they would be lovers. She was scared. If she'd had a lover before, he must have been a big disappointment, John thought.

"It's really time for me to leave Onijima," she said quietly.

She put the wine down. She found she couldn't finish it. She raised her eyes and looked into his, searching for something that he could never give her. She wanted him so much, she could barely sleep at night. Her heart beat faster whenever he came into the room. She found the happiest part of her day was the time they spent together, no matter what they were doing. She was falling in love with him. Madly in love. And he wanted her. Badly. She knew she couldn't resist much longer. Her common sense was withering away beneath the relentless heat of those deep blue eyes.

"I called George today."

"Oh?"

He had long since given her free access to the phone. He wasn't surprised, therefore, that she'd taken charge of her life again and had begun making plans to leave. Of course, he couldn't let her. Not until it was safe. Or until he could go with her and keep a watchful eye on her.

In addition to his concern for her physical safety, he was frustrated that she resisted every subtle overture that he made for her to linger awhile and resolve their personal needs, of the pheromonal variety.

Frankly, he doubted that he was going to enjoy hearing her next sentence on the subject of her future plans. However, years of stoicism supplied him with the calm to listen without displaying a glimmer of emotion.

"I've asked George to arrange a flight plan for me," she said quietly. "He's going to call back with the details sometime tomorrow."

A cold, hollow sensation opened up inside his guts. If he didn't know better, he would have called it loneliness. Damn it. He'd miss her when she finally went her own way. Not just her body that he had yet to enjoy, he thought wryly. He'd miss her mind. And her curiosity. Her laughter that sounded like wind chimes in the breeze.

"John?"

"What?"

"You . . . look strange."

He smiled and the cynical glint that always returned to his eyes gleamed there once again.

"I feel strange." His voice took on a more steely quality. "And you must be feeling rather peculiar yourself if you think it's safe for you to fly home under these circumstances."

Alyssa bristled.

"It may not be completely without risk," she conceded with great reluctance, "but I can't stay here."

He poured himself some more hot *sake* and swallowed it. Then he rolled the small cup between his palms and stared at it unblinking.

"Can I convince you to stay here at least until the mystery of who sabotaged the plane and switched the *tsuba* is solved?" he asked softly.

Alyssa saw the odd expression in his eyes. Since he wasn't looking at her, a bit of his inscrutable mask could be penetrated, by one who truly cared, at least. She thought the expression was pain. A pain that he intended not to acknowledge.

Alyssa's heart ached. She knew they needed each other. But she was afraid to give herself to him, afraid once they'd slaked their desires that he would tire of her. Afraid she would be heaped on the pile alongside his other discarded mistresses. That danger was almost as upsetting as the idea that someone might still try to do her harm.

"If I stay, we'll end up in bed," she pointed out, her voice almost breaking at the end.

His eyes met hers.

"And?" he challenged.

"I'm not sure I can handle an affair with you," she admitted bravely. "I've . . . never had one, you see. So, I don't have any practice at the good-bye part of it. I'd be without a clue," she exclaimed, laughing shakily.

"I'm gratified to hear you've given it that much thought," he said, his eyes softening as a wry grin spread across his face.

"Oh, I have," she admitted. Why did his damn eyes have to make her heart melt like this? she wondered forlornly. "I've thought about it, all right. You . . . make it awfully tempting."

He reached for her hand.

"Then don't resist."

She pulled free. She felt very shaky suddenly. Very vulnerable.

"I can't, John. I'm scared to death, to tell you the truth. You're out of my league." She smiled as best she could, trying to be philosophical about it. It was hard. God, it was harder still when she looked into his eyes and knew how desperately she wanted to yield. She could feel his arms around her. Feel his lips on her mouth. Every inch of her ached for him.

"Do you still want the sword?" He'd been thinking about that for quite a while now. It might give them the time they need and allow him to find out just how guilty George Bodney and Alasdair Jones were. It was the best card that he had to play, and he knew it.

Alyssa stared at him in complete surprise.

"Of course . . . but your father . . ."

"Father and I talked about your hopes, and he's had a change of heart."

"You're serious." She was stunned. She hadn't expected this.

"We want to find the original *tsuba*. From all you've said, it would appear that your business partner, George, is the likely culprit. But we need to find the *tsuba* to prove that. Or find the person he's sold it to. I've made discreet inquiries, and as far as I can tell, it hasn't been privately sold. Yet. That means it may still be in his possession. If you and I were to bring the *katana* to San Francisco, perhaps he could be tempted to try to steal it."

Alyssa frowned. She agreed that George seemed to be a likely suspect, but her sense of loyalty made her reluctant to find him guilty. And then there was the problem of traveling home with John Mori. That didn't sound like a way to keep out of his bed.

"Alyssa?"

She blinked and forced herself to have the courage to look at him again.

He smiled a bittersweet smile and caught her fingertips with his.

"Nothing will happen between us. Unless you are completely willing."

"That's hardly a persuasive argument." She sighed and bit her lip. "You'd let me show the sword?"

"Yes. As long as I stay with it. Father insists it not be out of my sight. That far he was willing to go."

"That's pretty far," she murmured.

"Yes, it is. Well? How far are you willing to go?"

Alyssa was afraid she knew the answer to that. She poured more *sake* into his cup and picked up hers.

"Wherever my karma will take me," she said with a rueful grin.

He swallowed his wine and smiled.

Chapter 12

Derrick Alsop flew back to Onijima a few days later. John was leaving his office near the airport when Derrick hopped down from the mail plane.

"Say, John!" he called out, waving an arm and grinning. "Everything shipshape here while I was gone?"

John stopped beside his car and waited for Derrick to reach him.

"Just a few minor illnesses," John said. "Did you enjoy your vacation?"

Derrick rolled his eyes back in ecstasy and smiled broadly.

"I'm in love, old man! Met the woman of my dreams. She's a nurse gone back to school to train to become a physician. She has two grown boys and is on her own. She's got a mind as sharp as a needle and a heart as warm as a summer day."

John laughed.

"You covered a lot of ground it appears," John said.

Derrick grinned contentedly.

"Covered more than ground, John, old boy. Ah! Makes me think of the joys of settling down. I could use a partner here on the island. Maybe she'd look on it as a possibility after she's finished her residency next year."

Derrick whistled cheerfully and got into John's car.

"Mind dropping me off?" Derrick asked, tossing his bag in the back seat.

"I guess not," John said with a laugh.

He had just gotten off the phone with Henry Chan, who was still holding a vigil at his sister's bedside. Her recovery had been slowed because of complications. She was still far too ill to talk about the attempt on her life, and Alyssa's. Pneumonia had set in. They'd nearly lost her. Her body had drawn down nearly all its reserves. Henry had been holding her hand and swearing at her to get better or he'd lecture her ashes for the rest of his life, never giving her a moment's peace.

Henry had wanted to talk to John longer, but he had to go back to the hospital for visiting hours. He intended to call again, from the hospital. That gave John more than enough time to drive home, so he'd told Henry to call him there.

A slight detour by the doctor's office wouldn't be much of a problem.

"So tell me about this lady doctor...." John said.

Alyssa was in her room when she heard Etsu talking with the guard outside Isamu Mori's room. From the tone, it sounded as if Etsu was worried, so Alyssa poked her head outside her door and looked to see what was going on. The conversation was in Japanese, but Etsu switched to English when she noticed Alyssa.

"Missy? You seen John? He come home?"

"I don't think so. I haven't seen him since we went down to Mariko's for lunch." Alyssa glanced at her watch. It was nearly eight-thirty at night. He'd missed dinner. And he hadn't called.

John had told her he had an important matter to take care of off the island and it would delay their departure for the States by two days. Alyssa wasn't clear on exactly what the matter was. Perhaps it had somehow delayed him? She wondered what duty he had to perform that could take him away from the other pressing matters they were grappling with.

"Maybe he had some last-minute work to take care of," Alyssa suggested. With business all over the world, John made calls and executed transactions at all hours of the day and night. Still, when they had parted after lunch, he had kissed her hand and said that he intended their last evening together to be a memorable one.

Something was wrong. He would have called.

"Henry Chan on phone," Etsu said crossly. "He call many times now. He say John told him call here. John not here. Henry say he call office, too. John not there, either. Where John?"

"Has anyone asked the guards?" Alyssa asked. There was quite a well-coordinated police force on the island, and they served as the Mori family guards at all locations around Onijima.

Etsu looked at the guard beside her with less than a charitable view.

"He know nothing. Say Kojiro gone to Tokyo for wedding of wife's nephew. Say nobody say nothing to him."

Alyssa went into John's office with Etsu at her heels. She picked up his Rolodex and looked for the main number of his business. She dialed but was told he'd left some time ago with Dr. Alsop.

She dialed the doctor.

"John? Why, he left long ago. Said he was expecting a call from Henry. Is something wrong, Alyssa?" Derrick asked, his voice sharpening with worry. "Look, I'll round up Mariko's son and we'll take her car up toward the house. Have a guard come down the mountain. If he's had car difficulty, we'll fix him up."

"But it's been hours! He could have walked home by now." Alyssa felt the cold grip of fear close around her heart.

"I know. Let's not cross any bridges till we get to them, though," he said grimly. "I'll bring my bag…just in case."

"Thank you, Derrick."

She hung up the phone.

"Etsu, could one of the guards help me look for John?"

Etsu nodded and they went in search of the man on duty at the security station behind the house.

He was slumped over his desk.

Etsu felt his throat. She looked shocked. "He dead!"

Alyssa rushed back to John's office and grabbed the set of keys to the car he'd loaned her.

"Etsu, stay by Mori-sama. Make sure no one comes near him unless you'd trust them with your life. And get the guard to call for help. I'll drive down the mountain and see if I can find John."

Etsu nodded and hurried down the hall.

Alyssa saw a small knife lying on John's desk. She picked it up and ran down the hall toward the front door. The knife, called a *tosu,* was the kind an assassin might hide up his sleeve. John used it as a letter opener.

It wasn't much of a weapon, but it was better than rushing into danger totally unarmed.

She flew down the front drive and jumped into the car, her heart pounding.

"Please be all right...." she whispered. She turned on the engine and slammed her foot on the gas. Pebbles shot out from beneath the tires as she tore out of the drive.

It didn't take long to find his car. It was halfway between the house and town, not far from the turnoff to the airport. She saw the underbrush where it had been run off the road. The silver metal was now scarred and covered with underbrush. It had smashed into a tree a few yards down one shoulder. Since there was rarely traffic passing by, no one would have seen it until the next day, when some of the guards shifted onto household duty and drove up from town.

Alyssa pointed her lights toward the wreck and jumped out of the car. She scrambled down the dirt, and brambles. The driver's door was open. John was not inside.

She heard a slight rustling in the tree to her right and whirled.

John Mori sat against the trunk. He looked like he had passed out and was just coming around. A few feet away lay the body of a young man she had never seen. He wasn't moving.

"John!" Alyssa ran to him, falling to her knees and taking his face between her hands. When his eyes opened and gradually focused on her, she felt a rush of pleasure that was indescribable. She pressed her mouth to his in a tender kiss. "Thank God!"

John stared at her, working to bring her more clearly into focus. He inched his spine up the tree until he was sitting more comfortably. He felt like he'd been used as the ball in a rugby game.

"You stay put," she ordered. "Is anything broken?"

"I don't know. I don't think so."

"What happened?" she said, sitting next to him and putting her arm around him to keep him warm and to keep herself sane.

He nodded toward the young man lying not too far away.

"He was standing in the road when I came around the corner. He ran straight toward the car. I had to swerve off the road to avoid hitting him. When I got out, he was coming at me with a knife."

Alyssa took a closer look at the stranger. There was a knife nearby and it had blood on it.

"I'm not an easy man to knife," John said grimly. "Someone should have told him that."

The sound of an approaching car got John's full attention.

"Get out of here," he growled, trying to push her into the woods. "That may be reinforcements." He didn't know what the hell was going on, but he had no intention of assuming it was the cavalry.

Alyssa pulled out her knife and knelt in front of him.

"You're in no shape to fight off any attackers," she argued, outraged that someone had tried to kill him.

John easily disarmed her with one hand and held her against his chest with the other. Their faces were close and she could see the strange expression in his eyes.

"Half-dead I can probably handle that knife more effectively than you can," he pointed out. The tenderness in his voice removed any possible sting.

Alyssa heard Derrick's and Mariko's son's voices and laid her cheek against John's.

"Probably so," she agreed shakily.

"Thanks anyway, tiger. The thought counts," he whispered. He pressed her head close and waited for the pair to reach them. He really didn't feel like moving quite yet. And it wasn't all due to his bruises.

The ghosts of the Mori clan must have been protecting him, John thought as he sat on his bed and allowed himself to be examined.

He was banged up from the car crash but his injuries would not be incapacitating. There was a bad bruise on his cheek and another near his temple where he'd been thrown against the car when it tumbled. He had a hell of a headache but his skull was intact.

His skin was scratched from the underbrush when he'd struggled with his attacker. Still groggy from being knocked out in the car, he'd fought in a haze. He barely remembered what happened. Only unerring instincts, years of battle-toughening training and fast reflexes had saved him.

He offered a silent thank-you to the many men who had taught him the arts of fighting over the years. They had literally saved his life tonight.

When the knife had come down, he'd grasped the assassin's wrist and broken it. After a short but brutal struggle, he'd forced the attacker down to the ground. The man had fallen on his own death. And John had staggered to the tree to sit down and fight off the wave of light-headedness that engulfed him. He'd passed out for a while but was just coming around when Alyssa's headlights appeared.

He was glad to know there were no broken bones, unless one of the bruised ribs turned out to have a hairline crack instead of just a bruise. And he hadn't been concussed, unless it was so mild that Derrick had missed the diagnosis. He intended to go to San Francisco even if he went on crutches. But he'd prefer having all his abilities in perfect working order. After all, they were baiting a trap.

And maybe the bait was already attracting attention, he thought.

The bodyguard in charge during Kojiro's absence arrived at the house in an anxious hurry. While Derrick checked his ribs again, John discussed new security arrangements on Onijima until they got to the bottom of the murder. Then one of the guards said he recognized John's dead attacker. The man had been delivering a dinner of steaming noddles to the dead guard from his favorite restaurant down in the village. A quick call to the restaurant owner yielded the fact that the deliveryman had just been hired today. He'd arrived from Japan on a fishing trawler that morning, claiming to be desperate for a job. The man had apparently splashed some poison into the broth and it had killed the guard within moments.

Someone said the man strongly resembled a sailor from one of Esau Holling's trawlers.

John looked at Alyssa, who'd been sitting in his office and watching through the open door.

"Esau Holling," John murmured angrily. "Then this is probably connected to the attacks on Alyssa."

The *tsuba* was the connection there. Perhaps the *katana* was the connection with the Moris. Someone wanted them both. And they'd hoped the sword was kept on display in the home. That would be normal. Someone had risked a great deal on that gamble, John thought. They'd smuggled an assassin onto the island, arranged a job so he could have access to the house as a deliveryman and they'd poisoned a guard to gain time to search the house and clear a route of escape.

Someone wanted the Takehira sword and its *tsuba* very much. John's eyes narrowed with cold fury.

"Tell Kojiro I want to know exactly where Esau Holling is," John said. The head guard bowed and said he'd see to it immediately.

A short time later, everyone withdrew except Etsu. John was getting very sleepy from one of the medications that Derrick had given him, and Etsu joined Alyssa in the office.

"Missy take nice bath, warm up, calm down."

Alyssa was about to protest. Etsu would have none of it.

"After you clean, you come back. Doctor say someone must stay with John, make sure he all right. I too old. Get sleepy."

Etsu looked at Alyssa expectantly.

Alyssa stood up and squeezed the old woman's hand in thanks.

"I'll stay with him."

Etsu nodded and stood by the door, her hands neatly folded, waiting for Alyssa to return.

"Maybe you get married sooner than you think," she told John, who was by now asleep.

The old woman grinned toothily and waited for Alyssa's return.

Alyssa sat in a chair near John's bed, watching him sleep. A small hint of moonlight filtered through the *shoji* window, etching the room in black and white.

She couldn't stop crying. The tears kept trickling down her cheeks. They welled up again. She brushed them away and blinked, trying once more to stem the silvery tide.

She heard the sheets rustle, and she watched as John turned from his side onto his back. His long legs moved restlessly beneath the light cover.

Anxiously, she got up and closed the small distance to the bed. Bending over him, she touched his brow, worried that he might develop a fever, like Suzie had. She had seen the knife next to the attacker. Seen the blood on it. Seen the ribbon of red so dangerously near John's jugular. She shuddered. Who knew what filth had been on that awful knife? What if John died? What if he had been killed outright?

A ghostly tear kissed John's hard cheek.

He opened his eyes and looked at her.

"I'm sorry," she murmured remorsefully. She wiped her tear from his cheek. "I didn't mean to wake you."

"What are you doing here?" he asked, trying to shake the last of the sleep from his mind. "Where's everyone else?"

"I'm keeping an eye on you to make sure you rest and get better. Everyone else is either asleep in bed or doing their job." She laid her hand on his cheek and her eyes softened tenderly. "Go back to sleep yourself. I'll be here if you need anything."

He smiled slightly and reached up to slide his fingers through her silky hair.

Alyssa closed her eyes in pleasure and smiled as his fingers slid down to the back of her neck. With gentle pressure, he touched the resilient flesh, releasing the tension one fingerprint at a time.

"Come here," he murmured, pulling her down onto the bed beside him.

She stretched out beside him, sighing with contentment as their bodies fit together. A sheet and some bedclothes lay between them, but the hard contours of his thigh, hip and ribs were satisfyingly vivid to Alyssa.

He turned his head, and they stared into one another's eyes for a long while. Time melted away. So did the room. And the house. Everything that ever was or ever would be. There was only the two of them and the profound realization that they had nearly lost one another to the cutting arm of death.

"I was so afraid," Alyssa whispered, her gray eyes wide with shock.

He pulled her into his arms and brought her cheek close to his. The warmth of his skin banished the chill of fear from her heart. He was warm and strong and alive. His heart beat against his chest so hard, she could feel it in her own. His breath came as hers did. She nuzzled his cheek and reveled in the scent and the feel and the taste of him.

When he began to caress her, she knew what would happen if she stayed. His fingertips touched her lightly at first. Moving from her shoulders down the taut muscles of her back to her hips.

"You're so beautiful," he murmured against her neck, nuzzling the tender flesh of her throat and sending warm tendrils of desire spiraling into her belly.

The nuzzling made her arch and curl into him and smile and reach out to slide her hands over his warm, muscled shoulders.

His torso was bare. She could explore him at will, she realized. She shyly splayed her hand and slid it over his muscled chest, turning his flat male nipples into pebbles.

"That's right," he murmured encouragingly as he pressed his lips against hers.

The touch of his mouth on hers made everything shatter. All her resistance and fears and repressed desires fell away. She opened her mouth and slid her arms around his neck and arched herself into his body.

She moaned with hunger as he grasped her head between his hands and slanted their mouths for an even more perfect fit. Then his velvet tongue was stroking the insides of her tender mouth and she felt waterfalls of desire cascading from her mouth straight through her belly only to coil tightly between her legs.

"Mmm."

"Mmm-hmm."

"Yesss."

"Yesss..."

The covers were pulled down, Alyssa's clothes peeled away. And then they were naked and in full-frontal contact. John ran his hands over her soft skin with increasing friction and speed. With their mouths still fused together in a passionate kiss, John slid his knee between hers, pushing her thighs apart.

"So soft...so beautiful...so brave..." he murmured, kissing her cheeks, her throat, the delicate hollow at the base of her throat.

His hand found her breast and he cupped it gently. Then he caressed it, sliding his thumb across her nipple as it pouted proudly.

When he bent his head and closed his mouth over it, Alyssa gasped in pleasure and caught his hair in her hands, holding him in place.

He smiled against the soft skin and slid his tongue over the tiny bud. Everything about her was incredibly arousing. Hell, she could be wearing a sack and he'd be hard as steel. But having her in his arms, her eyes big as moons at harvest, worried about him, sitting by him to make sure he was all right...

It made him want to show her how much pleasure they could share together. It filled his heart with an uneasy longing.

Her belly quivered beneath his hands. She was twisting with need.

"Ahh," he murmured against her breast as he kissed his way down her midline. "You're my own sun-goddess, burning my flesh with your sexy little pheromones. Can you feel the heat you've created?"

He brought her hand to his throbbing flesh. He held her shy fingers around the hard, velvety shaft and hissed with the effort it took him not to thrust.

Alyssa shivered at the intimacy. She felt as if she were drowning in a dream. She was spiraling down into deeper and deeper tension. At the same time she felt lethargic and warm and relaxed, as if she couldn't have moved off this bed to save her life.

They tangled their legs and kissed and caressed and murmured and sighed and entwined with one another until neither was fully aware of where one of them ended and the other began.

John pulled her on top of him and played with her soft breasts. Then he and Alyssa rolled over until he was on top of her and she was biting his shoulder playfully, finding goose bumps of excitement along his chest, feeling the throbbing press of his hard male shaft sliding over and over along her warm, slick cleft.

They rolled over again, telling each other how much they needed the other. How much she wanted to be his, how much he wanted her.

"Alyssa," he whispered hoarsely, raising himself on his hands and lying on her chest, his aching shaft taut against her damp satiny folds. "How far do you want to go? We can stop here...."

She smiled and slid her hands down to cup his firm, trim buttocks.

"You don't feel like you want to stop," she said shyly.

He kissed her mouth, sliding his tongue urgently into hers. Sucking and caressing and swirling heat into her body. When he raised his head, she was drowsy with desire, melting like soft candy in the hot summer sun.

He leaned away long enough to open a drawer beside his bed and find a foil packet. Opening it with his teeth, he removed the contents. They looked at each other.

"Last chance to say no, sweetheart," he whispered, pressing a tender kiss to her sensitive, slightly swollen lips.

"Do you want me to say no?"

"Hell, no."

"Good."

He found her mouth and kissed her deeply. When he lifted his head this time, his eyes glittered with determination. He slid on the condom and pressed her thighs apart with his, sliding his legs against her provocatively.

Alyssa moaned and he renewed his loving assault on her breasts. And he pressed rhythmically against the small cap of flesh that was the key to her deeper satisfaction. Reflexively, she gripped him with her thighs and moaned.

He could feel the tension sliding through her and he stroked the sources to keep it building. She was as responsive and trusting as a woman could be, he thought, treasuring that honesty and holding it dear. As much as he wanted to bury himself in her warm heat, he forced himself to wait. He wanted it to be good for her. So good that she would feel bonded to him.

"You belong to me," he murmured against her mouth as he began a slow thrust into her body.

The pressure was greater the deeper he went. The pain came about halfway.

"Alyssa . . ." he whispered regretfully.

She pressed her heels into the bed instinctively and lifted her hips, settling him fully inside her body.

This was the way it should be always, she thought. The two were made of one flesh. . . . She understood . . . she understood.

Red-hot pleasure washed up from the depths of her and she heard John murmuring sweet praise and words of tender encouragement. He was moving inside her, thrusting in slow, deep strokes. His mouth found hers and they kissed deeply as their bodies connected and withdrew.

At first the rhythmic undulating was steady and slow. They rolled to one side and John lifted her leg along his hips, keeping them joined. A sensitive nub of flesh sent a jolt of pleasure into her abdomen and she squeezed him with her arms, sliding her nails down his back to contain the sweet torment of it.

Then something happened deep inside. The early ripplings spread out, followed by wave after wave of more violent ripples. Alyssa cried out and John buried his face in the warm skin of her neck and thrust fast and furiously.

As the last convulsions seized her, his face contorted in naked pleasure and he threw back his head, gasping with joy.

Alyssa wrapped her arms around him and hugged him with her thighs as he relaxed on top of her.

I love you, she told him silently. She caressed his head with infinite tenderness.

He sighed and rolled over, taking her along so that she ended up on top.

They lay together in silence, as he gradually eased out of her body.

Eventually, John got up. When he came back, he sat on the bed, looking down at Alyssa. He traced her features with his fingertip.

If he could have welded her to him at that moment, he would have. He wanted her in his bed every night. This had been something beyond sexual satisfaction. She had fed the hunger of his mind, the loneliness of his heart as well as the raw, hard lust of his body.

She opened her eyes and looked at him questioningly.

"Are you sorry?" she asked uneasily. She swallowed hard. She'd die if he said yes to that.

He smiled.

"No." His smile faded and he lay down, pulling the sheet over them. He looked into her uncertain face and asked, "Are you sorry?"

He wasn't sure what he'd do if she was. Hell, he'd have to think of something. He didn't want her feeling guilty or remorseful about their being lovers.

Her gaze was steady and clear when she answered him, he was relieved to see.

"No. I'm not sorry. I'm fiercely glad."

His eyes lightened in faint amusement.

"You see, I couldn't bear going through life wondering what I'd missed by not becoming a part of you. Now I'm glad that I did. You see, I never knew what loneliness was until we made love. When you kiss me, when you come into me, when we hold each other so desperately that it feels like we're going to blend together and then explode, well ... I know what it is to be complete."

She leaned toward him and kissed him reverently on the mouth.

"Thank you for that gift," she murmured softly.

"You gave the same gift to me," he said quietly.

He took her in his arms and they lay together in the dark, peace moving through them like a river. Twining around them, binding them together, bringing the mind the emptiness that it craved.

John kissed Alyssa's temple and slowly caressed her.

He wasn't sure he'd be able to let her go.

Chapter 13

Through the mist of time they came together again. Two halves of one soul. Two hearts that beat as one.

He reached out for her, still half-asleep. She rolled into his arms and sighed.

Still hovering between waking and sleeping, he found her lips with his. Soft met hard, and each was altered. His mouth softened at her touch. And hers responded eagerly. Caress upon slow caress began the pleasure bond.

He murmured something she didn't understand.

"What?" she managed sleepily, sliding her thigh between his and arching as he pressed his thigh up, sending fireworks sparkling everywhere.

"I said you're silk against my skin...."

"Mmm," she murmured against his shoulder, her eyes closed, her sleepy smile felt by him.

Outside the dawn was spreading the sun's winter fire, warming the land and the sea. The bamboo fountain in the garden played its delicate song of falling water.

His strong arms enfolded her smooth, curved body and she moved sinuously against him, their hot skin adding friction to the newly reborn fire within. He pulled her hips close, mating with her in the eternal way, and suddenly the essence of life burned brightly.

Mouth sought mouth hungrily. Hand found hand in urgent need. Fingers laced. Thighs tightened. Each ragged breath, like oxygen bellowed into a raging furnace, fed the white-hot fire that was consuming them.

Her cries began. Blended with his. Shudder upon shudder forged the bond between them anew. Into the fire of life they had gone, with only the other to guide them. It was a walk of purest faith, of guileless trust, of urgent needs that only the other could soothe.

The molten feeling subsided slowly. Memory of the bone-fusing ecstasy remained.

He caressed her bare back in a long, slow stroke. She murmured his name in utter peace.

It was difficult to gauge how long they lay together like that, floating on the tranquil afterglow of violently satisfying passion.

The light filtered through the *shoji* window was little help. Finally John turned his head and reached for his watch. He read the time on it and laid the watch back down. Then he kissed Alyssa. It was a long, slow, thorough kiss.

It felt like longing and desire and honest appreciation to her. She opened her eyes and braved a look.

His expression was serious in spite of the lingering smoke of desire she detected in his eyes.

"Your eyes are like the winter sky," he whispered softly. "I've been at sea and looked into the heavens and seen that same soft color... a gray mist that beckons to a man and folds him in mystery."

She laid her head on his shoulder and slid her arms around him, hugging tight.

"I'm not sure you've left much of me to be discovered."

She felt him smile and felt the stirring of his flesh against hers. She laughed and kissed him hard.

"Well..." he murmured seductively. "If you're not leaving... maybe we could find something else to do...."

He found her most sensitive spot and pressed gently.

Alyssa groaned at the exquisite pleasure. She hadn't expected to want to, not so quickly. But he manipulated the flesh with such tenderness that she realized he wasn't the only one who was more than ready to walk through the fire again.

"Come with me," he murmured. "Now..." He thrust into her and she met him blow for blow.

It was natural between them. They each sensed the other's need, the other's pace. And the pace this time was hard and fast and ruthless. Like lightning it came, striking her and striking him. Shaking them like trees in a violent storm.

As the trembling eased, he murmured, "Come to Hong Kong with me."

"I thought that was a personal matter," she said surprised.

"It is."

She swallowed and felt the tears well up in her eyes again.

He sensed her emotion and raised his head to look at her. He kissed the tears off her lashes and cheeks, licking the silvery drops and sliding them across her tongue as he kissed her deeply on the mouth.

"I thought you never cry," he said softly. His dark eyes stared into hers, asking what was the matter.

"I never used to," she said, laughing tremulously.

He kissed her on the mouth again, playing with her lips with tender affection.

"I'd love to go with you," she whispered huskily.

He folded her in his arms and they rolled around on his bed. It was a joy to be close. To feel life in his arms. To bask in the warm tenderness of someone who cared for him. Of someone who was the other half of him.

He felt complete.

And so did she.

Their bags were loaded in the car and Kojiro was waiting for them. Inside, John knelt in his father's room and presented the sword before leaving.

Alyssa had worried they were making a mistake. When she'd suggested it might be too dangerous to take the sword and use it to attract their attacker, he had shrugged off her concern. When she'd worried that if anything happened to it, it would devastate his father, he looked at her and said he'd take care of everything. And when she told him if it came to his life or the sword, they could *have* the sword, he'd pulled her close and kissed her until they both were uncomfortably aroused.

"It will be all right, Alyssa," he said huskily, smoothing her mussed clothes and trying to cool down his libido.

She swallowed hard and tried to have faith. She knew he was capable of defending himself and guarding the sword. She was just very much afraid that whoever wanted it might go to any length to obtain it. And what could John do against a bullet?

He had clearly made up his mind, however, so, scared that this might turn into a huge mistake, she fell silent.

Alyssa watched from the door as the old man accepted the sword from his son, when it finally came time for the parting. Something passed between the two men, she thought. A silent communication. Their eyes met. Then Isamu Mori pulled the sword out a few centimeters and looked at the shining metal. He raised his eyes to his son and nodded curtly. With a sharp click, he slid the sword back into place.

"Good," Isamu said in Japanese. "Fight hard. Stand firm. Do your best to find our enemies and defeat them. *Gambatte!*"

"Hai!" John said, executing a short, formal bow of compliance. He accepted the sword from his father's hands.

Isamu looked across John's shoulder at Alyssa and smiled.

"Have a safe journey. I hope I will see you again very soon. There is still much to learn about our life here on Onijima, you know, Alyssa Jones. And there are many beautiful things to appreciate. I would be honored if you would allow me to show them to you one day."

Alyssa was deeply touched by the old man's sincerity and kindness.

"Thank you very much, Mori-sama. It would be a very great honor for your humble friend." Out of respect, she spoke in Japanese herself this time.

Both John and Isamu were startled by her fluency.

She grinned. "Perhaps there are a few things for you to learn about me, too," she suggested teasingly.

Isamu laughed. John nodded his head, and from the look in his eyes she had no doubt he'd make a point of finding out quite a bit more about her at the very first opportunity.

Alyssa had the strangest sensation that Isamu Mori knew that she and John were lovers. Did it show? she wondered, faintly embarrassed. Had John said something to him? Had they been seen?

Isamu seemed pleased, happily, so she relaxed. When John took her hand, she knew their cover was blown and she sighed. Such personal touching was rare among mere acquaintances.

"I suppose you get used to this," she whispered to him as they left the house.

"Used to what?"

"Walking around with everyone knowing what you're doing in the privacy of your own bed."

He glanced at her. "Shall we stop?" he asked. His face became momentarily blank of all emotion.

She tightened her grip on his hand.

"Not on your life!" she exclaimed, laughing. "I'll adjust. Just give me a few days to figure out how to take it all in stride."

He relaxed and pulled her close, squeezing her shoulder reassuringly.

"It'll get easier," he promised. "Just tell yourself it's none of their business. It's ours."

Ours. The word echoed comfortingly in her heart.

They said their good-byes to Etsu and the other staff and left for Onijima's airport by car. Kojiro, back from the wedding festivities, insisted on driving them personally.

He'd asked to accompany them to provide additional protection, but John had declined. Kojiro was needed on Onijima. John didn't want any more break-ins around Isamu. So Kojiro stood on the tarmac with some of the employees from John's company, waving goodbye as the plane rolled down the runway.

"Next stop Hong Kong," their pilot said as he prepared to take off.

"Speak any Chinese?" John asked casually. He looked out the window as Onijima dropped out of view.

"No."

"Your Japanese isn't bad," he grinned. "For a *gai-jin.*"

A *gai-jin* was a foreigner and not expected to understand.

"Arigato!" Thank you!

"Do itashimashte." You're welcome.

"This is why you had to make a detour through Hong Kong instead of flying back to Frisco with me?" Alyssa asked in amazement.

"Yes."

He led her up a narrow stone staircase that snaked up the overgrown hillside. Below and around lay a beehive of shops and streets and people. Traffic rushed everywhere. Noise of every description crescendoed to a frantic din.

But here where the solid rock and stubborn vegetation had hung on, lay an oasis in the midst of the human chaos. It was the Buddhist monastery where John had spent so many bruising years. Where he'd escaped from his mother's downward spiral into drinking after his father had been killed in disgrace. It was where he had found order and discipline for both his body and his mind. And it was where he had first met Isamu Mori.

They were greeted at the front door by a middle-aged priest wearing flowing robes and a serenely unconcerned countenance. When he recognized John, he smiled and motioned for them to come in.

"Today's a special day at the school. The students who have passed their studies are sent on to the next level," John explained.

Alyssa doubted that John would come simply to congratulate a bunch of children on moving to a higher grade. She eyed him curiously.

"Why did you come?" she asked.

They stood alongside a number of other adults and a scattering of children. The students' parents and brothers and sisters, Alyssa guessed, looking at the earnest expressions and neatly pressed clothes. They weren't a wealthy group, or if they were, they were unpretentious and didn't bother to buy expensive wardrobes.

John still hadn't answered her question, so she looked at him and repeated cautiously, "John? Why are we here?"

The students trooped in single file. Their faces were serious and each marched politely in his or her place. But every once in a while, an eye would rove as a student sought his family in the audience.

Alyssa and John sat down and listened to the monk in charge comment on the journey of youth to knowledge. Meanwhile his charges sat, trying not to squirm. When he'd finished a lengthy recital of each student's hard work and accomplishments, each pupil was presented with a small strip of paper with a calligraphy-inscribed meditation to keep for continued good luck in the future. Then the audience stood and thanked the monks for all that they had given to the students in the past year.

Finally, everyone was free to mingle.

The students dashed pell-mell to find their friends and relatives. One boy stayed alone.

John got up and waited. He stood out, both in bearing and in physical stature. It wasn't long before the boy saw John.

Alyssa had never seen a child's face light up with such delight. He raced toward John, his paper grasped tightly in his hand.

"Mr. Mori! You came!"

"Of course," John said, as if incensed that the boy would think otherwise. He smiled. "Congratulations. Your teacher says that you haven't missed a single day of school this quarter."

The boy grinned and shrugged.

Alyssa thought he couldn't be more than eight or nine, and he looked like a handful of energy. She looked around and saw no one else paying any attention to the child. He had no family or friends here. Except for John.

"Can I come to the Isle of Devils for the summer?" the boy asked eagerly.

Worry moved down the boy's happiness a couple of notches, but his tight little mouth made him look as if he were trying to be stoic about it. Alyssa bet that he would have denied any real interest in Onijima if John said no. The denial would have been a lie.

John held out his hand in friendship. The boy took it, wondering how to interpret the gesture.

"We'll shake on it," John said solemnly. "You kept your end of the bargain, so I'll keep mine."

The boy erupted in excitement and threw his arms around John in a burst of enthusiasm.

"Now... how about lunch in honor of your advancement?" John suggested casually.

"Yes! Yes. I know the best place."

John grinned. "I'll just bet you do. But no picking pockets or stealing silver."

The boy feigned innocence, but he laughed and shrugged. "Okay. You pay, right?"

"Right you are," John agreed. He glanced at Alyssa who had been trying to figure out exactly what the relationship was between these two. John grinned wolfishly. "But first I'd like to introduce you to a lady who's going to come with us."

The boy perked up and looked at Alyssa with considerable interest.

"Alyssa, meet my protégé, David. David, meet my friend, Alyssa."

While they sat in the airport bar, waiting to catch the flight out of Hong Kong, Alyssa finally had a chance to ask.

"So... how did you meet David?" she asked. She hadn't expected John to have a meeting with a child. She was still recovering from her surprise and wondering why John would come so far out of his way for one small boy.

"One of the monks told me that they had a kid who needed a sponsor."

"Like you once needed one...." she said softly, as realization dawned on her.

"Yes. If Isamu Mori hadn't paid for my education, shown an interest in me, taken pride in me when I had no pride in myself... I never would have made anything of my life."

"I think you underestimate yourself," she said, swirling her drink till the ice clinked.

"Perhaps, but when I saw that boy, I saw myself. The Buddhists teach that life is hard and full of challenges," he noted, staring blindly at the highball he held between his palms. "Everyone needs a little compassion along the way." He took a long, cold swallow and slowly set the drink down, pushing it away.

"He seems to be thriving," Alyssa said. "You must be very pleased for him."

"Yes. I think we got him just in time. Another year and he would be a professional thief." John grinned, shrugging off the intimate conversation as if it were getting a little too close to his own secrets for comfort. "Bloody hell, with my financing, the boy ought to at least be able to practice robbery in a more socially acceptable fashion, by joining a legitimate profession of some stripe."

Alyssa laughed.

A comfortable silence settle between them. Alyssa slid around the table to be a little closer to him. She wanted to have a private conversation, one she was certain could not be overheard.

"Suzie Chan told me you had a tough time as a child."

He shrugged noncommittally.

"*Tough* is a relative term," he said smoothly.

"She said everyone on Onijima knew what your childhood was like. Even everyone in Hong Kong."

John laughed bitterly.

"That's a fact."

"I don't live on Onijima. And I never lived in Hong Kong. Would you tell me what it was like for you then?" When he hesitated, she gently laid her hand on his forearm and added, "Please?"

His face became shuttered again. That hurt her. They'd been so close that she'd forgotten how distant he could be when he stepped behind those castle walls of his.

"My father was a very successful man. An entrepreneur. One of the best of his day. There was a slight problem, regrettably. His line of work, running guns throughout Asia, was not terribly popular with everyone. Especially when it was done under the table, as he occasionally did. My mother was a beautiful woman who'd grown up cared for in manicured homes in Manila and Hong Kong. She'd attended Catholic girls' schools and been sent off to a women's college that more resembled a cloister than an academic environment. When she burst into the social whirl, she fell into his hands like an innocent."

"So you remember them?"

"Oh, yes. They were unforgettable," he said darkly. "Even a child of three or four was impressed by their colorful ways."

"That's how old you were?" she probed gently.

"Yes. My father had one unfortunate weakness. He couldn't resist chasing women. And one year, he chased the wrong one. She was the bored wife of a middleman in the gun trade out of mainland China. But her husband didn't give a damn if she was bored. He wanted her faithful. When he found her in bed with my father, he slaughtered them both on the spot with one stroke of his machete. Poetic justice, one stroke for two adulterers. That's what he said at his trial. He was acquitted. My mother, however, served the sentence for that crime, even though she had absolutely nothing to do with it."

His jaw tightened and the look in his eyes was dark with the memory of a boy's impotent rage and desperate anguish.

"My father was good at manipulating figures. Unfortunately, he wasn't good at hanging on to his earnings. When he died, it took less than a year for us to become destitute. Mother's family had disowned her when she married, and she was too proud to go to them for help."

"Oh, John...how awful for you...for both of you...."

"No crying," he warned with a half smile. "If I see a tear, I quit talking. Agreed?" He still couldn't stand a hint of pity directed toward his tough childhood. It was a stubborn edge of pride he'd built a whole life around. He wasn't going to let it go now.

Alyssa swallowed hard and pressed her fingertips hard on her eyes. She nodded, hoping she could hang on to herself long enough.

"Agreed," she said huskily. "No tears."

"She got a job as an assistant manager of a restaurant and bar. But she found she enjoyed the bar and the drinks and the clientele more than the restaurant. Gradually, she stopped managing the bar and managed the patrons. Many were businessmen with money and expense accounts, and she quickly learned how to get them spent on her."

"Who took care of you while she worked?" she asked worriedly.

"Whatever neighbor woman happened to be home and willing. That breeds self-sufficiency fast in a child," he pointed out dryly.

And bitterness, Alyssa thought, aching for him and wishing she hadn't promised not to cry.

"One drink would lead to another, one man to another, one bar to another," he said without emotion. "She slid into the bottle and drowned there. I was five, nearly six, when I came home one afternoon to find her on the floor with her dress around her shoulders and a man I'd never seen, with his trousers around his ankles, lying between her thighs. I'd told kids she wasn't a drunk. And I'd gone crazy fighting bigger kids who kept taunting me that she was a whore. But a child gives up his fantasies slowly. And I hung on to mine like a fool to the bitter end."

Alyssa found his hand and held on tightly.

"That's a credit to you," she said sincerely. "Some people never let themselves have a dream. Others let go without a fight."

His lips lifted in a crooked smile.

"Maybe," he conceded.

"What happened?" Alyssa asked, feeling sick at what John had faced all alone and so very young.

"I tried to beat the hell out of the bloke. I thought the bastard was trying to hurt my mother. I landed on his back and bit on his neck, beat his shoulders and kicked him in the groin."

"You're lucky you didn't get killed," Alyssa whispered in horror.

John laughed shortly.

"I nearly did. By my mother. She was in the final throes apparently and was so drunk she didn't realize who was interrupting matters. When the son of a bitch grabbed me and tossed me over my head, she was swinging her shoe in my direction for good measure. When she saw it was me, she started screaming for me to get out. Get out in a hurry."

When he stopped, Alyssa didn't dare ask anything. She could see the raw pain buried deep inside the layers of the passing years. John had never forgiven his mother for crushing his dreams, she thought. An experience like that would make an angel cynical. John had turned out remarkably fair-minded, considering what he'd had to deal with long ago.

John glanced at her, saw the warmth and empathy in Alyssa's eyes and sighed. Something painful untied inside him. One knot of many.

"I ran down to the boats, intending to become a sailor and see the world," John said with a sober and straight face. "One of the monks was there, buying some kelp to make a broth for dinner. He sat me down to discuss my nautical aspirations...."

Alyssa giggled. She could just envision one of the smooth-faced Buddhists engaged in serious discussion with a distraught boy determined to run away.

"He convinced me that cabin boy was the post to which I aspired, but those positions weren't available in the modern age. The best a person with my scant muscle and stature could hope for would be cook's helper. When I told him I couldn't take that job because all I knew how to cook was rice, he offered to teach me cooking...if I enrolled in his school and took a few other minor courses in my free time."

"Such as language and writing and mathematics?" Alyssa guessed.

"And cricket and soccer and music." John took another sip of his drink and called for the tab. After he paid, he turned and put his arm along the back of the chair she was sitting in. His eyes were dark and serious now. "That man saved me. And he mentioned my poverty to Isamu. And Isamu saved me. They gave me the golden opportunities out of which I have been able to fashion a life that I find both interesting and highly rewarding.''

"So you are doing the same.''

"Yes.''

"John?''

"What?''

"Would you be willing to tell me what happened to your mother?''

"Why not? It isn't a secret.'' He laughed and a trace of the old bitterness came back to haunt him. "She was happy to have me in the Buddhist school. It kept me out of surprise visits to the house. She'd learned she could earn more on her back than standing up, and she wanted to make it while she still had something to sell.''

Alyssa paled. She was amazed at how straightforwardly John could tell this sordid tale. He was incredibly strong, she thought. Many would have been crushed beneath that seamy beginning.

"She thought she'd hit the jackpot when she developed a relationship with a strange man flashing a lot of cash one summer. I was fifteen. Isamu came to see me graduate to a higher level in *kendo* studies at the monastery. Because I had done so well, he gave me my own sword. It was made by a man living north of Tokyo. It wasn't an antique or a national treasure, but it was magnificent. And it was very valuable. Mother needed some money....''

"Oh, no....'' Alyssa felt a stab of pain in the region of her heart.

"Oh, yes,'' John said, smiling cynically. "Leave it to her to finance her fantasy cruise by pawning my gift from Isamu. I was beside myself. I'd never hated her so much, or despaired for her so deeply. She spent the money on clothes in the hope that her newest beau would decide to marry her.''

"And ... did he?''

"No. He killed her.''

"John, no!'' .

"He strangled her, tossed her body in the ocean and fled with her cash and jewelry. They caught up with him down in Indonesia somewhere. He got a prison term.''

The announcer was calling their flight. John looked at her and smiled dryly.

"That was many years ago, Alyssa. I got over it. People do. You can't hang on to tragedy forever. You have to let it go."

"Yes," she murmured. But sometimes it didn't let *you* go, she thought.

As they got on the plane, she turned to ask, "What did you say to Isamu when he came back and you didn't have the sword?"

"Nothing. He patted me on the shoulder and said he regretted the death of my unfortunate mother. Then we went out and purchased back the sword from the pawnshop. A little while later, he asked if I would be interested in being his son, since I had no parent and he had no child."

Alyssa sighed and wiped away tears.

John laughed as they sat down and fastened their seat belts.

"Bloody hell! You held back till I'd spilled my guts."

She caught his hand in hers and brushed a kiss discreetly on his cheek.

"It was the hardest thing I've ever done, John Mori."

They flew on to San Francisco, into the yawning jaws of fate.

Chapter 14

Alyssa's gallery threw a gala opening of the traveling *samurai* art exhibit and the Mori sword was made the center attraction.

Betsy De Laguna, exhausted from forty-eight hours solid of coordination and last-minute snafu resolving, beamed in every direction as people ambled through the rooms.

"This is the best Japanese art to be assembled in California since the Daimyo exhibit," Betsy said, gushing.

"The Daimyo exhibit?" Alyssa said doubtfully. "I'm certainly happy that you think so, Betsy, but, I don't know...."

The Daimyo had been sponsored by the Japanese government and a number of international businesses, and it had been spectacular.

"Naturally, if you know the descendants of all those Japanese nobles and *shoguns,* it's a lot easier to ask them to loan their priceless antiquities to your museum," Betsy said nonchalantly. "But you had to go it alone, with just your credentials and your rep! Wow!"

"I, uh, did pull a few old strings," Alyssa admitted. "And George, of course, loaned us quite a few magnificent pieces from his own personal collection."

"Did somebody mention my name?"

George Bodney moved smoothly around a pair of ladies and presented himself at Alyssa's elbow. He smiled and made a warm sweeping appraisal of Alyssa's strapless black evening dress.

"My dear, your legs are ravishing," he murmured, glancing admiringly at the thigh-high split and glimpse of black silk stockings.

George lifted Alyssa's hand and pressed it to his lips. Seeing John's complete lack of emotion, George smiled and slanted him a look of subtle challenge.

"Your friend has put on his face of stone again. Have you noticed it happens whenever I get overly familiar with you, dear?"

Alyssa shook her head.

"No, George, I hadn't noticed." She looked him straight in the eye and forced herself not to blink.

George's smile expanded.

"Careful, Alyssa, your pretty nose will grow longer if you don't watch out. While your urge to protect is laudable, I'm sure it's quite unnecessary. John here is quite adept at protecting his own back. Aren't you, John?"

John didn't comment. He didn't smile, either.

Alyssa stared at her partner, appalled. He had said something to that effect once before, insinuating that John had been responsible for someone's death. She never found a way to ask John about that. Of course, she didn't believe it. She simply wanted to know what these two men were struggling over.

"Ah, there are the happy threesome," her brother, Alasdair, said, sauntering into the room.

"Happy threesome" was not how Alyssa would describe them.

She could smell brandy on Alasdair's breath when he bent to kiss her cheek. His eyes were bloodshot. He looked exhausted.

"Alasdair? Are you all right?" she asked quietly.

"All right? Why, of course I'm all right. I've got the whole apartment to myself, thanks to your boyfriend over there with the stony personality. Tell me, Alyssa, is he warmer in the sack than he looks standing around with exhibitors?"

"Alasdair, please..."

"Alasdair, please. Alasdair, please," he mimicked. "When are you going to can that whine, huh, Alyssa? Do you know how irritating it is to have your sister constantly pulling the rug out from under you? Constantly being praised as a combination of a saint and a missionary for taking care of you? No. You probably don't." He sighed. Then he ran a hand through his hair and muttered, "I can see you've launched another coup, dear sister. Let me congratulate you on your victory."

He aimed a cool glance at John, who was listening with growing irritation but admirable personal restraint.

Alasdair bent close to Alyssa's ear and murmured something private. Alyssa blushed. Alasdair laughed. John wondered what was said.

"Well, I can see I'd better start circulating," Alasdair remarked, his speech still slightly slurred.

Alyssa watched him leave and tried to remember what tranquillity felt like. Alasdair didn't make it easy. And he'd been especially irritable ever since she'd returned with John.

She smiled and shook hands with several visitors, feeling her nerves stretch in the building pressure.

When she had originally conceived of this exhibit, Alyssa had been so excited she could hardly stop talking about it. This should have been her moment of crowning glory. The show was terrific. The items were sensational. The facility had never looked more elegant. Betsy had midwifed Alyssa's idea and the results were bringing in lots of enthusiastic compliments.

There were serenely simple tea bowls, brilliantly colored *Kabuki kimonos,* pale *Noh* masks, graceful ink brush calligraphy and several beautiful examples of *ukiyo-e* prints.

The tour de force of the exhibit was the sword rooms. There were examples of various types of swords from the flowering of the Heian Period in the Middle Ages all the way up to the banning of the sword during the nineteenth-century Meiji Period. The gallery had managed to acquire the loan of a particularly elegant Masamune sword by

Masamune, one of the foremost sword makers of feudal Japan.

The Mori family sword, O Takehira, was displayed in a pool of light, its scabbard and the fake *tsuba* nearby.

It drew a great deal of murmured discussion, Alyssa noted.

"Do you think anyone else has noticed that the *tsuba* is bogus?" John asked under his breath when they had a free moment.

Alyssa kept smiling across the room at people as she replied. "Not yet. Although, I held my breath when Dr. Shirazawa was examining the display. There was a look of puzzlement in his eyes. Then, thank heavens, George drew him off to show him his latest prize acquisition in the other room."

"George is no fool," John muttered. "He can't afford any unexpected challenges to the *tsuba*'s authenticity. He's probably sweating out every day, praying you don't realize what's happened, wondering when you'll have the time to take a good, close look and get suspicious yourself. What are the odds that someone will raise a question tonight, Alyssa?"

"I don't know. That depends on our luck, I'm afraid. Fortunately, no one has ever seen a verified Takehira, so it will be even harder than usual to identify a fraud. Also," she added with a grin, "I am considered an honorable person by most of these people, so they'd hesitate to question something of mine. And don't forget, they can tell that the other pieces are clearly authentic, so they may dismiss any misgivings they might have about my *tsuba*. For a while, anyway."

"It pays to lead a clean life," John observed dryly.

Alyssa laughed.

"I suppose it does," she conceded.

The crowd pressed closer and for a few moments, it became impossible for them to talk privately. When they got another break from the crush, John noticed Alasdair staring at him murderously from the main entrance.

"Your brother looks as if he'd like to slit my throat." John whispered in her ear.

Alyssa forced the smile to stay; someone else was coming along.

"Alasdair is a little jealous I think." She sighed. "And also a lot drunk. I'm about at my wits' end with him. And since I'm not home much, I can't keep the stuff away from him."

Alyssa rarely went to either of her own homes, and when she did, John accompanied her. She'd given up trying to convince him her brother wouldn't harm her. They'd just have to disagree about that, she had decided fatalistically. Time would prove one of them right. She hoped it would be her. She hoped she'd be proved right about George, too.

She had asked John to stay at her apartment, but he hadn't been interested in sleeping under the same roof with her brother. He had no desire to be knifed in his sleep or poisoned when his back was turned. And having the sword there might have been more temptation than even discreet George could have resisted. Alyssa had eventually agreed that staying in the apartment wouldn't work.

They had briefly contemplated staying at her beach house, but it was too far to commute daily to the gallery for the duration of the exhibit. Carrying the sword over those deserted stretches of highway might have been asking for more trouble than even John was prepared to handle. All a thief would need was a rifle with a good telescopic sight on it. So that had been ruled out.

And John refused to let her go off on her own.

"You're staying with me until we put away the person who tried to kill you," he said flatly. His hard stare and rigid stance had made his determination clear. Neither she nor the sword would be released from his watchful eyes.

Alyssa hadn't even bothered to put up an argument. Besides, she didn't really wish to be apart from him. His company was addictive, and she wanted more of it every day.

In the end, John had arranged for a suite of rooms at a well-located, rather expensive hotel. They both stayed there. And so did the sword. Not all their time was spent in planning for the exhibit and the care of the *katana*, either. John's kisses were aphrodisiacs. It was impossible to have just one.

Every night ended in deeper pleasure. And every morning brought more of the same magical delight.

Alyssa went to the gallery feeling as if she were walking on air. John, who was personally carrying the sword to the exhibit and removing it when the gallery closed in the evening, never strayed from her side.

It was strange to be so happy while waiting for something deadly to happen, but Alyssa stopped trying to make sense of it. Love was crazy, she decided philosophically. And probably so was she.

At the end of the gala opening, Alyssa wasn't sure she had the energy left to leave the gallery.

Betsy was sitting in the office with her head on her arm and her arm on a desk. She was sound asleep. And snoring.

Her husband came and woke her up. She staggered after him, trying to get her eyes into focus.

"That leaves us," John said, leaning against the door-jamb. He had the sword. It was in the scabbard, and neatly tied to his waist hung the *tsuba*.

Alyssa turned off the lights and pulled on her coat.

"Have you had any word about Esau?" she asked uneasily. It had been too uneventful ever since they'd left Onijima. Not knowing what had happened to Holling was making her want to look over her shoulder all day long.

John didn't appear perturbed.

"Kojiro is still looking for him. He arrived in Melbourne, but then he disappeared. He might be trying out all the flavors in the local whorehouses...."

"Or he might be coming after us," Alyssa murmured.

She looked at the sword and lifted her eyes to look into John's enigmatic blue gaze. He always stood back from her when she began airing her worries about their safety. Well...that was too bad, she thought, throwing caution and polite manners to the wind.

"John, shouldn't we have some sort of help? Could we explain the situation to the authorities? Ask for an investigation?"

He turned off the lights for her as they walked to the front door.

"We've been over this before," he said tersely. "The authorities have no reason to get involved yet. They may take a report and file it, but they can't act, because we have no evidence of a local crime. The only injuries occurred in another country. Onijima. Our best hope lies in tempting the person behind this to come after O Takehira. Only this time, we'll catch him in the act."

Alyssa grabbed his arm urgently.

"That's what worries me. What if..."

He laid a finger on her mouth and gave her a weak smile.

"Let me worry."

Alyssa glared at him.

"That's just the problem! You *don't* worry."

He looked unconcerned.

Alyssa sighed and locked the doors behind them.

"Alyssa, I want you to tell Alasdair and George Bodney that I've had second thoughts about permitting the sword to stay on display."

"What?" Her head came up sharply.

"Word will travel fast among those who are interested in swords. Whoever wants O Takehira badly enough to murder for it will hear about it."

"All right," she agreed, feeling as if she would be stepping off into an abyss. "What will you do?"

"Accept the gallery owner's generous offer to let me visit her charming seaside beach house."

"But the beach house is even more isolated than the hotel!" she protested. "That's a terrible place to fight."

John unlocked the doors to her car and slid in with the carefully wrapped scabbard and sword. When they were settled, he looked at her.

"I want to force his hand. A forced hand is more likely to have a misplayed card."

Alyssa dearly hoped John was right.

When they arrived at the hotel they varied their route to his suite, as they always did. When he was satisfied that the suite was in the same condition as it was when they'd left it, he turned his attention fully on her.

"That was quite a selection of the Bay Area's upper crust."

"Yes, I guess it was."

"Are they friends or just people who come to art events?"

"A few are friends."

He offered her a drink and poured one for himself.

John took a long swallow of the neat whiskey and contemplated the amber liquid remaining in the small glass.

She had never been on the wrong side of the tracks in life, he thought. In spite of the tragedy of her parents' marriage, she'd moved in the upper levels of society, gone to all the right places, done the expected things.

How could a woman like that tolerate his past? he wondered.

He felt her arms come around his middle, and he closed his eyes.

"I was getting lonely," she said hesitantly. "I ached but there was no one to heal the hurt." She smiled as his arms tightened around her protectively. "Ahh...that's what I need...."

He tilted her face back with one hand and covered her mouth with his.

"I don't want you going back there tonight," he said, placing soft kisses along her lips.

Alyssa had rarely felt less like going home herself.

"I can't keep staying here forever," she murmured as he kissed his way slowly over her.

"I know," he muttered, lifting his head and frowning. "That's why I'm going out to the beach house tomorrow." He braced himself for what he knew would come next. "And I'll go alone. You stay here till I send you the all clear."

"Oh, no!" She closed her fists and laid them on his chest. "I want to help. John...you can't face the unknown all alone."

"Damn it, Alyssa, you know bloody well that you've helped," he said, growing angry. "And if your brother is involved, it would be easier if you didn't have to stand there and witness it."

"He's got problems," she conceded, "but Alasdair would never agree to anything that could harm me. My Lord, John...that plane crash could have killed me! Alasdair wouldn't have done that to me. I just can't believe he would."

"For your sake, sweetheart, I hope you're right."

She flattened her palms against his chest and laid her cheek against his.

"Tomorrow night at the exhibit, you'll make the sad announcement about the curtailing of the sword's display. I'll drive to your beach house, and we'll make sure people assume I have the sword with me. We'll have made a switch, however, and you'll have O Takehira in your trunk."

"It's the next part I don't think I'm going to like," she sighed.

He gave her a friendly swat on the bottom.

"You don't have to like everything in life. As a matter of fact, it's generally guaranteed that there'll be plenty that you'll hate to swallow."

"This being one of them."

"I'll continue on to the beach house and see if I can catch a sword lover hungering for my unique piece of steel."

"What about a backup? Police always call for backup. Why shouldn't you?"

"Don't worry," he said with a smile. "I'll have some backup. But it's not going to be you! I want you safely hidden away and out of the line of fire. And my *backup* will be in place before I arrive. Will that be good enough to suit you?"

"It sounds a little better than it did a few minutes ago," she conceded.

They each turned toward the other at the same moment. Mouths met and kissed and held.

There was an urgency in John that Alyssa felt immediately. The tense tremor in his thigh when he pressed between her legs . . . the almost frenzied way that he took her mouth in one soul-wrenching kiss after another.

The boiling heat was contagious. Her own needs sharpened like claws on a cat as it scratches the bark of a tree.

His hands were inside her clothes, sliding away the coverings over her tender breasts. When he lowered his mouth to tease her nipple, it was already pouting tautly, as if to kiss him back. He lowered his zipper, and she wiggled out of the thin scrap of nylon and he thrust into her as he pushed her shoulders against the hotel wall.

Their groans came in synchrony. The sound inflamed their desire.

She slid her thighs higher and he plunged into her until the fever gripped. Deep in her abdomen a rocket uncoiled. Faster and faster and faster it went.

"John! Oh, my darling! Yes! Yes! Yes!"

He wrapped her shuddering body in a bone-crushing grip as his thundering climax overtook him. He stood there, holding her in his arms, impaling her with his body, shaking with the force of their lovemaking.

It had *never* been like this, he thought. Only with her. Drained of all tension. Satisfied to the bone. At peace with life. And with himself.

He slid his hands through her damp hair and found her mouth.

His kiss spoke of tenderness and of a yearning too deep for words.

Alyssa wrapped her arms around his neck and squeezed her thighs, hugging him, holding him deep inside.

"Did your mistresses ever say 'I love you'?" she whispered, still shaking from their incredible lovemaking.

"Yes. But the words came easily to them," he murmured. He kissed her lips, her cheek, her jaw.

She pressed her lips close to his ear and murmured, "Come back to me, John Mori. *Come back.*"

He let her ease down off his body and then lifted her in his arms and carried her to his bed.

"We have a while yet," he said, eyes darkened with something more than physical passion.

"Yes, my love. Yes..."

It all went as planned in the beginning. The public discussion of O Takehira's removal spread like wildfire among the people attending the exhibit.

They made the switch in an alley behind a police station.

John grabbed her by the back of the head, planted a quick hard kiss on her mouth and told her to go to his hotel room and wait for him.

Alyssa watched his taillights disappear into the sea of traffic as he pulled onto the street. In an hour or so, he'd be at the beach house.

Back in the hotel room, all she could do was wait.

Waiting was pure hell.

Pacing didn't help.

Watching the television news didn't, either.

She kept watching the phone, wishing it would ring, hoping it would be John telling her everything was all right.

The sound of a key in the door sent a chill through her.

Alasdair walked in.

"Alasdair! How did you get a key?" she asked in surprise.

He smiled coldly.

"Why, from the man who's staying here."

His eyes hardened into ice and Alyssa's fear thickened.

"What do you mean?" she asked.

"You'll see. You're coming with me. You're our trading card, sister dear."

He grasped her by the arm and pulled her toward the hall.

"Where's John?" she asked.

"Don't bother with the big-sister-knows-best tone, Lyssa," he said bitterly. "That won't work this time. I got myself into something even you can't get me out of. So forget the sweet persuasion, the logical reasoning, the emotional pleading for me to walk the good old straight and narrow."

He hustled her down the back stairwell and into the alley where his car was waiting. He shoved her inside, and she fell onto the seat from the force of it. She looked at him and saw a stranger staring back at her.

When she would have jumped back out again, someone locked the doors from the driver's seat control.

She looked up to see George. He was watching her in the rearview mirror.

"Hello, Alyssa," he said in those smooth, even tones that marked him as a well-educated man. He pulled away as Alasdair fastened his seat belt in the seat beside Alyssa.

"If you're calm and cooperative, things will go much more easily for all of us," he said.

How could he sound so appallingly reasonable? She looked at him in fury.

"What are you doing? How did you get John's key?"

George smiled apologetically.

"Well…we weren't very gentlemanly about it, I'm afraid. I'll spare you the details, dear."

Alyssa felt as if a part of her had died. What were they saying? Had they… She was afraid to even think the word. No. No. As long as he's alive in my mind, he's alive, she cried out in silent agony.

Her brother looked exhausted. George looked as unruffled as he always did.

George. Every inch a gentleman, George.

"Is he alive?" she asked, unable to bear not knowing.

Her brother looked away from her. Terrified that that meant the worst, she grabbed her brother's hand and held it till her nails indented his flesh.

"Alasdair! For the love of God, tell me the truth. Is he alive?"

Alasdair looked into her eyes and for a moment, she thought he was going to tell her. But he glanced toward George, seeking guidance, obviously.

George made a slight, negative motion.

Alasdair remained silent and looked away from her.

"What have you done to my brother?" she cried, wishing she could do something impressively painful to George Bodney.

George shrugged.

"I've been helping him develop his independence, my dear. You used to appreciate that. Remember?"

"I obviously made a terrible mistake," she said acidly.

"Just sit back, Alyssa. We'll be there soon. There's no point in struggling. You're outnumbered."

Chapter 15

The beach house sat on a rolling slope of land in the rocky bluffs overlooking the ocean. As they turned onto the winding road that led to the property, Alyssa stared out the window and looked at the sea. It stretched like a rippling black satin sheet, glistening in the starlight. She had bought the place as a refuge, but now all she felt was a horrible sense of impending doom.

They pulled up in front of the carport. John's rental car was already there.

Alyssa felt a wave of pain engulf her heart. John...what have they done to you?

George turned off the headlights and killed the ignition. "Shall we go inside and bring this drama to a conclusion, my dear?" he said as he released the electronic locks on the doors and got out of the car, carrying a long, cloth-wrapped, cylindrical object.

Alasdair grabbed her hand and pulled her across the seat, making her get out on his side of the car. They had no interest in chasing her on foot through the rough, untamed terrain.

The front door was locked. George pulled the key out of his pocket and laid the covered package against the smooth cedar wall of the house.

"How did you get a key to my house?" Alyssa asked angrily. Anger helped her temporarily disregard how afraid she was, and she embraced it eagerly.

"From John Mori." George smiled. "Not consciously."

Alasdair laughed.

Alyssa irately wished that she understood the joke. As soon as they stepped into the living room, she grasped the bleak reference. John was sprawled out unconscious on the floor.

"No!" Alyssa cried out, angrily pulling free of her brother's grasp and running to kneel at John's side. "Oh, my darling," she murmured, running trembling hands over his shoulder, finding the vein in his neck that would tell her whether he was dead or alive.

A slow, faint throbbing told her what she had so desperately yearned for. He was alive. Alive!

She bowed her head in relief and murmured against his cheek, "I love you. I love you so."

She knew that he couldn't hear her, and it didn't matter. She couldn't hold the words back anymore. She kissed his shoulder and positioned herself so that he was behind her.

George and Alasdair had been standing in the middle of the room watching, George in cool amusement, Alasdair in irritation.

"How poignant," George observed with his customary air of sophisticated detachment. "What a pity he can't hear you."

Alyssa put her hand on John, instinctively trying to shield him from any hurt. Her fingers brushed his throat. It seemed to her that his pulse had quickened. His cool skin was slightly warmer to the touch.

"What did you do to him, George?"

"Do you see that pot of tea on the table behind him? We merely saw to it that something was added to the leaves that would get your shadowy warrior out of our way for a few hours."

"He'll recover, then?" Alyssa felt the first small glimmer of joy and hope.

"Long enough to fall down the mountainside into the ocean and drown. After I've had a small measure of revenge, of course."

"What do you mean?" Alyssa's joy faded and fear gnawed at her heart anew.

"I warned you to stay away from him," George pointed out with a faint tone of censure. "He murdered a man once. In a *kendo* match. Well, afterward, to be perfectly honest. He had a grudge against the man and used the match as an excuse to hunt him down and assassinate him."

"I don't believe you, John Mori wouldn't do that. You don't know him as I do, George!"

"Do you know John Mori as well as you thought you knew me, my dear?" He smiled cruelly.

"I thought I knew who you were," Alyssa admitted unhappily, "I trusted you, became partners with you and let you become a confidant and mentor to my brother—a man who needed that. Obviously I made a tragic mistake. But John is a different matter."

"Because you slept with him?"

Alyssa was shocked at George's bluntness. She wondered how he knew about John and her.

"Frankly," George said, as though musing aloud, "I was startled to hear about that. You were always such a vestal virgin here in San Francisco. Tell me, was it the mystery and the atmosphere on that wretched island that loosened your knees?"

"No! It was the man," she said angrily. "Not that it's any of your business." She shot a critical look at Alasdair. "I suppose it was Dair who told you about John and me."

Alasdair appeared to be both defiantly proud of himself and vaguely uneasy.

"Of course," George acknowledged. He walked over to her and leaned down to touch John's neck. "His pulse is picking up. He'll be conscious again soon." He smiled but the smile was more condescending and self-satisfied than anything else.

Alyssa shoved George's hand away from John's neck and leaned protectively over his body.

George walked across the room to the black lacquer scabbard and its sword. John had placed it on its black display stand in a corner of the living room. George lifted the sword and removed it from its scabbard with the fluid motion of an experienced handler.

"This is what I have been waiting for," he said fervently.

"You'd risk people's lives for a weapon?" Alyssa cried in disgust. "You've lost your mind, George! Give it up. Now. It isn't too late. I'll find some way to help you if you'll just stop!"

"Not just for a weapon, my dear Alyssa," George said calmly as he examined the blade. He frowned and carried the sword closer to a lamp. George Bodney swore viciously and looked across the room at John Mori's still form sprawled on the floor.

"Where the hell is the Takehira?" George exploded. He ran to them and kicked John in the ribs. "Mori! Wake up! What have you done with my sword?"

John rolled over very slowly. Alyssa hovered over him, fiercely protective. When his eyes opened, his gaze found Alyssa's first.

There was a warmth in the dark blue that she hadn't expected. She was half lying across his arm and chest, now that he had moved. To her surprise she felt his hand close over hers. He felt warm and strong. The hard grip surely couldn't belong to a man who had been drugged, she thought incredulously. Then his eyes seemed to go blank, and when he turned his head so he could look up at George, his body went limp again.

"Where is the Takehira *katana?*" George repeated. His normally easygoing demeanor was fast being consumed in fury.

John squinted blearily, as if trying to bring George into focus. He shook his head and pressed the heels of his hands against his temples.

"What the hell . . . did you slip . . . me?" he said hoarsely.

"Never mind about that. If you don't tell me where the sword is, you'll have worse things to worry about than a headache."

"It'll take . . . few minutes." John shook his head, as if to shake loose the somnolence.

Alasdair paced back and forth nervously.

"Holling's supposed to be here soon. Hurry up, George." He shot a suspicious look John's way. "He's waking up too fast, if you ask me. Maybe we didn't give him enough."

"You were here, Alasdair. That was your responsibility," George said coldly. "Did you do what I told you to do?"

"Yes, of course! I told him that the tea was from Lyssa and I brought it to make amends for distrusting him and wanting him out of our lives. Then I took the hotel room key and the house key off the table when he passed out on the floor."

"Then stop bellyaching, Alasdair. Everything's going as we planned. Except for one unfortunate delay." George stared hard at Alyssa. "After he took the sword from the gallery, where did the two of you go?"

"Drop dead, George. I wouldn't help you for all the swords in the Orient!" She put her arm behind John's shoulder as he struggled to a sitting position. She kept it there and hugged him protectively, desperately wishing she had some weapon to use to defend them.

The phone rang.

Everyone became stone still.

It rang again and again. The answering machine came on. They listened to hear who was calling. It was Betsy De Laguna. Alyssa had never been so glad to hear her voice. If only she could get some sort of message to her. . . .

"Alyssa? Alyssa? I know you're there. I've called everywhere else. Someone saw John leave with you earlier in the day at the hotel. I have to talk to you! God, if I don't, I just don't know what I'll do!" She was sobbing.

George looked thoroughly disgusted. Alasdair whispered, "Betsy hangs on like a sand chigger." He gave his sister another contemptible look. "Lyssa just can't resist trying to be a human crutch."

"I'll come out there right now..." Betsy was saying between gulps and sniffles. "Maybe you're down along the beach and can't hear me. I'm sorry if I'm interrupting anything private, but I'm so desperate, I don't know what I'm going to do. Please, Alyssa? Is it okay if I come? Can you hear me? Are you anywhere near the phone?"

"Tell her not to come," George ordered coldly. He stared straight through Alyssa. "And be very careful what you say. If you try to call for help, I'll test this sword on your bedmate there."

He lowered the point of the sword until it was six inches from John's abdomen.

Alyssa fought off the sickening wave of fear that tumbled through her. The image of John being sliced open by that deadly weapon made her blood run cold. She squeezed his shoulder as she stood up, as much to draw comfort for herself as to communicate hope to him.

She picked up the phone and turned off the answering machine. "Betsy?" Alyssa said evenly. "Uh...what's the matter?"

"We...we're pregnant!" Betsy burst into tears.

"That's wonderful. That's what you've been wanting for so long!" Alyssa saw the impatience in George's face and wondered how she could communicate her desperate situation to Betsy without George or Alasdair being aware of it.

Betsy began talking quickly. "I wasn't sure until this morning. I was so thrilled! You know what hell we've gone through."

"Betsy..."

"So I picked my husband up at the airport tonight to surprise him with the news! But before I could tell him, he told me he wanted to call it quits!" She burst into tears again.

Alyssa was in agony. She didn't want Betsy to do something dreadful, something hurtful to herself, but she was staring at the gleaming steel hovering with such deadly intent so very near to John's belly. She had little choice. She had to trust that beneath the emotional crucifixion that Betsy was suffering, she still had a level head. *Please, Betsy,* Alyssa prayed. *Figure this out....*

"Betsy. I'm really sorry, but I can't talk right now. Maybe you could call one of the other girls?"

"Alyssa! Didn't you hear what I just said? My husband wants a divorce! He's giving up on our whole life together just when our dearest dream is coming true! I need your shoulder to cry on, Alyssa!" His dismay was clear.

"I'm sorry, Betsy, but this is really an awkward time. Call your doctor. Remember what a sympathetic listener he is? He told you to call anytime you really needed him. Remember?"

"Alyssa?" Betsy sounded puzzled. Her tears were drying up.

Her doctor was well-known for his lack of sympathy. "Don't say a thing more," Alyssa warned, fearing that Betsy had sensed there was a problem and was about to proceed to ask Alyssa what was wrong. "I can't talk now. I've got my hands full." She held her breath as she added, "Too full." She laughed hoping George would think it was a joke. Alyssa prayed that Betsy was getting the real message. Alyssa had never refused to help Betsy through a crisis like this before. She'd broken dates, been late to social events, dressed and done her hair with Betsy crying on her bed. She'd even cancelled business appointments to keep Betsy sane in the midst of her grief.

"Alyssa?" Betsy said, sounding even more confused and uncertain. "I would do anything for you. You know that, don't you? You've been such a friend to me. Even now, when everything looks so hopeless." There was a split second of silence, as if Betsy were struggling to think clearly enough to know what to say. "Is there anything I can do for you?"

"Just don't give up quite yet. Things aren't always as they seem."

"Can I come out there, Alyssa?" Betsy asked. This time her voice was incredibly steady.

"I don't think that would be a good idea, Betsy."

"Tomorrow, then?"

"I'm afraid not." Alyssa had never refused to come up with an alternative time or date for them to get together.

This was a complete rejection of all contact in the immediate future.

"Alyssa?"

"Yes?"

"Maybe I should call Josie. What do you think?"

Alyssa could have kissed Betsy. Josie was the new lady policewoman who patrolled near the gallery. They'd had coffee with her recently at the corner café. Neither Alasdair nor George went there and neither knew the woman.

"I think that would be an excellent choice of confidantes," Alyssa said with a sigh. "Good luck, Betsy."

"Same to you, Lyssa," Betsy whispered.

Alyssa hung up the phone.

George poked John in the rib with the tip of the sword, not hard enough to draw blood. John stared up at him. He looked wider awake, but still less than fully in control of himself.

"Tell me where the sword is."

"In the trunk of a car." John stared back at George, his eyes narrowing. "Now tell me why you're trying to steal it."

George smiled and shrugged.

"Why not? It will be a pleasure knowing that you hear its fate before you go on to your reward."

"Thank you," John said ironically. He stood up slowly. The sword point hovered near his belly. He moved with care.

"I love the swords, as Alyssa has explained. I have one of the finest collections in the world. Unfortunately, it does not generate much income. And I like to live rather well. I have been forced to find something valuable to sell. There are men of incredible wealth who would give great sums to possess something that is one of a kind." George looked at Alyssa and smiled faintly. "I'm sure you know what I mean, Mori."

John looked at Alyssa, and she felt the leap of fire between them in spite of the desperate situation in the room. His gaze never left her face as he murmured, "Yes."

George looked calm and amused again. He lowered the sword and walked away from John.

"I happened to come across Alyssa and Alasdair a few years ago, and realizing the phenomenal treasure that she had in the Takehira *tsuba,* I began making discreet inquiries around the Far East, Europe and the Americas, seeking a buyer who would pay well and not mind keeping his purchase to himself.''

"Did you take the *tsuba* already?" John asked, moving slowly across the room toward Alyssa.

"Yes." George looked at Alasdair as one might stare at a puppy who hadn't quite gotten his lessons right. "Alasdair pocketed it one day when Alyssa opened the bank vault. She assumed he had put it back in the box, trusting soul that she is."

Alyssa looked at her brother and the disappointment in her eyes could have filled an ocean.

Alasdair bristled.

"I wanted more money," he said defiantly. "You don't know what it's like having to go through every day hearing how wonderful your sister is," he said, sneering. "How hardworking, how selfless, how perfect!" He grabbed his hair in his fists, torn with pain. "I wanted enough money to be free of you, to be free of that damned trust fund." He laughed bitterly. "Who wants his puritan sister to be the trustee of his damned money? What man wants to be a child forever to his damned sister?"

"I'm sorry, Dair," Alyssa whispered. Tears filled her eyes. "I had no idea that you felt so bitterly about this. It wasn't my idea...being the trustee. Please, we can find some solution to this. You're my brother, Dair! My brother! Help me. I'll do whatever you want if you'll just come to your senses before it's too late!"

Alasdair looked at her for a long time. There was a small glimmer of the tender bond that had existed between them when he was small and had depended on her for everything. But the resentment of the man rolled back over him. He turned away and shook his head, gritting his teeth in determination.

George lifted his brows fatalistically. "It's too late, Alyssa."

Alasdair frowned and glanced back at her. But he said nothing.

"Where's the *tsuba*?" John asked, his voice still soft and roughened.

"In my personal collection," George said with a modest smile.

"You had a copy made and slipped it back into Alyssa's bank deposit box the next time she got into it," John guessed.

"Exactly. We knew that it was essential we get a good enough copy to pass expert scrutiny. That was not an easy task, believe me, and we couldn't afford to let Alyssa take a close look at our copy. If we had failed, she would be the one person most likely to detect some flaw in our duplicate. I arranged for the expert replication, for a considerable sum, I might add, and Alasdair got it in and out of the bank under his trusting sister's nose."

Alyssa flinched. Her brother looked both defiant and somewhat humiliated by George's frank admissions. Defiant was definitely uppermost, though. She felt a wave of nausea at her brother's betrayal. How could he? How *could* he?

"I wasn't sure we would be able to fool other experts," George conceded with a rare trace of humility. He smiled coldly. "But we did. None of them questioned it at the gallery. Not one! That was a real triumph. Of course, none of them had ever seen it or anything by Takehira, so..." He shrugged and let the sentence go unfinished.

"If I had only *looked* at the *tsuba* before I got on that plane," Alyssa whispered.

"But you didn't," George pointed out. "We kept you busy and kept emphasizing the need to keep the *tsuba* out of sight until you were with Mori senior."

Alyssa realized why now. She glared at her deceitful partner.

"Loathing doesn't begin to describe how I feel about what you've done, George," she hissed.

George didn't look as if he particularly cared.

John, who had quietly edged closer, spoke again.

"I assume you arranged for someone to tamper with the plane that Alyssa took," John murmured. He was within a few feet of Alyssa now.

"Right again." George managed to appear somewhat apologetic about the plane crash.

Alasdair stared at George.

"You didn't tell me that," Alasdair said, shocked. "You said it was a fluke—that the buyer got nervous and did it without your knowledge. I didn't know..."

"Shut up, Alasdair," George ordered coolly.

Alyssa was glad that her brother hadn't actually tried to have her killed. He'd really been upset about her near miss, she thought, recalling what bad shape he'd been in when she finally got him at home. Maybe there was a faint ray of hope left for him after all.

"Why did you try to kill her?" John asked softly.

"I wasn't so much trying to kill Alyssa as I was trying to get rid of that copy of the *tsuba*," George explained. He gave Alyssa an apologetic smile. "She simply wouldn't be parted from it and we didn't have a chance to replace the copy with the original before she flew to Onijima. You see, the *tsuba* copy was a test for my forger. If he could copy it to satisfy me, he would be asked to copy the *katana* when we finally got access to it. But I knew that the copy of the *tsuba* would not fool your father. He had seen the original for years. And those old monks on Onijima know how to authenticate swords and their fittings. I wanted to make copies of the Takehira sword and its *tsuba* and leave them with Alyssa. It would give us a few months before anyone would realize what had happened. The fakes would be on display at galleries all over the world. And the originals would be finding their new home. By the time the copy was returned to Onijima, the trail would be cold."

"But you couldn't switch the *tsuba*s before she got on the plane," John said coldly.

Alyssa stepped closer to him. When he put his arm around her she clung to his waist. He still seemed a little unsteady, but he was telling her he was going to be there for her when the time came. She closed her eyes and leaned close to his shoulder for a second, absorbing some of his latent strength. Even half-drugged, she'd take John Mori as her champion any day.

"That is correct. But it didn't matter, did it? When you dredged it up, you thought it was the real thing. I suppose it never occurred to you that a copy could have been made, since it didn't seem like there was opportunity. Or maybe that old man and his monks have been too long in the mists of that devils' island of yours and they've forgotten the fine points of telling a treasure from a fake," George said with a cynical smile.

"Identifying genuine antique swords, *meito* as they call them, is a rare art," John said softly.

"True. As is mastering the skill of handling them. Tell me, Mori, would you care to test your skills with me before you fall down those rocks into the sea?"

"Now, why would you want to do that?" John asked softly. He blinked his eyes, as if trying to sharpen the focus.

"Because that man you killed years ago was my brother."

"I didn't kill him. He was trying to kill me. After the match. I had no choice but to defend myself." John shook his head, as if still plagued by an inner fog from the drugs they'd put in his tea.

"I'm glad you at least remember," George said bitterly.

"He was the only man I've ever killed with a sword," John murmured seriously. "That makes it relatively easy."

"I suppose it would. Pity. I had hoped it would have been the guilt that made you recall."

John pulled Alyssa a little behind him. His eyes narrowed and his body radiated increasing strength and danger.

"I regret your brother's death, Bodney," John said quietly. "I had no intention of killing him. You know that. The inquest was quite clear about it. He wouldn't back off. If I hadn't fought flat-out, he would have done his damnedest to kill me for besting him. His ego and arrogance killed him. Not me."

"Well, I have ego and arrogance such as he possessed," George muttered coldly. "And I loved my brother, unlike Alasdair and Alyssa here." He flexed the sword, testing its flexibility and admiring its weight and feel. "This isn't the

Takehira, but until you remember where you put it, I think I'll test this one on you, my friend.''

"No!" Alyssa cried as George lunged forward, sword extended.

John whistled and suddenly the lights went out.

She was being rolled across the floor and under the table as George reached in his pocket and pulled out a gun.

"If you won't stand and fight, Mori, I'll have to shoot you." George snarled dangerously.

John was hustling her back on their bellies in the darkness. They were cloaked in black since the curtains were drawn. When they reached the edge of the room, John grabbed her hand and pulled her toward the front door. They were outside before George realized where they were going.

"Oh, John," she whispered in terror, clinging to his hand as they raced out into the rocky, scrub-dotted landscape.

"It'll be all right," he whispered against her ear as he pulled her into some sheltering rocks. He pushed her against the rocks and covered her body protectively with his. "Trust me."

She wrapped her arms around his muscled strength and felt the first surge of real hope. John had raised his head to listen, and it occurred to her that he had made a remarkable recovery from the effect of the drugs. She looked up, and when he gazed down at her she saw the glitter in his dark eyes.

"I should have known you wouldn't have drunk tea that Alasdair brought," she said in a soft whisper only audible to him.

He smiled slightly and caught her chin with one, warm hand. Then he kissed her deeply, pulling her close, so close he seemed to be making her part of his body.

There was a sound at the door. John released her and laid his finger across her lips indicating that she should be silent. She nodded.

"Alyssa?" called out George. "I don't know what trick your friend is trying to pull, but if you value your brother's life, come out now. I'm willing to let you go, if you give me Mori. I hadn't intended to leave but obviously I'm going to have to change my immediate plans. The man who wants to buy this sword can see to it that I have relocation in his country. New identification won't be hard to get. But I want the sword. Give me Mori, and I'll give you your brother." There was a pause. "What do you say, Alyssa?"

She wrapped her arms more tightly against John's waist, and he squeezed her comfortingly.

There was a scream of pain.

It came from Alasdair.

Alyssa shuddered and raised her head. She looked up at John and saw the hard, grim expression on his face.

"Alyssa!" Alasdair screamed. "He's got me against the wall. There's nowhere for me to go! He's slicing me up with than damned sword!" There was another scream.

Alyssa shook, feeling the pain herself. He was still her baby brother, the boy she had comforted and bandaged and soothed all her life. Tears filled her eyes and rolled down her cheeks. John lifted her chin and stared down into her suffering. He raised his eyebrows and tilted his head questioningly in the direction of George and Alasdair.

He was volunteering to go to face George, she realized.

Alyssa wrapped her arms around him more tightly and fiercely shook her head. Racked with silent sobs, she clung to him. She wouldn't let him face death for her brother. She loved them both. Alasdair could not kill a lifetime of love, no matter how bad he was. In the end, he was her brother, and she would be loyal to him to the last. But she wouldn't give George the life of the one man she loved above all else. Not even for her beloved, pitiful Dair.

There was a long scream.

"He'll bleed to death if you don't come out, Alyssa," George said. "I'm afraid I'm running out of time. Holling will be waiting in his boat offshore. If I don't bring the sword and the *tsuba,* he may leave. I can't have that. Tell me where Mori is and I'll let you go. You can bind Alasdair's wounds while I take care of Mori and pick up the sword. After I've left, you can walk to a neighbor and get help. I'll have to eliminate your phone, of course. And whoever else Mori has out here to disconnect the electricity."

There was a shot from the gun. Some rocks cascaded near the back of the house.

"Perhaps I won't have to worry about that person after all," George said unpleasantly.

Alyssa looked through tear-filled eyes at John.

One of my men came with me, he mouthed.

Alyssa saw the grim lines around John's mouth. He didn't know whether his man had been badly hurt or not by that shot.

John looked down into Alyssa's face and saw the love and trust that he had never believed he would find. She wasn't going to reveal their position to George, even if it cost her brother's life. No man could have been given a greater sacrifice, he thought. He knew how dearly she loved Alasdair, in spite of everything. He found her mouth and kissed her. Not gently. Not tenderly. It was too filled with pain and desperation and the hope for a way out of this to be gentle.

Alyssa rose to meet his harshness with a desperation of her own. When he finally broke the kiss, she looked at him in wide-eyed fear as he kissed away each tear on her cheek.

"Stay here," John whispered. "Don't give your position away. I'll take care of George."

And from the tempered steel of his voice, Alyssa thought he actually would. Heart in her throat, she touched his cheek and ached as he pulled silently away, melting into the darkness.

Chapter 16

Alyssa wrapped her arms around herself and strained to hear what was happening. Naturally, she couldn't hear John move. She hoped George couldn't, either.

There was a sound of a scuffle and she ventured to look around the rock. It was too dark to tell what was happening. She told herself she had to stay put. John had told her to. She should do what he asked. She knew she should.

Someone screamed. There was a loud grunt and a long moan.

Alyssa couldn't bear it. She bolted out from behind the rock and ran as silently as she could toward the house.

If John was hurt, perhaps she wouldn't be too late to save him, she told her pounding heart. And if the sounds were coming from George, everything would be all right. She'd be perfectly safe. Until John noticed that she'd disobeyed his order.

She'd deal with that when she had to, she told herself, fighting fear and trying desperately to hang on to her courage.

There were two men fighting on the front steps. One had a sword, the other nothing at all.

Alyssa stopped in her tracks and wanted to scream. How could an unarmed man defeat someone wielding a sword?

John sidestepped a wild slash and moved in fast as lightning. A quick twist of his body and he'd disarmed George. George screamed as his wrist snapped. John settled his forearm around George's neck, caught the man's back with his knee and pulled hard. George cried in agony and stopped fighting.

"My back!" George screamed in a blood-curdling voice. "You're breaking my back!"

Alyssa drew near. Seeing her brother in a heap a few yards away from the fighting men, she rushed to kneel at his side and start applying pressure to his bleeding wound.

"Alyssa!" George screamed. "Tell him to stop!"

"I *should* break your back," John said through teeth clenched in rage. "Then I should take you apart slowly, piece by piece for what you've done to her. Believe me, Bodney, it requires every ounce of control I have to resist the temptation."

John's gaze met Alyssa's and her heart turned over at what she saw in his.

"You can thank Alyssa Jones for your life," John said tersely. "Somehow I don't think she'd appreciate having your death as a memory. Jail, however, is something else again."

A shadowy figure scrambled down to join them. A man wrapped in Mori black. He unwrapped the cloth covering his face.

"Kojiro!" Alyssa exclaimed in surprise. "I thought you were on Onijima!"

"John-san want me here. I come."

"You all right?" John asked Kojiro.

Kojiro nodded. "He bad shot."

"The man's bad—period." John shoved George to the ground.

There was a sound of tires on the drive, and all of them turned to see who had pulled in.

It was a police car.

Josie was driving. And Betsy had come along.

"Betsy caught me as I was going off-duty," the police-woman explained. "We thought we'd just drive up and see if everything was all right." She looked over the situation, seeing Alyssa's relief. Then she eyed John, standing over George and looking more than a little annoyed. "I assume this is that man of yours, Alyssa? Maybe someone could tell us what's going on."

"With pleasure." Alyssa sighed. "First, could you call an ambulance? George has cut my brother pretty badly. And, uh, George might need a little patching up. Before you take him to jail for attempted murder, that is."

Josie got on the radio and notified the appropriate authorities that they needed an ambulance and the police. This was out of her jurisdiction. George didn't know that, of course.

Alyssa looked at John as they waited for help to come.

And he looked down at her, brooding.

She wondered what he would say when they finally could be alone again. Something was eating at him. She wondered whether is was how to say good-bye. She swallowed hard and fought off a new ripple of tears. God, and to think she never used to cry! she thought hysterically.

The dawn was breaking over the rocks and boulders, sending its long golden rays out across the vast blue ocean. Through the large picture windows the light chased night from the beach house. Alyssa's aged *bonsai* sat in its flat container, a lonely sentinel as the sea turned to molten gold.

Alyssa was lying on the bed fully clothed. John lay next to her, still wearing what he'd had on the night before. The past two days had been exhausting. When they'd gotten back to the beach house, they'd fallen into bed and slept.

Alyssa opened her eyes and stared blindly into the future, wondering what lay in store for her and for John. There had been no time to talk of themselves. Time was elusive quicksilver that slipped away before you realized it, she thought wistfully. What she wouldn't give for a few more days, a few more hours even, with John before he had to go.

The hospital had assured her that Alasdair's physical wounds would not be fatal. A counselor and a physician had recommended involving him in alcoholism treatment as soon as possible, though. She recalled how he leaned on alcohol and wondered if that had contributed to George's ability to manipulate him. If that was true, maybe there was some slim hope for Dair yet.

George was a different matter, of course. She felt her hatred for him deepen, in spite of her best effort to remain calm. Well, he had a lawyer. But she doubted the best attorney on the planet would be able to get him out of this. John assured her that he'd see to it that George's accomplices—Esau Holling and the wealthy buyer and the forger—were pursued, as well.

John rolled over, leaning on his elbow to gaze down at her. His eyes were filled with a tenderness that made her heart ache with yearning. He ran a hand over her hair, sliding his fingers through the soft silky strands. Then he trailed a tender path down to her blouse and began tugging loose the buttons and finding warm, supple flesh.

His eyes darkened and he bent over her. His warmth enveloped her, and then his mouth fastened on hers.

Alyssa moaned at the familiar warmth spreading dangerously through her body. Like dawn it stole over her, heating her blood and bringing her lonely heart the joy of another day.

He rustled the warm yellow and orange-brown folds of her print silk blouse, loosened the fastenings of her dark brown slacks, used his stockinged feet to push her low heels onto the floor next to his black dress shoes.

"Did you mean what you said that night, Alyssa?" he murmured against her cheek as he kissed her soft skin and caressed her in slow, unhurried strokes.

Her eyes closed in the deep lethargy of pleasure he gave her, she murmured, "What night?"

He pulled her under him and she slid her hands along his warm, muscled chest. He'd already unbuttoned his shirt, and she willingly slid it off.

"When you thought I was unconscious and said that you loved me," he told her quietly.

Alyssa stared at him, completely vulnerable.

She swallowed hard and cupped his dear face between her soft hands. How could she ever explain how she felt about him? How could he believe what had happened to her? It sounded foolish somehow.

"Yes," she murmured huskily. "I don't know how it happened. I couldn't believe it at first. But somehow I stepped into your life and discovered that I'd lost my heart when I wasn't looking."

His eyes were as dark as two pools of midnight sky. She felt his body hardening against her thighs. She smiled wistfully.

"I hope you don't mind," she murmured, pulling his head down so that she could find comfort in his lips.

He groaned and wrapped her in his arms so tightly that she couldn't breathe. "Alyssa," he whispered. "Alyssa..."

The flare of heat between them suddenly sizzled along their skin. Alyssa felt something in him change, become intent and hungry and unable to hold back.

"Yes," she gasped, as he ripped the last of her clothes away, as she felt the last of his go, as well. His hard body, his trembling hand, his urgent kisses said what she wanted to hear.

Even if he didn't love her the way she loved him, she knew that he needed her. Not just now, not just physically, but at a deeper level. There was a hunger in him that only she could fill, and she gave herself to him completely, wanting to ease that hunger so badly that she hurt with it.

Like two parts of one soul they found each other. Everywhere he touched her, fire burned her flesh. And everywhere he kissed her, she ached for more and still more.

He couldn't wait and eagerly she opened her thighs, gasping as he held her hips and thrust deep inside. His groan of satisfaction sent electricity like a shower of needles over her breasts and belly and into her innermost core.

He held himself still and buried his face in her neck, struggling for control. He lifted his head and looked down into her eyes, the dark need in him like a torment deep in his soul. He grasped her face between his two large, strong hands and kissed her deeply.

As he began slowly to move, she felt the wave of ancient pleasure begin deep within her body. She felt treasured and cared for and passionately desired. With each firm stroke and every warm caress she felt her heart break with a love so deep, she couldn't hold it back.

Tears slid down her cheeks as he murmured endearments and found the hot core of her need.

"You are mine," he groaned, shaking as the waves of pleasure began their inevitable crash. "Mine...mine... mine..."

They held on to one another as the tide of love crested and crashed upon the shore. As it subsided, he realized that she was crying, and he looked down into her tear-streaked face with uneasy concern.

"The girl who never cries?" he teased softly. "You'd have a hard time convincing me. Or is it me? Do I bring out all this sadness?"

Alyssa shook her head.

She smiled bravely.

"I'm crying because I feel so much emotion that it has to come out somehow, and so it comes out in tears."

He wiped the tears away with his fingers, then tenderly kissed her swollen lips. He rolled onto his back, carrying her with him, keeping her warm, relaxed body draped intimately over his.

"I never believed in love," he said. He caressed her slowly, savoring the satin of her skin, the satisfaction it gave him simply to lie with her like this. "I thought love was for other people. Maybe for one who had been born with all the right things in life. Even after I was old enough to realize that I didn't have to be miserable simply because my mother had been a dead loss, I found it impossible to believe that any woman was worth losing your head over."

Alyssa sighed, resigned to hearing that she was about to be given the usual parameters. No long-term expectations. That's what he'd told his mistresses. She leaned on her elbows and looked down into his strong, masculine face. His dark hair was endearingly mussed and he looked strangely vulnerable, she thought in surprise. She straightened his hair

with a tender caress and braced herself to say what she
wanted to say.

"You don't have to love me back," she whispered unsteadily. The darned tears threatened and she swallowed
hard to fight them off. "Not that I don't wish that you did,"
she added, choking on the words.

"Alyssa..." he said huskily.

She shook her head.

"It's all right," she lied, trying hard to be able to mean it.
"I'm in love enough for both of us. It must be that island... I'm hopelessly enchanted. So, if you would be willing to consider me for the post of mistress... which I know
you think I'm unqualified for, but the post is vacant... last
I heard..." She hesitated and looked at him in momentary
terror.

He was staring at her in surprise. Pain lightninged across
his features and he grabbed her head firmly.

"Alyssa," he said quite distinctly. "I wasn't going to ask
you to be my mistress."

"Oh," she said in a small, terribly deflated voice. "I don't
suppose we could just lie here and not say anything at all?
You see, I'm having a hard time imagining how I'll ever say
good-bye...."

The pain in his face was just like the one she felt, she
thought.

"Someday you'll fall in love," she whispered, laying her
face next to his and curling her arms around him. She
couldn't bear the hurt that she saw in him. The deep, ago-
nized suffering. "She'll be the luckiest woman in the world,
too," Alyssa said, her voice barely a wisp of sound. She was
shaking, she hurt so badly.

John sighed and rolled her onto her back and lifted her
hand to his lips. He kissed her and looked into her tear-filled
eyes and said, "I am in love."

Alyssa's heart stopped, and she stared into the heat and
determination simmering in his eyes.

"She fell into my life like a star from the night sky," he
said softly. "She brought light where there had been only
darkness. Her laughter made me remember how to smile

from joy, and her courage taught me that not everyone with a warrior's heart came in a big, tough package.''

He kissed her on the lips, warmly, intimately for a moment. When he raised his head, he slid his fingers into her hair and gazed deeply into her widened gray eyes.

''I don't want you for just a mistress, Alyssa Jones,'' he murmured huskily. He caught her legs beneath his thighs protectively. ''It wouldn't be enough.''

He smiled slightly at her look of shock.

''You aren't the only one who's been feeling foolish, sweetheart.'' He sighed. ''I've been trying to figure out what's wrong with me since we met. My mind is only empty of all turmoil when you're safely in my arms. If I let you go, I'll be a hell of failure when it's time to meditate.'' He kissed her lightly, smiling at her shock and her stunned realization that he was serious.

She pulled him into her arms and they were silent.

He whispered in her ear.

Heat flooded her and she turned to see his face. ''What did you say?''

''I said I love you,'' he repeated seriously. ''And I'll be damned if I'm going back to Onijima without you.''

He held her close and savored the peace of folding her in his arms.

''Onijima is going to be coming out of isolation,'' he said. ''We'll be joining the world of nations eventually, once we finally leave our lawless reputation behind. But for the next few years it will still have a lot of the old mystique. Would you be willing to come back with me? To be there while we fight our way into the next century?''

Alyssa was afraid to believe it. Maybe she was hearing what she longed for.

''You have never wanted to complicate your life with a woman before,'' she said huskily. ''And, I know you've loved some of them . . .''

''Not like this.'' He sighed. He looked at her lips and his eyes darkened. He raised his eyes until their gazes met again.

''I never gave any serious thought to marriage, Alyssa.'' He grinned wryly. ''And it wasn't for lack of Etsu's trying to set me on the proper path, obviously.''

Alyssa smiled, but she was too confused by her own feelings to feel much like laughing at the moment.

"I want to marry you, Alyssa Jones."

She stared at him. He sounded deadly serious. And John was generally rather serious, anyway, in her opinion.

"You needn't look quite so shocked," he objected, laughing.

"I just didn't really expect you to feel that way."

He bent his head to her shoulder and caressed her skin with his lips.

"I can't imagine why," he murmured. "I've been doing my damnedest to seduce you."

"Seduction isn't the same as marriage," she pointed out in a whispery voice.

He cupped her head tenderly between his hands as his eyes darkened further with emotion.

"I want to hear you say that you'll come back with me," he said in a rough voice. "I need you, Alyssa. And, damn it all, I'm not a man accustomed to needing people. I've made a life of being an island unto myself. Onijima was tailor-made for someone like me. But it isn't going to be the same. I'll know what I'm missing now. Know the sweet tenderness, the fierce desire, the humor, the arguing that's almost as much fun as the loving...."

Her heart ached and her eyes brimmed with tears.

He ran a finger along the lashes and collected them.

"I always seem to make you cry," he said, frowning. "Maybe it wouldn't be good for you there. It's full of ghosts from the past..."

She fiercely threw her arms around him and stopped fighting the tears of joy that fell in spite of his tender kisses.

"I love you like crazy, John Mori," she cried. "And if you don't take me back and marry me and raise children with me, I'll come back and haunt you myself someday, like all those ghosts you've already got!"

She felt him sigh with relief and then was crushed in the strength of his embrace.

Their lips met and their bodies entwined. Two lovers made one. Two lives made into a single, joyful whole.

"I love you," he whispered.

She smiled amidst the tears.

"Show me how much again?"

He didn't quite laugh. There was pain mixed with his joy. This was a new road for him, this being part of another's life.

"When we go back, you'll tell me all the tales of Onijima?" she coaxed him.

"Yes, love," he murmured between kisses on her lips. "And we'll make tales of our own that our great-grandchildren will recount someday. I promise you."

And as he bent to kiss her again, the sun stretched out its golden fingers, carrying the warmth of life out across the vast and rolling Pacific.

Far away stood the island of legend, Onijima, wrapped in its mysterious mists, rising above the ancient waves, waiting for the return of its master.

And of his chosen woman. The other half of his heart. The part of his soul that had been missing. The two who would go on together as one, forged in the fire of love.

* * * * *

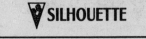

▼ SILHOUETTE

Sensation

COMING NEXT MONTH

RESTLESS WIND
Nikki Benjamin

Taylor Brannigan hadn't listened to the warning that
she was a target for a ruthless criminal. Now
kidnapped and alone with the enigmatic, magnetic
Ross MacGregor, it looked as if that mistake might be
her last. Just as disturbing, Taylor couldn't understand
the strange longing she felt for her abductor…

POINT OF NO RETURN
Rachel Lee

Under Blue Wyoming Skies

Sheriff Nathan Tate was hunting desperate criminals,
but he was also facing trouble at home. A tall, dark,
handsome younger man was threatening the love he'd
thought could withstand anything. Could his wife have
betrayed him?

SILHOUETTE

Sensation

COMING NEXT MONTH

NIGHTSHADE
Nora Roberts

He Who Dares & Night Tales

Colt Nightshade was looking for a friend's young daughter and he needed local police help, Althea Grayson's help (some of you may remember Althea from Night Shift). Althea was all business, even though Colt was being distracted by thoughts of mutual pleasure. How was he to woo this serious lady?

STILL MARRIED
Diana Whitney

Suddenly, here was Kelsey, only a signature away from being his ex-wife, back in Luke Sontag's life again. Asking him to help her. Forcing him to face the passion and heartache that was their past. What of the future?

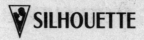

COMING NEXT MONTH FROM

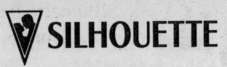 **SILHOUETTE**

Intrigue

*Danger, deception and desire—
new from Silhouette...*

UNDER THE KNIFE Tess Gerritsen
RISKY BUSINESS M.J. Rodgers
GUILTY AS SIN Cathy Gillen Thacker
PRIVATE EYES Madeline St. Claire

Special Edition

Satisfying romances packed with emotion

A MAN FOR MUM Gina Ferris Wilkins
A SECRET AND A BRIDAL PLEDGE Andrea Edwards
DOES ANYONE KNOW WHO ALLISON IS?
Tracy Sinclair
TRULY MARRIED Phyllis Halldorson
A STRANGER IN THE FAMILY Patricia McLinn
A PERFECT SURPRISE Caroline Peak

Desire

*Provocative, sensual love stories for the
woman of today*

MYSTERIOUS MOUNTAIN MAN Annette Broadrick
IMPULSE Lass Small
THE COP AND THE CHORUS GIRL Nancy Martin
DREAM WEDDING Pamela Macaluso
HEAVEN CAN'T WAIT Linda Turner
FORSAKEN FATHER Kelly Jamison

A years supply of Silhouette Desires – absolutely free!

Would you like to win a years supply of seductive and breathtaking romances? Well, you can and they're FREE! All you have to do is complete the wordsearch puzzle below and send it to us by 31st March 1996. The first 5 correct entries picked after that date will win a years supply of Silhouette Desire novels (six books every month – worth over £150). What could be easier?

STOCKHOLM	PARIS	HELSINKI	ANKARA
REYKJAVIK	LONDON	ROME	AMSTERDAM
COPENHAGEN	PRAGUE	VIENNA	OSLO
MADRID	ATHENS	LIMA	

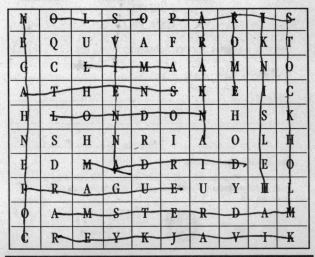

N	O	L	S	O	P	A	R	I	S
E	Q	U	V	A	F	R	O	K	T
G	C	L	I	M	A	A	M	N	O
A	T	H	E	N	S	K	E	I	C
H	L	O	N	D	O	N	H	S	K
N	S	H	N	R	I	A	O	L	H
E	D	M	A	D	R	I	D	E	O
P	R	A	G	U	E	U	Y	I	L
O	A	M	S	T	E	R	D	A	M
C	R	E	Y	K	J	A	V	I	K

Please turn over for details on how to enter ➡

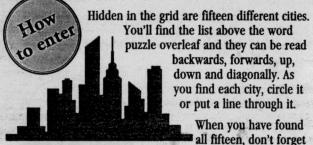

How to enter

Hidden in the grid are fifteen different cities. You'll find the list above the word puzzle overleaf and they can be read backwards, forwards, up, down and diagonally. As you find each city, circle it or put a line through it.

When you have found all fifteen, don't forget to fill in your name and address in the space provided below and pop this page in an envelope (you don't need a stamp) and post it today. Hurry – competition ends 31st March 1996.

Silhouette Capital Wordsearch
FREEPOST
Croydon
Surrey
CR9 3WZ

Are you a Reader Service Subscriber?   Yes ❑   No ❑

Ms/Mrs/Miss/Mr _____

Address _____

_____

_____ Postcode _____

One application per household.

You may be mailed with other offers from other reputable companies as a result of this application. If you would prefer not to receive such offers, please tick box.   ❑

COMP295
C